BRING
HER
HOME

BRING HER HOME

S.A.DUNPHY

bookouture

Published by Bookouture in 2021

An imprint of Storyfire Ltd.
Carmelite House
50 Victoria Embankment
London EC4Y 0DZ

www.bookouture.com

ISBN: 978-1-80019-645-2
eBook ISBN: 978-1-80019-644-5

PROLOGUE

Uruz – ᚢ

September 2018

'Uruz is the runic symbol of the aurochs, the Scandinavian wild bison. It is a reminder that the untamed powers of creativity are not without danger.'

Poetic Edda

I left his body where I knew it would be found, nestled gently in the tidal mud of the Thames in the shadow of the Tate Modern in Southwark. He had been a strong one, had William, and breaking him had taken skill and patience. In the last moments of his life, as I brought him to his final crisis, I came to believe we had bonded in a special way, he and I.

I almost loved him, at the end.

And as I released him after such a long struggle, I think he loved me too.

In the dark and quiet hours before dawn, I rowed slowly and silently up the great river, the husk that had once been a man wrapped in a tarpaulin at my feet. I have studied my beloved Thames for years and knew how to guide my craft into a current that would carry it to just the right spot, a point where I could ease the barque out of the channel and allow it to sit atop the silt and filth near the shoreline while I unwrapped my gift and laid it out in all its ragged glory to await the rising sun.

With gentle shifting of my weight, I nudged the boat back into the flow, and then I was gone, William's bloodied, raw remains enshrined in the freezing, dank-smelling ooze, waiting patiently to be discovered.

And now, here I sit at my vantage point, a quarter of a mile away, my telescope trained on the mudflats as day dawns, and I wait too.

A lone kayaker finds him. She is almost past the body before she realises what she has seen and articulates a wide arc in the water, coming alongside and using her paddle to pause until she is certain. Through my high-powered lens I see her lean over the side and vomit. Then she produces a mobile phone that was Velcroed to her arm and rings it in.

After that everything happens quickly.

Here they come, the police with their flashing lights and their motorboats and their frogmen in scuba equipment. Such a lot of fuss. By now, one would think they'd have learned that all I ever leave is the body. It says all I need to say. William is my work of art, as were all the others. He is my magnum opus. My symphony. They all are.

A cordon is placed around the area. I watch the forensic investigators arrive at Bankside, their white, sterile outfits stark against the grey concrete of the waterfront. And finally, I spy *her*, the one I have been waiting for, climbing out of her orange 1973 MGB GT – such a flashy vehicle for so spartan a woman.

Jessie Boyle, the criminal behavioural specialist.

This is the investigator who came so close to catching me but was too blinded by her own prejudices to comprehend what was right in front of her.

Now she will know. Today she will see.

I wish I could be closer. I long to hear her breathing quicken as she makes her way down the steps from street level, taking them two, sometimes three, at a time. Jessie has long legs and the jeans she wears show them off to fine effect, even though she is almost always draped in that long, grey woollen overcoat, which I have always believed is meant to make her seem less feminine.

I focus my attention on her face: sharp cheekbones, a long, aquiline nose, slate-grey eyes. In the dawn light, her expression is solemn and stoic, but do I discern a slight quiver around the thin-lipped mouth? In another attempt to subvert any perceived softness, Jessie Boyle has cut her hair short and close to her head. There is a smattering of grey if one looks closely – she is forty-five years old, after all – and I know she has the words *Is mise an stoirm* tattooed in Celtic script on her left shoulder blade. It is a phrase in the native Irish tongue, for Ms Boyle was born in Dublin. The saying has its origins in an ancient Irish fable. Allow me to share it with you.

The Devil comes upon an old Celtic warrior preparing for war. Sneaking up on him as he prepares for battle, the Devil whispers in his ear: 'You are old and frail. You will never withstand the coming storm.' And the old warrior turns, looks the Devil in the eye and retorts: '*Is mise an stoirm!*' I am the storm.

I like that. Today I will teach her that she is wrong, of course. Jessie Boyle has never truly experienced a storm before. This morning, she will feel the full force of the hurricane.

Without so much as a pause, she wades out into the mud, the viscous, black, foul-smelling ooze splashing and staining her clothes as she fights her way forward. On reaching the crime-scene tape she stops. Through my eyepiece I can see she is panting with exertion, her shoulders rising and falling, sweat dappling her brow, even though it is very cold. Those grey eyes are wide as she peers at the flayed body in the mud, now only a few feet away.

I made sure to leave his face untouched. I wanted there to be no doubt as to who this cadaver once was.

As I watch, I see the emotions dance across her features in a shadowplay of horror. She knows it is William Briggs, the man who was her partner, both in the Violent Crime Task Force of the London Metropolitan Police and in a variety of personal and intimate ways too.

I see recognition settle in, followed rapidly by a fierce and immediate denial. It is her partner, friend, lover... but she doesn't want it to be. The colour runs out of her face as she takes in what I have done to him. She fights to keep her composure, but tears begin to well in her eyes, and she lunges forward, breaking through the tape in a bid to reach him.

One of the police divers grabs at her and brings her up short, but she fights him, driving an elbow into his gut and surging forward again.

Jessie Boyle is almost on top of what is left of the man she loves when she sees the message I left her, and it is beautiful to know that just as I broke William Briggs, so too have I broken her. As far away as I am, I fancy I can hear her screams of anger and pain.

Her beloved William is dead, and she knows that it was me who took it all from her. She knows because I left my signature, my calling card, carved into the plains of his chest.

Just before he died, I cut the Uruz rune – ᚢ – into his flesh. The Uruz is the ancient Scandinavian bison. The symbol speaks of manifestation, regeneration and endurance, the divine power that laces up the skin but can also slash it wide open. Such violence, when correctly channelled, sustains the spirit and can be used to protect the soul from trauma.

And it can be used to inflict trauma too. Such beautiful trauma.

The last thing I see before packing up my telescope and disappearing into the catacomb-like streets of the seething city is Jessie

Boyle sinking to her knees in the sludge, tears streaming down her face as the love of her life is zipped into a body bag.

It is an image I will return to time and time again in the time to come. It will give me strength.

PART ONE

A Sort of Homecoming

October 2018

'We serial killers are your sons, we are your husbands, we are everywhere. And there will be more of your children dead tomorrow.'

Ted Bundy

CHAPTER ONE

It felt like Dublin had been waiting for her to return, as if the city had held its breath while she was away. Jessie couldn't work out whether the thought was comforting or foreboding, and eventually decided it didn't matter – she had come home for better or worse, and no amount of navel-gazing was going to change that.

She took a room in the Grand Canal Hotel in Ringsend, a ten-minute walk from where she had grown up. When Jessie was a kid in the Ireland of the 1980s, Ringsend had been a crumbling collection of tiny, terraced houses set amid factories and mills huddled along the southern bank of the River Liffey. Back then, what industry there was in Ringsend was experiencing its death rattles as the economy tipped into free fall. But that had all changed in the boom of the twenty-first century.

Now a large swathe of the suburb was going through a gentrification. The canal that wound down to the Liffey had been cleaned up and adorned with a walkway and a cycle path, and newly opened coffee docks sold almond-milk lattes to the bearded and top-knotted executives who seemed to be everywhere.

But all the luxury apartment blocks in the world couldn't disguise the area's true identity from Jessie – this was old Dublin, through and through.

Yet she was unable to take any pleasure from the knowledge. In truth, Jessie had only come home because she didn't know where else to go.

A case she had been working had gone badly wrong. A man she cared for, possibly more than she cared for herself, had died horribly. It took her all of five days after she helped pull his body from the sludge of the Thames to realise that police work had lost all its pleasure for her. That, in fact, she could not stand to be around the buildings and people and locales she had once relished.

Every single one of them now carried memories she wanted to forget. She would open a door to a room she had been in hundreds of times before and be assailed by a recollection of a conversation or a joke or simply a sense of being with Will, and she would be reduced to a trembling wreck.

It was intolerable. And more than that, it was unsustainable.

She fought it for another week, but she already knew what she needed to do. A fortnight to the day after they found Will's body, she handed in her resignation, and that night she was on a plane bound for Dublin.

After Jessie had booked into the hotel, she slept for two days straight, the welcome cloak of oblivion keeping the self-recrimination and anger that were the mental soundtrack to her waking hours at bay.

On the third day, she slowly drifted back to consciousness and was surprised to find she was starving – she'd had no appetite since Will died.

In the breakfast room of the hotel, she ate mechanically, barely aware of what she was consuming, and when the meal was finished, she realised that, for the first time in two decades, she had nothing to do.

So she walked.

Jessie wandered the city of her birth for hours, first making her way along the river until she hit O'Connell Bridge. She paused for a moment, looking to her left towards her old alma mater, Trinity College, before crossing the river to the Northside, still following the Liffey's curve until it brought her to the Phoenix Park, where she lost herself among the trees for a time. As the shadows grew longer, she left the green coolness and crossed back over the river before executing a wide loop past St James's Hospital, by the Guinness Brewery and finally back to the docks.

She had just arrived in the lobby of her hotel when her mobile phone buzzed in her pocket: a text message. She opened it as she got into the elevator. It was from a number she didn't recognise.

I want you to know that William screamed. In the final moments, he begged for it to end. And I was glad to grant his wish – eventually. Bye for now. Ո

Jessie Boyle, applied social psychologist and criminal behavioural specialist, late of the Violent Crime Task Force of the London Metropolitan Police, read the message as she walked to her room on the second floor of the hotel. She closed the door behind her, sank to the floor, buried her head in her hands and wept.

CHAPTER TWO

Jessie woke two hours later to someone knocking on the door of her room.

Fumbling for her phone in the dark, she checked the time and found it was nine thirty. She listened for a moment, wondering if she might have dreamed the banging, but within moments three smart raps sounded again, so she dragged herself upright and switched on the lamp.

Jessie peered through the door's peephole, wondering who her visitor might be, seeing as no one knew she was even in Ireland. The individual she saw on the other side of the door was probably the last person she would have expected, and for a moment she thought about pretending she wasn't in and just going back to bed.

'Jessie, I know you're in there,' the visitor said sharply in a pronounced Northern Irish accent. 'Open the fucking door. I need to talk to you.'

Heaving a deep sigh, Jessie turned the handle.

Dawn Wilson was the same age as Jessie at forty-five and an inch and a half taller at six foot two. Her long red hair was brought up in a neat bun at the back of her head, and even though she had recently been appointed Police Commissioner of Ireland, tonight she was dressed in plain clothes – a modest black trouser suit over a blue shirt.

'You look like shit,' she told Jessie, who was clad in a baggy Dire Straits T-shirt and leggings.

'Thanks.'

'Can I come in? I've got a bottle of Bushmills in my handbag.'

'When you put it like that, how could I refuse?'

Grinning, the commissioner pushed past her.

When they were seated at the room's small table with large whiskeys in two waterglasses, Jessie asked, 'How did you know I was here?'

'I called the Met looking for you. They told me you'd resigned.'

'Did they tell you why?'

'I'd like to hear it from you.'

Jessie swallowed the contents of her glass and poured another. 'How'd you find me?'

'You've been working in law enforcement at one level or another for more than two decades, so you know as well as I do that phone you've got on your bedside locker is effectively a tracking device. It wasn't hard to work out you were in Dublin, and I figured that if you were here, you'd probably be drawn to your old stomping grounds. It was a simple enough matter to ring the few hotels in the area to find out which one you were staying at. I think the whole process took me ten minutes. Possibly even less.'

'Very clever.'

'Not really. Why'd you pack in the job at the Met?'

'I'd had enough.'

'You and I have known one another a long time, Jessie. This was your dream job.'

Jessie had met Dawn Wilson when they were students of the applied psychology department at Trinity College, Dublin, in the mid-1990s. They had quickly bonded – both were from working-class backgrounds, and they had each secured their places through scholarships – Jessie's from Dublin City Council, Dawn's through the Centre for Peace and Reconciliation, which had been established to build relations between the communities on either side of the border.

Despite their friendship and mutual respect, their relationship always had a sharp edge, one honed by competition. They had been the only female students in their degree class, and, friends or not, each had declared that they wanted to work in the field of policing.

Painfully aware their gender would limit their career options, they had to be ruthless in their ambitions. It was one of the reasons Jessie had decided to move to London for her postgraduate studies.

'I screwed up,' Jessie told her old friend. 'Badly.'

'How so?'

Jessie sighed, running her fingers through her short dark hair. 'I made a stupid mistake, and someone I cared about died as a result.'

Dawn stood up, went to the window and pushed it open. As they were on the second floor it didn't open much, barely a crack really, and Dawn looked at it glumly.

'William Briggs.'

'He was lead investigator for my unit.'

'I'm sorry.'

Jessie waved the condolence away.

'If you stay in this job for any length of time, you lose people,' Dawn continued. 'Police officers put themselves in harm's way every single day. Policing is one of the few professions where you're trained to run towards danger, not away from it. Your DI Briggs would have known that.'

Jessie shook her head. 'He died hard, Dawn,' she said. 'And it was my fault.'

'You can't be sure of that.'

'Yes, I can.'

'Don't flatter yourself.' The commissioner took a pack of Silk Cut Purple cigarettes from her jacket pocket and tapped one out. 'You worked as part of a team – we all do on the force. And with good reason. If I fuck up, there are three people standing behind me whose job it is to catch that error and fix it.'

'Did I say you could smoke?'

'Did I ask?'

'For God's sake, Dawn, will you leave me alone? I'm not looking for a shoulder to cry on.'

'What are you looking for then?'

'I don't know. To be honest, I don't even know who I am anymore.'

'You're the best fucking profiler I've ever met,' Dawn said, lighting her smoke using a bronze Zippo. 'That's who you are.'

'The facts suggest otherwise,' Jessie said. 'This man – this *predator* – was right under my nose and I didn't see it. Looking back, it was so obvious. But I was focused on another suspect, and I didn't realise my mistake until it was too late. And by then, William was already gone.'

'I spoke with your bosses,' Dawn said, blowing smoke rings at the gap created by the small open window – some went out; most didn't. 'Whatever you did or didn't do, no one is bringing charges of negligence or dereliction of duty against you. In fact, I talked to your chief inspector earlier today, and he told me how disappointed he is you've packed in your job. So it seems the only person who blames you for whatever happened is *you*.'

Jessie laughed bitterly. 'Maybe they just don't want to see the truth.'

The commissioner took a final pull on her smoke, and flicking the butt into the night, she closed the window.

'I think you're hurt, and you're angry,' she said, sitting back down opposite Jessie, 'and I'm sorry you're feeling like that. But I'm here because I need your help.'

'To do what?'

'To do what you do best – I need you to look at a case for me.'

Jessie gasped in surprised horror. 'Jesus Christ, Dawn. Haven't you listened to a single word I've said? I'm done. I have nothing left.'

'I don't agree.'

'No!' Jessie was almost shouting. 'I am declining your request!'

Dawn poured them both another drink, pushing Jessie's glass across the table so it was right in front of her.

'I don't think you've understood me very clearly,' she said gently. 'I'm not asking you.'

'What?'

'You owe me, Jessie Boyle. You owe me fucking big, and you know it. I'm really, really sorry to have to do this, but you haven't given me any choice.'

Jessie looked at the commissioner in disbelief. 'Tell me you're not doing this.'

'I am. I'm calling in that debt.'

Jessie opened her mouth to respond, but no words came.

'Let's you and me catch a very bad man,' Dawn said, and raised her glass in a toast to the venture.

Dawn Wilson

She had been an outsider all her life.

Growing up in rural Antrim in the 1980s, surrounded by political and religious division, Dawn made the decision to remain removed from the Troubles as far as was practically possible.

The fact was, she had troubles of her own to contend with.

Dawn's father was a devout Catholic: he believed there was an all-forgiving God of love who held people in the palm of his hand, sheltering them from harm. He was also, without the vaguest sense of irony, free and easy with his fists.

It didn't happen every day, or even every week. To the outside eye, Benjie Wilson was a kind, gently spoken, spiritual man. But a couple of times a year, frustration and anger would build up, and when that happened, he would turn into something terrifying, and Dawn and her mother would bear the brunt of it.

The experience made Fiona Wilson a timid, nervous creature who jumped at shadows.

It just made Dawn angry and determined never to compromise.

Probably in an attempt to hurt her father, religion was one of the first aspects of her life where she drew a line in the sand.

Dawn saw no evidence of a benevolent being who offered succour and comfort. If anything, the pain and poverty and conflict she observed as she went about her life in this small pocket of the British Empire led her to conclude that, if there was a God, he was at best an absentee landlord, at worst wilfully perverse.

She wanted no part of any collective that laid their trust in something so apparently arbitrary, and after a series of rows that became increasingly bitter and culminated in her father beating her senseless on her fourteenth birthday, there was an unspoken agreement that she was no longer required to attend Mass.

It was a relief for all of them.

The beatings didn't stop, but Dawn's lack of faith was no longer one of the sparks that set Benjie off.

Individualism and independence of thought became Dawn's defining personality traits. The other young people in her community were drawn to careers in agriculture or teaching or community development. For her, it was always going to be the law.

Policing seemed the only way she could effect the changes she wanted to make. The heroes in the comic books she read by torchlight in the evenings were vigilantes: Wonder Woman and Black Canary and the Huntress – they struck a blow for the disenfranchised and the oppressed, and they did it without allying themselves with any formally endorsed command structure.

In the Northern Ireland of the 1980s, they had a different name for someone who responded to social tensions in that way: they called them paramilitaries. The newsreaders called them terrorists.

Dawn Wilson was damned if she was ever going to be one of those. If she was going to alter the institutions of her world, it would have to be from within, and to stand any chance of achieving a high rank, she needed a degree.

Her family barely made enough money to survive. The only way for Dawn to get to college was through a scholarship, and the local librarian – the same one who loaned her graphic novels – helped her to complete an application for just such an award under the cross-border initiative for peace and reconciliation.

She never thought she would actually be successful.

When the letter arrived informing her she was being offered a place, it was in Dublin, in the lower twenty-six counties of what her father referred to as the 'Free State'.

She felt guilty leaving her mother behind, but despite that, a sense of wild abandon filled her heart as the bus pulled away from the kerb in Antrim Town and headed south. She came home the first three weekends, but her father barely acknowledged her, and her mother seemed unsure how to behave.

Finally, a Friday came, and when it was her turn to step onto the bus, her legs wouldn't move. As she watched it drive away up Nassau Street, she knew it was the right decision. From then on Dawn made her grant money stretch and got a job in a bar on Dame Street, and her new life began.

It was twelve years before she saw Antrim again.

Attending Trinity College was like living a bizarre dream of how her life might have been. There was only one other female student in her class, but Dawn was used to being singled out as unusual, so having someone in a similar situation made the whole experience much easier.

She and Jessie Boyle became firm friends.

It was the third week of their course when she noted Jessie arriving into class with a black eye hastily – and unsuccessfully – hidden behind some concealer.

'What the fuck happened to you?'

'Nothing.'

'Oh, right. So you're just trying out some new cosmetic techniques, are you?'

Jessie fell quiet before saying, 'If I wanted to talk about it, I would, okay?'

Dawn looked at her friend and said softly, 'If this was just a one-off thing – you were in a brawl in a pub or you got mugged – tell me to fuck off and I will not be offended.'

Jessie looked away, but Dawn knew she was listening.

'If someone who is a constant in your life did it – your da or your boyfriend or your brother – that's a different thing. You can't let that go, because they'll keep doing it. They'll promise they won't, but I'm here to tell you they will.'

That was the end of the conversation. That time.

Two weeks later, Jessie came in with her arm in a sling and her eye so swollen no amount of make-up could cover it.

Dawn looked at her long and hard. She didn't have to say anything. Jessie stared back, and over lunch, she told her friend what was going on at home.

They drank several cups of the strong tea they brewed in the student canteen while they made a plan.

What followed changed their lives irrevocably.

CHAPTER THREE

Ten thirty the following morning found Jessie seated in a conference room in police headquarters in Harcourt Street. The HQ complex was situated only a five-minute walk from Grafton Street, a hugely popular pedestrianised shopping area and for many the beating heart of Dublin City, and St Stephen's Green, a beautifully maintained park where families strolled and students from nearby Trinity College met for al fresco lunches.

Jessie mused as she was admitted by the security guard that the bustling shoppers and happy families who came and went nearby had no idea of the macabre nature of some of the cases the detectives based in this nondescript building worked. And that was probably just as well.

The HQ complex consisted of three red-bricked office blocks containing the bases of operation for specialist units like the Criminal Assets Bureau, the Garda Armed Support Unit and the National Bureau of Criminal Investigation, Ireland's equivalent of the FBI.

It was to this latter group's nerve centre that Jessie had been summoned. The room was long and characterless: blank walls painted magnolia; a single, long halogen lightbulb that buzzed intermittently illuminating a table covered in grey Formica around which had been set four chairs.

Jessie had been in countless rooms like this during the years she had worked for the London Met, and she understood the logic of its design: there was nothing here to distract the occupants from the task at hand, whatever problem they had gathered to solve. Meeting rooms like this were a blank slate upon which plans of action were written.

Dawn Wilson, today clad in the commissioner's navy-blue uniform, with its distinctive red Garda insignia to denote her elevated rank, was at the front of the room, setting up what appeared to be an old-school video cassette recorder, running a cable from where the machine sat on a small rolling table to a flat-screen TV attached by a bracket to the wall.

Jessie noted the older technology and was annoyed that she did. She didn't want to be there, but her analytic mind was already paying attention, despite itself.

This was the type of thing most police commissioners would have a technician do, but Jessie knew Dawn had no patience for such conceits and preferred to do even the most mundane tasks herself. The commissioner liked to think this made her accessible and 'just another one of the rank and file', but Jessie knew it was really because she was a control freak.

Seated at the nondescript table was a young man in a cheap grey suit, his cream shirt open at the collar and a red striped tie hanging askew. The commissioner had introduced him to Jessie as Detective Seamus Keneally. Jessie thought he looked to be in his mid-twenties, although his eyes betrayed a maturity far beyond those years.

Last among the room's occupants was a man Jessie had recognised immediately, and whose presence made her extremely curious. Dominic O'Dwyer had been Taoiseach – Prime Minister – of Ireland from 1993 until 1998, and while party politics, by its nature, made him as divisive an individual as any politician, the fact that he had piloted the country through the beginnings of the economic boom – the 'rising tide that lifted all ships', as one of his ministers had put it – caused him to be remembered with a degree of fondness by those old enough to have an opinion on such things.

O'Dwyer was a tall, slim man, sporting a well-tailored black pinstriped suit, complete with a pink tie and pocket square. His grey hair was brushed straight back from his forehead, and the jawline of his long face was coloured by the blue shadow of a beard, even though Jessie knew he must have only shaved a couple of hours ago.

His carefully maintained dress could not mask the turmoil the man was going through, however. Dominic O'Dwyer was seventy-five years old, and he looked every day of it. His features were lined with worry, and there were deep bags beneath his green eyes. Jessie reasoned she would learn the cause of his anxiety soon enough, and this almost made her glad she had made the trip to police HQ that morning. Jessie, regardless of the emotional upheaval she was in, still loved a mystery.

And she had a sense this was going to be an interesting one.

'Okay, let's get started,' Dawn said, sitting down at the top of the table, a remote control for the TV and VCR in front of her. 'Mr O'Dwyer, thank you for joining us. I know you and your family are going through a lot at the moment, but I think your insights can only be useful.'

'I'm glad you invited me,' the older man said in a voice which, despite whatever stress he was experiencing, was rich and resonant.

'All right then. Let me introduce you to Jessie Boyle. Jessie is a criminal behavioural specialist who has worked for the London Metropolitan Police service for the past twenty years. During that time, she was instrumental in securing the capture of quite a number of very high-profile – which is to say extremely dangerous – criminals. Most recently she led the team that caught Cyril Shaw, known in the press by the charming moniker of the Clapham Cleaver.'

'Thank you for being here, Ms Boyle,' O'Dwyer said, reaching over and shaking her hand.

'I'm glad to be of help,' Jessie replied, trying to set aside her resentment at being called back to the front line.

'And also with us is Detective Seamus Keneally. Seamus has recently been promoted to the NBCI due to marked bravery during an attack on a prison transfer.'

'Congratulations, Detective,' O'Dwyer said, shaking the younger man's hand and squeezing his arm – a move Jessie remembered seeing him do on the campaign trail.

'Detective Keneally is here because he is originally from the West of Ireland and has local knowledge we think may be valuable – he's actually from the locality where the events took place, so is a very important resource.'

'I'll do what I can, boss,' Seamus said.

Jessie caught a strong accent, but she did not know enough about the West to tell what part it originated from.

Dawn picked up the remote control and pushed a button. The television flickered to life.

'Mr O'Dwyer has seen this, but you two haven't,' she said to Jessie and Seamus.

The TV screen was filled with an image of the front page of the *Irish Times*, the date clearly visible: 17 October 2018 – two days ago. The newspaper was lowered, revealing a figure completely in shadow. Jessie could make out an upper torso – effectively a chest, shoulders and head – but nothing else. The lighting and camera position had been set up to place the person completely in silhouette. Behind the figure was a blank wall – it looked to have been painted grey or was possibly bare concrete.

'I am the one who has taken Penelope O'Dwyer.'

The voice had been distorted using some kind of audio filter. It was a droning growl that sounded like it came from deep within the earth. Jessie thought that if a real person spoke like that, talking would be an agony.

'*You do not know who I am, but please believe me when I tell you that killing this young woman would cost me nothing. Her life is meaningless to me. However, I am going to give you a chance to win her back. You have until the eve of Samhain to find her. If you do not, I will end her life. And it will not be a good end.*'

A shadow-wreathed arm reached forward, and the camera was turned to reveal a young woman who looked to be in her early thirties. Her blonde hair was matted and stuck to her head with sweat and grime, and her eyes – green like her father's – were wide with terror. Brown packing tape had been fixed over her mouth, but Jessie could hear muffled sounds as she tried to call out for help, for comfort, for a way out of the nightmare she was trapped in.

'*Proof of life,*' the droning voice said. '*You have until the eve of Samhain. The sand is running through the hourglass. Each grain is a heartbeat closer to the end. When the last one falls, so does my blade.*'

And the screen went blank.

Dawn Wilson turned to look at Jessie. 'Thoughts?'

'Why haven't I heard about this in the press?'

'We've managed to keep it out of the media.'

'You won't be able to for much longer.'

'I know. It's why we need to act quickly before it all turns into a shitstorm.'

The commissioner mouthed an apology at O'Dwyer, who waved the expletive away.

'When is Samhain?' Jessie asked. 'Is it Hallowe'en?'

'It is: the thirty-first of October. If we're playing the game according to his rules, we have twelve days.'

'What are the circumstances of the abduction?'

'Ms O'Dwyer was in Cahirsiveen, in County Kerry, visiting a client – she's a financial advisor. She went out to dinner on the night of the fifteenth. She was seen by her client leaving the restaurant and walking in the direction of her hotel, which was three minutes away. She never got there.'

'So she's been missing for four days?' Jessie asked.

'Exactly.'

'And what have you been doing during that time?'

She saw the young detective bristle. 'Almost everyone in the town has been interviewed at least once; some of those who were in the vicinity of the abduction have been spoken to several times. Forensics have combed the entire main street of the town and we have closely analysed Ms O'Dwyer's movements in the days preceding the abduction to see if there could be possible connections.'

'CCTV of the area?'

'There are six cameras along that route, all of which stopped working for ten minutes around the time of her disappearance.'

'All of them? Shops, traffic lights, street cameras?'

'I have done this work before, Ms Boyle,' Seamus said. 'We checked all available recordings.'

'Any other eyewitnesses?'

'None that we've been able to locate,' Dawn said. 'Every shop owner, restaurateur and publican who was working at the time has been questioned. Seamus has compiled a list of every customer, diner and drinker who was out and about on the night of the fifteenth, and not a single one of them claims to have seen Penelope O'Dwyer during her walk back to the hotel.'

'There are four side streets between the wine bar and the hotel where Ms O'Dwyer was headed,' Seamus added. 'She could have been lured up any one of those.'

'Have you interviewed family members?' Jessie asked. 'What about her close friends? Does she have any enemies? Is it possible what's happened is connected with something in her private life?'

Dominic O'Dwyer seemed unsettled at the suggestion. 'My daughter is as kind, honest and sweet-natured a young woman as you could hope to meet,' he said. 'She has no enemies I am aware of, and I would be surprised if you managed to unearth anyone who has a bad word to say about her.'

'Detective Keneally?' Jessie looked at Seamus. 'Does this correspond with what you've learned?'

'Everyone at her firm says she's well liked. She's risen through the ranks reasonably quickly, but no one seems annoyed about that. I've interviewed some girlfriends of hers, and they all reported that she lives for her work. Doesn't really socialise outside of it.'

'And no romantic partners?'

'None that have been reported.'

'Had she seemed upset? Nervous? Alarmed?' Jessie pressed.

'The last time I spoke to Penelope she seemed relaxed and at ease,' O'Dwyer said. 'We talked about how her work was going, about some projects I'm involved in as a director – she was attentive, interested, animated… She seemed very happy and content. She and I planned to have dinner when she got back from Kerry.'

'Her colleagues say much the same. No one reported her presenting as any different to her usual self.'

'No new clients?'

'No. All was business as usual.'

Jessie nodded slowly, turning over what she had just heard, looking for anything that might offer a line of inquiry. Finally she said, 'The person in the video knows who she is. Mr O'Dwyer, we have to assume this is someone who has an axe to grind against you.'

The former Taoiseach sighed, the sound seeming to come from deep within himself.

'Of course I thought the same thing,' the man said. 'I have given the commissioner a list of people who may bear grudges or who have threatened me in the past. I was involved in politics for thirty years. So, as you can probably imagine, we are not short of suspects.'

'Who are the front runners?' Jessie asked. 'I'm immediately thinking of a group like the Continuity IRA, who have good reason to be irritated at you due to your involvement in the peace process.'

'I have some people from counter-terrorism looking into that,' Dawn said.

'The lad in the video didn't name Mr O'Dwyer,' Seamus observed. 'If this is a way of getting at him, don't you think he'd have addressed him directly?'

Jessie pondered that for a moment – it was a good point, and the young detective immediately went up a notch in her estimation.

'You say she's a financial advisor?' Jessie asked O'Dwyer.

'Yes. She's quite successful. Works for Bandon, Ludlow and Murphy.'

'I don't know them.'

'Suffice it to say they get paid the big bucks,' Dawn said.

'Do we know what Ms O'Dwyer was working on in Cahirsiveen?'

'I believe she was talking to a client about broadening their stock portfolio,' Seamus said. 'Whatever that means.'

'It was just a routine job,' the missing woman's father said. 'At the level Penny works, there is an expectation of the personal touch. She spends a lot of time travelling to meet clients all over Ireland, and often outside of it.'

'Have you looked into her caseload to see if there's anything there?'

'The firm have begrudgingly cooperated,' Dawn said. 'Client confidentiality and all that jazz. But they have handed over the relevant files. So far we've found nothing out of the ordinary, but the forensic accountant is giving them another sweep as we speak.'

'According to her friends, Penelope is not currently in a relationship?' Jessie said to the former Taoiseach.

'Not that I'm aware of.'

'Any exes who may be upset at the way things ended?'

'I have to admit, I don't know much about my daughter's romantic life.'

'Would your wife be better informed?'

'I am a widower, Ms Boyle,' he replied, sounding a little surprised Jessie didn't know this about him.

'I'm sorry to hear that. Does your daughter have a stepmother?'

'I never remarried, and I am not in a serious relationship at present.'

'I've already asked that question of all her friends,' Seamus said, his voice betraying an edge of annoyance. 'There are no angry exes. Ms O'Dwyer hasn't really had any serious relationships. That line of investigation is a dead end.'

Jessie nodded.

'Ms Boyle, what can you tell us about this man who has taken my daughter?' O'Dwyer looked at Jessie intently as he spoke.

She could feel the force of his gaze and for a moment understood why he had risen to the position he had – there was a charisma and energy about him that was almost tangible.

'You have to understand that whatever I say at this stage is guesswork.'

'Yes, but it is conjecture based on years of experience hunting people like this,' the former Taoiseach said. 'I want to know what you think. Please.'

Jessie took a deep breath and felt an internal trip switch clicking into place. The side of Jessie Boyle that could see into the dark places, the aspect of herself that saw the shadows others did not want to name, slowly shook itself into wakefulness. She both loved and loathed this version of herself.

Today, she thought the hatred was very much to the fore.

'He's thorough,' she began. 'There is not a single feature in the video to identify him. Even the fact that he sent a videotape – old-school, analogue technology, meaning there are no digital signatures we can trace. I'm assuming there were no fingerprints on it?'

'There was one,' Dawn said.

'Penelope O'Dwyer's,' Jessie guessed.

'Bingo,' the commissioner said drolly.

'The fact that he used old technology doesn't mean he has no grasp of modern tech – he was able to knock out the CCTV cameras on an entire street, which shows a pretty advanced level of skill and suggests he either has a command of technology himself or had a crew containing someone else who does – either way, he understands how important it is.'

'Do you think he's working with a team?' Seamus wanted to know. He was watching her closely, a notebook in his hand.

'I wouldn't rule it out, but I'd be surprised if he's not working alone. If you listen to the language used, it's all "I" and "me". People working with someone else instinctively use "we" and "us".'

'Why the challenge?' Dawn asked. 'Why does he want us to try and find her?'

'That could be down to any number of reasons,' Jessie said. 'My guess would be the challenge of it attracts him. He wants to pit himself against us.'

'Against the police?' O'Dwyer asked. 'Against me?'

'Probably both,' Jessie said. 'The key is to try and draw him out as much as we can. Use what knowledge we can garner against him.'

'But we don't know anything about him!' O'Dwyer said, despair evident in his voice.

'We have that tape,' Jessie said. 'It offers us a few clues.'

'What clues?'

'I bet there's something in the reference to Samhain – why draw attention to that? And that second-last line: each grain is a heartbeat closer to the end. I'm prepared to bet that's a quote from something.'

'It's from a fantasy novel,' Seamus said. '*When Battle Falls* by Joseph Jack Stephens.'

'Fantasy? Like *Lord of the Rings* or *Game of Thrones*?' Jessie asked.

'Yeah. It's book two of a five-book saga. And each novel is about eight hundred pages.'

'Is the author Irish?'

'He's American, and a recluse. I think we can rule him out.'

'Will this man make good on his threat?' O'Dwyer cut in, his tone communicating the urgency of the question.

'We have to assume he will,' Jessie said. 'I wish I could deliver better news, but this is a crime that has been planned and executed flawlessly. No ransom has been sought. Until we know otherwise, we have to work on the premise that a predator has taken your daughter and is working to some personal pathology.'

'I don't know what that means,' the older man said.

'It means that if we find her, he'll let her go, as promised. If we don't, he will almost certainly take her life.'

'We're *going* to find her, sir,' Seamus said.

'We're going to do our very best,' the commissioner corrected, throwing the detective a stern look.

'Well, call me if there's anything else I can do,' Jessie said, pushing back her chair.

'There is,' the commissioner replied.

'Okay,' Jessie said. 'I'm listening.'

'My office was contacted by a confidential informant yesterday morning, claiming to have intelligence on the abductor.'

'Well, that's wonderful!' O'Dwyer said. 'Who is this person, and can we go and talk to them immediately?'

'He says he won't talk to you,' Dawn said. 'Nor will he talk to me.'

'Who will he do business with then?' Seamus asked wryly.

'The only person with whom he will share what he knows is Jessie.'

Jessie blinked, taken aback. 'But up until this morning, no one even knew I was in the country.'

'I'm as puzzled as you are,' Dawn said. 'This informant is the reason why I came looking for you, and why I couldn't take no for an answer.'

'Who is it?' Jessie asked.

'You're not going to be happy.' The commissioner looked about the small group, a grim expression on her face. 'None of you are going to be happy.'

'Who is our secret conspirator, Commissioner Wilson?' O'Dwyer pressed.

'His name is Frederick Morgan,' Dawn said.

'Then my daughter is as good as dead,' Dominic O'Dwyer said, the words heavy with emotion.

Penelope O'Dwyer

Penny loved her parents. Her mother had been a beautiful and accomplished woman who did a lot of charity work and made sure her daughter understood that the image you presented to the world was as important as the reality behind that image. Penny understood that this was not lying but a way of protecting yourself. Your inner truth didn't have to be public property, even when the man whom you called Dad was a household name.

And that was important, because Penny grew up in a world where everyone knew who she was because of her father. Due to his prominence, she never knew who her friends really were, which made relationships difficult. Some of the girls in her school seemed to fawn over her, others kept her at arm's length, while still others bullied her mercilessly.

Penny learned to keep the part of herself that was vulnerable buried deep within her centre. If she did that, no one could hurt her.

Finally, she decided to ignore the social aspect of school and instead focus on her classes. Economics was never her favourite subject, yet in spite of finding it dry and not terribly exciting, money somehow made sense to her. Penny understood it, could predict its movements and the subtleties of its behaviour. Money to her was a living, breathing, thinking creature, and when she allowed herself to pause long enough to truly get to know it, she grew to love it.

Because Penny O'Dwyer grasped a profound and compelling truth: money was power.

And that caused her to think about the nature of power itself.

Penny's father was a politician, and a successful one at that. He had, on two occasions, been Minister for Finance, and you could be forgiven for thinking that meant he was the person who ultimately controlled the ebb and flow of capital in Ireland. By the time he was Taoiseach, she was convinced he virtually ran Ireland.

Penny grew up believing her father's job allowed him to do good things. To make the world a better place. This was something she thought she might like to do too, and asked if she could go to work with him one day, confessing she was considering her career options and wondering if politics might be the path for her.

Beaming with pride, Dominic O'Dwyer brought her to Leinster House with him, and to her dismay she saw that, in fact, her dad was nothing more than a mouthpiece for an army of men in suits who instructed him on what to think and, most importantly, what to say. As party leader he did not even really get to express his opinion, as every single member of the house and all the ministers were always surrounded by a throng of drab-clothed, nondescript advisors, all with their own agendas.

Penny returned to the Irish houses of government with her dad several times, and it was on her fourth visit that she discovered what it was she was seeking: she learned who the person was who really called the shots.

She never found out his name, but forever after, she thought of him as The Chief Advisor.

When she looked back on it later, she couldn't work out what it was about him that told her he was different. He was older, certainly – not as old as her dad but perhaps not far off. Maybe it was the way he carried himself – the other advisors and assistants always looked as if they were trying to blend into the background, like they desperately did not want to be identified as important. This man, on the other hand, walked upright and erect, and when he spoke even the most vociferous of the suits shut up and listened.

He had been at a meeting with her father. During these events, Penny was usually asked to go to the Dáil cafeteria. On this occasion, however, she hung back in the corridor outside her dad's office and waited.

When the meeting was over, the man came out and strode down the corridor towards the Dáil bar. She followed.

He was ordering a glass of beer when she caught up.

'Can I ask you a question?' she said, trying to catch her breath.

The man turned his gaze on her. He was not terribly tall, perhaps five foot nine or ten, and though he was slender, he looked strong. His hair was dark and streaked with white, almost as if the paler tones had been purposely applied. His suit was of a plain blue, but Penny could tell it had been expertly tailored and would not have been bought cheaply.

'You can ask me whatever you like,' he said. 'But if I answer, you must keep whatever I say to yourself. It cannot find its way to your father. Do we have a deal?'

Penny was shocked at this response but also more than a little thrilled by it.

'I want to make a difference,' she said.

He nodded, sipping the golden beverage in his glass. Penny noted he had not ordered a pint. Somehow, his restraint made him seem more sophisticated. More controlled.

'That's a fine ambition to have,' he said.

'I mean a real *difference though,' she said. 'Not like him.'*

She gestured with her head towards a junior minister who was laughing raucously at his own joke on the other side of the room.

'Like your father then?' the man asked.

She knew it was a test.

'No. I want to have influence. I want to be the one who decides what should happen. So I can help people.'

'The most influential people are the ones who advise,' the man said. 'If you speak with wisdom and authority, others may listen and heed you. But then, they may not. Never underestimate the stupidity of those around you, Penelope O'Dwyer.'

'You think I should be an advisor then? Like you?'

He smiled, and in that moment, she thought he may have been the most attractive man she had ever seen. She was only sixteen, and he was probably in his late forties, but just then she experienced the first real surge of sexual lust she had ever known.

'This is only a small part of what I do,' the man said. 'And I would not suggest you be one of the sheep who devotes their lives to politics. It is a futile exercise, if ever there was one.'

'What should I do then?'

'The people who truly control the world are the businessmen,' he said. 'Bankers. Corporations. Entrepreneurs. Your father and his ilk are in complete thrall to them. Make yourself an advisor to those who ply their trade in the business world and you'll truly have the power to change the world.'

'Thank you,' she said.

He nodded and turned back to the bar. 'Remember, your father need not know we had this conversation. I doubt he would approve.'

He turned his gaze on her then, for the final time. 'And you gave me your word.'

She never did tell her dad about what she had learned in the Dáil bar that day.

And she never saw that man again.

Though she thought of him often.

CHAPTER FOUR

Ireland's Central Mental Hospital was based in Dundrum, a suburb just south of Dublin City. It had been in operation since 1850 and was the first secure psychiatric facility in Europe, catering to patients referred either by the courts or the prison system.

The hospital building itself, while considered a forward-thinking and benevolent institution, appeared at first glance to be every inch a Victorian asylum. Jessie had to admit, as she piloted a rental car up the long driveway, that she found the place architecturally and historically fascinating. But she wasn't there to sightsee.

As soon as the meeting with Dominic O'Dwyer had finished, she'd made her way directly here, to talk to the man who claimed to have information on Penelope O'Dwyer's abduction.

Containing ninety-four beds, the hospital treated patients in low-, medium- and high-security conditions. While not meant as a long-term residency, there were a number of patients who have called the Central Mental Hospital home for many years.

And it was one of these that Jessie had come to see.

Frederick Morgan was one of Ireland's most high-profile and infamous psychiatric patients. A merchant banker by profession, in 1984, the year he was committed, he'd been engaged to the daughter of the country's attorney general and a close friend of various serving politicians. A well-known society figure and a regular fixture of the gossip columns, Morgan had been considered charming and debonair – a man destined for greatness.

Yet something was not quite right. Reports in the Irish newspapers would later claim there had been rumours for some time about his violent temper and unprovoked rages. An office worker in his employ stated he had threatened to murder her when she had incorrectly filed a report, and his fiancée had hinted at dark sexual appetites.

Whatever the truth of these assertions, what was certain was that on the evening of 3 August 1984, Frederick Morgan had gone on a killing spree.

While driving through County Wicklow, he had picked up a German hitchhiker and brought her to a wooded area in the Glen of the Downs where he'd raped and strangled her, leaving her body barely concealed in a shallow grave.

He'd then booked into a hotel in the small town of Arklow, where at about 3 a.m. – the hotel did not have CCTV, so this was a rough estimate – Morgan had used a paperclip to pick the lock of the room next door to his, where a middle-aged couple were sleeping, and stabbed them both to death with a butcher's knife. The attack was so quick and so vicious, neither of the two victims even had time to scream.

Naked, and bathed in blood, Morgan had proceeded to the next room along the corridor. This time, he had not felt the need for subtlety and simply kicked the door in. The noise roused the man who was sleeping inside, a retired fireman. He'd managed to keep Morgan at bay using a chair and sustained only superficial injuries before the night porter arrived on the scene and subdued the by now completely deranged banker by hitting him over the head with a fire extinguisher.

The former fireman had tied Morgan's hands and feet using torn-up bedsheets, and the police had been called.

It seemed that something in Frederick Morgan had snapped, yet other guests at the hotel noted the man had eaten his dinner in the restaurant that evening and had a couple of brandies at the bar as if everything was completely normal, despite the fact he had killed and was planning on killing again.

The psychiatrists at the Central Mental Hospital, after much testing and months of interviews and observation, had diagnosed Morgan as having an antisocial personality disorder and pronounced narcissistic traits.

He was, in layman's terms, a sociopath.

Morgan was, despite now being seventy-nine years old, a completely lethal and deeply disturbed individual. And, somehow, he believed he had information about an abduction that had occurred 350 kilometres away while he was incarcerated in a secure mental hospital. And the only person he would share this knowledge with was a behaviourist he shouldn't have known was even in Ireland.

Jessie begrudgingly conceded that Dawn Wilson had been right to track her down. Morgan may have simply been toying with them, but the stakes were too high to risk it.

Once she was buzzed in, passed through a metal detector and had been sniffed by a German shepherd trained to detect both drugs and explosives, a barrel-chested male nurse showed Jessie to the office of Dr Benjamin Kealy, the CMH's chief psychiatrist. As they made their way down one long corridor after another, Jessie was surprised to find the building in a state of disrepair: paint cracked and peeling, windows loose in their frames and some visible patches of black mould in the upper corners of some of the walls.

'We're supposed to be moving to another location next year,' her guide informed her in a voice so deep it positively rumbled. 'They're building us a new hospital complex in Portrane. It'll hold twice as many patients, and we're told there'll be state-of-the-art equipment.'

'Sounds wonderful,' Jessie offered.

'Sounds too bloody good to be true if you ask me,' the nurse growled. 'Dr Kealy is in there. He's expecting you.'

The psychiatrist was a bookish-looking man in his late forties. He peered out at Jessie through thick, plastic-framed glasses and wore an old-fashioned tweed suit. His large office was dominated by an enormous desk made of dark-stained wood.

'Are you familiar with Frederick Morgan's case?' he asked her when they were both seated.

'Yes. I've actually met him before.'

'Really? When was that?'

'I was given permission to interview him for my undergraduate dissertation.'

'That was extremely ambitious, if you don't mind my saying so.'

Jessie shrugged. 'At the time he was the only clinically diagnosed sociopath in the Irish system.'

'How did you find him?'

'He was very charming.'

Kealy smiled. 'He must have liked you.'

'I don't know about that. He didn't say much about his own case that wasn't in the papers. But he did talk a lot about other things.'

'Charming. Well, I'd better show you to the visitor's room. He's been quite calm these past five years, but just in case, there will be security staff present, and he'll be wearing restraints.'

'I appreciate that.'

Kealy stood and led her to the door beyond which a killer waited.

CHAPTER FIVE

Frederick Morgan was sitting in a padded chair with a metal frame, his arms and legs held fast to it by leather straps. Seated, it was impossible to get a sense of his height, although Jessie knew from his file that he was half an inch shy of six feet. Jessie was surprised at how slender he appeared: his waist seemed impossibly narrow, and his shoulders created only the slightest of ledges. He had fine bone structure – despite his age, he remained a handsome man. A full head of white hair was swept back from a domed forehead, his nose straight and well formed.

He's in this room today, trussed up like a basting chicken, because he wants to be, she pondered.

And the thought made her deeply uncomfortable.

Morgan surveyed Jessie and Benjamin Kealy through heavily lidded eyes, and a wry smile played about sensuous lips. He rolled his shoulders, as if loosening the muscles there after strenuous exercise, and said, 'Jessie Boyle. It's wonderful to see you.' His voice was calm, rich and sonorous.

Jessie knew the man spent most of his days separated from the other patients – he was considered too dangerous to mix with the general population – and probably didn't have much opportunity for conversation. Yet his vocal cords showed no signs of lack of use.

Two security guards stood just behind Morgan, literally within arm's reach, so they could bring him down without delay should the situation call for it. Jessie was glad they were there.

The long, high-ceilinged space, at the centre of which sat Morgan's tethered form, smelled of dust and damp. It had once been a ward but looked to Jessie like it hadn't been used in years. A couple of bedframes were stacked on their sides against the bare stone wall at the far end, but other than that, the only furniture was the chair the murderer was shackled to and a seat for Jessie ten feet in front of him. As the small windows that were set at regular intervals close to the ceiling let in very little light, the grim scene was illuminated by a single bare bulb suspended directly above Morgan's head. It cast a glow about his chair but did little to permeate the gloom that shrouded the rest of the area.

Jessie had to admit it was a particularly bleak setting.

'It's good to see you again, Mr Morgan,' she said, remaining just inside the door but maintaining a relaxed eye contact.

'Likewise, my dear. I've been following your career with interest. You've made quite the name for yourself since last we met.'

'I've been lucky. Right place, right time.'

Morgan tutted indulgently.

His gaze drifted to the psychiatrist, and Jessie felt a subtle change in mood, a slight bristling. It was as if the air was suddenly filled with a static charge.

'Dr Kealy, please leave us,' Morgan said, and while the volume of his voice did not change, the words were heavy with aggression. It was chilling to hear, and Jessie was struck by the suddenness of it. 'I can bask in your delightful company any time. I have important information to share with Ms Boyle, and I have no doubt she will give you a detailed account of it before she departs, so you do not need to eavesdrop.'

Kealy held the shackled man's gaze for a moment, apparently unmoved by the ire they had both witnessed.

'I'll wait outside. Security has been informed to subdue him if he so much as blinks out of turn.'

Morgan snorted loudly at this, as if he found the idea that two guards could control him ludicrous.

'Thank you, Doctor,' Jessie said gently.

'For your own safety, remain seated in the chair provided,' Kealy continued, 'and do not approach him, no matter what he says or does to coerce you.'

'I understand.'

The psychiatrist threw the killer a weary look, nodded once at Jessie and strode out the glass-panelled door. As it clicked shut, Morgan turned his gaze full on Jessie. The force of his attention was almost a physical vibration.

With the halo of light around Morgan and the rest of the long room in gloom, it was as if they were alone amid a great emptiness. Jessie had a horrible feeling, just for a moment, of having been lured into a trap and tried to shrug it off and focus on the matter at hand.

'Alone at last,' Morgan purred.

Jessie kept her expression neutral, but inside she was seething.

It was a creature like this who butchered Will. Who took the man I loved from me, she thought. *What the hell am I doing here?*

But as the thought crossed her mind, another entered too – a cooler, calmer voice.

You're here because a woman is in danger and you might be able to do something about it. If Will could talk to you, he'd say he wants you to be here. So shove all the grief and the anger aside, and get this creep to talk.

'I've been told you have information pertaining to a crime,' Jessie said, getting straight to the point.

The doubt and pain she felt was, momentarily at least, gone. She would return to it later, but for now, it was walled off in her unconscious.

'That I do,' Morgan said.

'Do you wish to trade that information for extra privileges?'

'Do you think I would set my price so low? Come now.'

Jessie cocked an eyebrow. 'You want to be discharged?'

'I am an old man, Ms Boyle. I have been a guest of the state much longer than I ever intended to be. I have a niece I do not know who has expressed a desire to get to know me. I want to walk on the beach and visit libraries and museums and eat delectable food with utensils made of something other than flimsy plastic.'

'I can't grant a demand of that size, regardless of what you tell me.'

'I never thought you could. But your old friend, Commissioner Wilson – I expect she wields significant influence.'

'Mr Morgan, the crime you claim to have knowledge of has not been reported in the newspapers.'

'I know.' Morgan winked lasciviously. 'Intriguing, isn't it?'

'Not at all,' Jessie said mildly.

Morgan feigned surprise. 'I hope you're not going to ruin my fun, Ms Boyle.'

'The only way you could have come by such intelligence would be through communication with one of the perpetrators.'

'That would seem probable,' Morgan agreed amiably. 'But how might that have happened?'

'Why don't you tell me and save us all some time?'

'Your people have already explored the large quantity of mail I receive daily. Did they learn anything from it?'

This had, in fact, been done before Jessie was even aware of the case and had yielded not a single clue. Wherever Morgan had come by his information, it wasn't from the letters sent by misguided people seeking a vicarious thrill through communication with a serial killer.

'I'm sure you've considered,' she put to the man sitting opposite her, 'that withholding information that could aid the police in their inquiries makes you an accessory.'

Morgan shook his head and tutted. 'Jessie, you wound me.'

'You're made of sterner stuff than that,' she retorted. 'Do you understand what I'm saying to you, Mr Morgan? Failure to be utterly candid with me today *will* result in loss of privileges. I can make your stay here much less comfortable.'

'Look about you, Ms Boyle. Can it *get* more uncomfortable?'

'No more letters. No more books. No writing material. Need I go on?'

Morgan sighed deeply. 'I'm in a therapeutic environment, Jessie. I don't believe such sanctions are very ethical. What about my rights under the Patients' Charter?'

'Try me, Mr Morgan.'

She could see the cogs turning as the predator considered his position. Seconds passed, and then he smiled and said, the words dripping with sincerity, 'Would I have asked you to come if I didn't intend to share?'

'I'm not going to attempt to guess your motivations.'

Even with his limbs constrained, Frederick Morgan could be enormously expressive. He gave a magnanimous roll of his head, expertly portraying a man shucking off a negative experience.

'Why don't we start again? Will you permit me the opportunity to explain the situation we currently find ourselves in? If you are unhappy with my exposition, by all means walk away and apply whatever sanctions you feel are appropriate.'

Jessie gave a slow nod. 'I'm listening, Mr Morgan.'

And he told her the story of how he came to know the man behind the abduction of Penelope O'Dwyer.

By the time he was finished, Jessie knew he was telling the truth.

And she was certain the missing girl was in even graver peril than she had at first believed.

CHAPTER SIX

'When I first came to the hallowed halls of this bijou residence, I was on my best behaviour,' Morgan began. 'I cooperated with the various therapies. I engaged in group work. I exercised in the grounds. I lay on the couch and I talked about my relationship with my mother. You know the sort of thing.'

Jessie nodded. And waited. He'd get to the point in his own time. If she didn't know better, she would have been convinced he knew the Gardai were on a deadline and was stalling on purpose.

'At first I had a room to myself, but after five years of full compliance, during which time I even did some menial jobs about the place, my medical team thought it would be a good idea to give me a roommate.'

'This would be James O'Leary?'

Morgan made a clicking sound with his tongue – if his hands had been free, he probably would have accompanied it with a thumbs up.

'You've done your homework.'

'In fairness, you've only had one roommate.'

'James was a predator,' Morgan said. 'A good old-fashioned serial killer who, in my humble opinion, would have remained undetected if he hadn't lost control of himself. That can happen, you know. The impulses get too strong. It's how I was caught, after all.'

'If he was a serial killer, he must have murdered at least three people,' Jessie said. 'He was only convicted of one murder.'

'Oh, he killed many, many times.'

'It's unlike you to be so vague.'

'He wasn't sure how many,' Morgan said. 'My estimate would be that he killed upwards of fifteen women.'

'In a country as small as Ireland, I find it very hard to believe such a toll could go undetected. You're one of our most well-known criminal figures, and you only clocked up three before getting caught.'

'James was careful in the victims he chose.'

'In what way?'

'He preyed on the homeless. On prostitutes. On the old woman who lives alone and receives no visitors. People who exist below the radar of society. If you pluck one of those pieces of overripe fruit, Ms Boyle, no one notices.'

'What does any of this have to do with Penelope O'Dwyer, Mr Morgan?'

'Quite a lot, actually.'

'Please get to the point.'

'On St Patrick's Day of 1983, James O'Leary was contacted by a person who, for a time, elevated his predations from the mundane acts they had always been to something more refined.'

'You're saying…'

'Oh, yes. James found himself a mentor. Or perhaps more accurately, the teacher found the student.'

'Please be more specific.'

'James told me that the Devil reached out of the darkness and called to him. My roommate was not inclined to poetry, but he did become florid when he spoke of Balor.'

'Balor?'

'Yes. That's what this person, if person they are, calls themselves.'

'The name has a familiar ring to it.'

'Of course it has. Balor appears in Celtic mythology. He is the leader of the Fomorians, a demonic army eventually defeated by the Tuatha Dé Danann. Balor is a cyclops, whose enormous eye sees all, a talent that gives him and his minions knowledge of everything that goes on in the world, which by logical extension means they can never be surprised or beaten on tactics alone – the only way to fight them is in open confrontation, and the only hope of victory is through sheer force of arms.'

'Charming little story,' Jessie said.

'Quite. Celtic scholars describe Balor as a kind of fire-demon. Some even say he is the Celtic equivalent of Satan.'

'I doubt Beelzebub is bothered with a small farmer from the West of Ireland,' Jessie deadpanned.

'Be that as it may, James believed he was dealing with something that was… other than human.'

'You're telling me James O'Leary thought Satan was speaking to him?'

'That is exactly what I'm telling you, Ms Boyle. And I've asked you here today because Satan has a message for you too.'

CHAPTER SEVEN

Jessie did not try to hide her disbelief. Or her scorn.

'This is a man you met in a psychiatric hospital, Mr Morgan,' she retorted. 'We probably shouldn't take his opinion too much to heart.'

'I should be insulted by that,' Morgan said. 'But allow me to continue with the story. There is much still to tell.'

'All right. I'm listening.'

'In their first conversation, Balor told James he had been watching him and wanted to help him. He said that, if he accepted his guidance, he would turn him into something special. Something beautiful.'

'Did O'Leary know what he meant by that?'

'The only thing that made James O'Leary different to anyone else was killing.'

'The implication being that Balor was going to help him be a better killer.'

'Exactly.'

'What form did this help take?'

'He *taught* him. Instructed him. Showed him how to be better than he was.'

'So this was an apprenticeship?'

'That's a very good description.'

'Tell me more about Balor. What did he look like, what age was he, where did they conduct their affairs…?'

'That's the fascinating part of it all – old James never met him.'

Jessie shook her head. 'I don't follow.'

'Every piece of instruction James received came in the form of letters left where he would find them. He was instructed to dial a number from a particular payphone – never the same number or telephone twice – and Balor would answer. Other times he might be told to be at a certain location and look under a rock or go to a hollow in a tree, and there would be a notebook with details of a victim, information that would have required months of surveillance. He said there was a Bronze Age burial mound ten miles from where he lived that was a regular drop point. He waited there once ten hours ahead of the time he was supposed to arrive to collect a bundle. No one showed. When he went to the cave where the package was to be left for him, there it was.'

'How many victims did he kill with this person?'

'Nine.'

'Was he still hunting with him when he was arrested?'

'Haven't you been listening to me? James O'Leary was arrested in 1990. The last time he heard from Balor was 1989.'

'Why? What happened?'

'He didn't know. The communications just stopped.'

'Out of the blue? No warning, no wind-down?'

'None.'

'Do you have a theory as to why?'

'I think he kept on working, but with a different accomplice.'

Jessie gazed at the sociopath, who was smiling warmly at her from his chair ten feet away.

'And you've come to this conclusion how?'

'It wasn't just me. James thought it too. We made a project of it, you see. Used our library access to research the newspapers. Kept an eye and an ear on TV and radio news broadcasts. Once we knew what we were looking for, it was easy. We soon discovered that Balor had been killing women along the West Coast of Ireland for more than a decade before he reached out to James. And he hasn't stopped. I suspect once you begin investigating the case, you'll find that there has been at least one other apprentice. An individual with access to particular resources or with a skill set Balor needs.'

'Mr Morgan, to be very clear, are you telling me…?'

'Penelope O'Dwyer has been taken by Balor's latest protégé.'

Jessie narrowed her eyes. 'How could you possibly know that?'

'We are a community, Ms Boyle. We… special people.'

'You're not making sense. The community you're a member of is locked up twenty-four-seven.'

'You see me in very narrow terms, Jessie.'

'I'm supposed to take this story on face value? You've ensured I can't question James O'Leary about any of it. You drowned him in the toilet.'

'After the flow of verbal excrement I'd endured for three years, it seemed a rather apt retort.'

'I'm starting to know how you felt. My patience is running thin.'

The manacled man sighed. 'Very well. I'll show you my hand – some of it anyway. Balor didn't reach out himself, but he got a message to me through another. Someone you've worked with recently, in fact.'

Jessie felt cold fingers creep up her spine. 'What are you talking about?'

'Uruz says hello.' Frederick Morgan grinned.

And then he began to laugh.

He was still laughing when the guards took him away.

PART TWO

The Writing on the Stone

'I robbed them, and I killed them as cold as ice, and I would do it again. And I know I would kill another person because I've hated humans for a long time.'

Aileen Wuornos

CHAPTER EIGHT

Three hours later

'Explain it to me again,' Seamus Keneally said, staring at Jessie across the table in the food court in the Stephen's Green Shopping Centre.

It was just after three, and the place was thronged with people rushing to eat, shop, meet friends or just grab five minutes over a sandwich with a book or their favourite podcast. Jessie and Seamus had managed to get a table by the window, and the young detective was gazing with warm affection at a baguette filled with shreds of beef, jalapeños, fried onions and some kind of green sauce that smelled as if it would corrode metal. Jessie's appetite had vanished since her meeting with Frederick Morgan, so she was nursing a black coffee that was now virtually cold.

Her companion had no such digestive complaints and applied himself to his lunch with gusto.

Seamus Keneally was tall, a couple of inches over six feet, and had the slim, wiry build of an athlete. His auburn hair was worn short – Jessie reckoned he got what her mother would have called a crew cut every couple of months and didn't think about it in between. Tufts were sticking up here and there, and she guessed his daily grooming regimen probably involved running his fingers through the mop each morning after his shower. Up close, she could also discern that his suit looked like it could do with being pressed, and his shirt was obviously unironed. The young detective's expressive eyes showed a keen intelligence though, and he had one of those faces where every thought and emotion was displayed in a pantomime of vivid expression.

Seamus Keneally would make a terrible poker player.

'One of the hospital cleaners had been smuggling notes to Morgan,' Jessie told him as he used a plastic fork to make sure the meat and peppers were evenly dispersed across the length of the bread roll. 'When Dr Kealy had his room searched, we also found a burner phone wedged into a hole in his mattress. The phone contained no records of calls so Morgan must have deleted them each time he used it, and they haven't been able to locate a SIM card as yet. I don't expect they will either. It'll be long gone. Morgan just wanted us to know he had it.'

'The notes were all from this Uruz character? You know, I hate calling him that. It seems very feckin' pretentious, if you don't mind my saying.'

Seamus took an enormous bite of his sandwich. Jessie mused that if she had been eating it, she would have got most of the filling down her front. The detective, in a display of almost superhuman dexterity, spilled not so much as a drop of sauce, and, nodding in appreciation, put the colossus back on his plate without misadventure.

'I know what you mean about the name, but we don't have anything else to call him just now, so it'll have to do,' Jessie said. 'Only one note was found in Morgan's room. I don't think we can doubt there were others, probably many of them, but he destroyed the lot.'

'Any signs of ashes, scraps of paper, that sort of thing?'

'In all likelihood he ate them. Morgan is no fool. There won't be any evidence.'

Seamus nodded and took a slug from a bottle of water.

'You and Uruz have had dealings in the past?'

Jessie felt herself stiffen but pushed the feeling aside.

'Yes. During my last case with the London Met. He… he got away. Obviously.'

Seamus nodded, shrugged. 'Sure, you can't catch them all.'

'That does not offer me much comfort.'

'Don't s'pose it does. The note made reference to Penelope O'Dwyer?'

'Yes. Directly. We'll have a copy this afternoon: forensics has it now, but it'll be clean. In short, it says that Balor has taken another apprentice, and that Penelope will be the first of many. It refers to the women as "female beasts to be culled".'

'That phrase mean anything to you?'

'No. Just the usual misogynistic bullshit I've come to expect.'

'Might be a reference to something – you never know with these boyos.'

'We'll check it, don't worry.'

Seamus picked up his baguette again. It looked like it should require two hands, but he seemed quite capable of managing it with one.

'You said no one knew you were in Ireland,' he said, screwing up his eyes as if he was considering the implications.

'It seems I was wrong.'

'Uruz clearly wants you involved in this case. I mean, he instructed Morgan to ask for you, didn't he?'

'Yes, he did.'

'That probably isn't a good thing.'

Jessie sighed and picked up her coffee, but even the smell of it turned her stomach, and she set it aside.

'What this all hints at is a network of killers,' she said. 'Uruz seems to have had contact with Balor *and* Morgan, and Morgan, who was aware of Balor's existence through James O'Leary, had probably already reached out to him long before Penelope O'Dwyer was taken.'

'Do you reckon so?'

'I do. Which makes me wonder if the three of them are in communication with others.'

'You're painting a picture of an international support group for psychos?'

'Doesn't bear thinking about, does it?'

'Seems a bit over the top,' Seamus said. 'Isn't it more likely we're dealing with some kind of fantasy Morgan has cooked up since he's been locked away?'

'That's possible too, of course.'

'And you're saying Morgan is certain this Balor lad has been coordinating the kidnap and maybe the murder of women in the West of Ireland since the 1970s?'

'He's convinced of it, yes.'

'And you believe him?'

'Before I left the Central Mental Hospital, he gave me a list of twenty-eight women he says Balor has taken.'

'Doesn't mean they're all real people. I could think of twenty-eight names off the top of my head if I had to.'

'I've only started to go through them, but from what I can tell, they're all genuine. The earliest, Melissa Murphy, dates back to 1978. She was twenty-two years old when she disappeared on her way home from her job in the supermarket in Douglas, in Cork.'

'I know where Douglas is.'

The detective took another enormous bite. This time a glob of sauce escaped the end of the sandwich and hung ominously, looking as if it were about to ooze onto his tie. Unmoved by the threat, the young man, in an easy, unhurried motion, tilted the bread and its contents to just the correct angle. The sauce seeped back from whence it came, and the threat was nullified. Jessie was impressed, despite herself.

'Okay, so these women are missing,' the detective continued, oblivious to his new colleague's inner monologue. 'But just because they're not around doesn't mean anyone killed them. Ireland was not a good place to be a woman in the 1970s. Or '80s, for that matter.'

'Seamus, for a good part of the 1990s, it was pretty shit too.'

'I was born in 1990, and I'm sorry to say I didn't pay a lot of attention to the feminist struggle during my early childhood.'

Jessie decided to ignore the fact that she was technically old enough to be Seamus's mother.

'You're making my point for me though,' the young man went on. 'These women could have been running away from unwanted pregnancies, abusive husbands, parents who wanted to marry them off to the seventy-year-old farmer down the road – there's dozens of sensible reasons for them to head for greener pastures without telling anyone.'

'Morgan doesn't have any reason to lie to us though.'

'He's a deranged sociopath. Does he need a reason?'

'He doesn't work like that. Frederick Morgan is a classic narcissist. It would devastate him if we proved him wrong.'

'Not if he set out to lead us on a wild goose chase. He could well be messing with us, Jessie.'

Jessie shook her head. 'Not this time. Morgan wants out. He's going to drip-feed us information in the hope that, by cooperating, the commissioner will arrange an early release.'

'That'll never happen,' Seamus spluttered around a mouthful of meat and peppers.

'The life of the daughter of a former leader of our nation is on the line,' Jessie said. 'Strings could be pulled by people we aren't even aware of in back rooms we never knew existed. I reckon all bets might be off on this one.'

Seamus put the remnants of his lunch back on his plate, looking deeply annoyed. 'That is enough to put a man off his food, so it is.'

Jessie guffawed. 'Seamus, what you've eaten in the past twenty minutes would keep a small village going for a month!'

The detective looked offended. 'I get low blood sugar,' he said stiffly. 'My mother says I get awfully contrary if I let myself get hungry, and believe me, Jessie Boyle, you don't want that!'

'I'm sure I don't. Come on, let's get back to HQ. Uniform are picking up the cleaner who was passing notes to Morgan, and you can help me encourage him to reflect on his life choices.'

'Right you are.'

'I'd also very much like to be able to track down Penelope well before the time we've been given on our own merits,' Jessie said. 'I *really* don't want to give Morgan the satisfaction of being able to say he helped us.'

'I'm right with you on that,' Seamus said.

She had gone a few yards through the crowd when she realized he wasn't following. Looking back, Jessie saw Seamus was busily wrapping up the last wedge of the sandwich.

'For the three o'clock slump,' he said, jogging to catch her up.

'I thought you'd lost your appetite!'

'Interviewing accomplices always makes me hungry,' he said, shoving the food in his pocket.

'Good to know,' Jessie said, and they made their way back to Harcourt Street.

Seamus Keneally

He wasn't even supposed to be doing the prisoner transfer that day. That he was there was one of those bizarre accidents of fate.

He still woke up with a start at night, drenched in sweat, the taste of blood and fear in his mouth, his muscles tensed for action. Sometimes he sat in the dark for an hour, going over the events in his head, wondering if there was any way it could have gone differently. More than a year later, and he still couldn't see a chain of events where Goff and the others didn't die.

That he, Seamus, had survived made no sense to him. He could recall every second of those awful few minutes, remember every move he'd made. And what amazed him every time he replayed it in his head was that it had all occurred without conscious thought.

Seamus Keneally had received commendations and a promotion for performing acts of bravery. Yet everything he had done occurred while he was functioning on autopilot. And that didn't seem right.

He'd talked to his mother about it, and she'd told him not to be daft.

'Whisht, a mhic,' she'd said in the native Irish that was always spoken in the Keneally family home. 'Hush, my son. Bravery isn't about not being afraid. It's about being scared out of your wits but doing what has to be done anyway.'

He'd told her he knew she was right.

Although he still struggled to believe it.

And in the dark hours of the night, the events of that day whirled about his head.

Seamus had been posted to the Pearse Street Station in Dublin's city centre right after graduating from the Garda College in Templemore, and he'd loved working there. It wasn't glamorous and it wasn't fast-paced – the work he did was community policing in its purest form.

He got to know the local shopkeepers. He spent time fostering friendships with the homeless community that orbited around the Pearse railway station. He offered support to the sex workers who plied their trade on the streets in his part of the city. They were initially suspicious of him but soon came to understand he only wanted to keep them safe.

In the year he worked the inner-city beat, he felt more like a social worker than the kind of cop he had always thought he would be, chasing down murderers and crooks. But to his surprise, this role was deeply satisfying.

On the day it happened, he and Cheryl, his partner, were supposed to patrol the shopping area off James Street. There was a market there where a gang of pickpockets had embedded themselves. Seamus knew the gang leaders and had asked his sergeant for the assignment.

'These kids aren't bad,' he had said at the briefing that morning. 'They're not stealing to fence the goods for big money. They're trying to feed themselves.'

Seamus was about to head over to that old part of Dublin when the sarge called him to his office.

'You're wanted in the motor pool. Change of plan.'

The sergeant was an enormous bear of a man with a barrel chest and a thick black moustache.

'I don't follow, boss.'

'The roster's changed, Seamus. Davies was supposed to be helping out with the transfer of a prisoner from Mountjoy to Portlaoise. He's called in sick – again – so you're going to have to step in.'

Seamus was disappointed but knew better than to argue. 'Anything I need to know?'

'All I've been told is that the convict is a member of one of the *Limerick gangs. His sentence was handed down in the Special Criminal Court yesterday, and they had a bugger of a time making the charges stick – witness intimidation, evidence tampering, you name it. This is a bad man, Seamus.'*

'What's our roll?'

'He's being transferred by prison van with a two-car escort. One *from here, one from the Organised Crime Unit. There's not much more to it than that. We're just making a show of force to dissuade any of this villain's cronies from trying anything stupid.'*

It all sounded so easy.

A cop named Goff was driving the car, his hard, round beer gut pressing right into the steering wheel. They arrived at the gate of Mountjoy and parked opposite; the SUV driven by the Organised Crime Unit was already in place. Seamus could see the angular face of the man behind the wheel and waved, receiving a nod in return.

The gates opened and the van pulled out, grey and nondescript, no marking insignia save for the metal grilles across the windows. The SUV dropped in front; Goff manoeuvred their car behind.

'Mind if I put on some music?' Seamus asked.

'Long as you don't have it too loud.'

Seamus fiddled with the radio until he found Raidió na Gaeltachta, an Irish-language station that was playing traditional Irish music – jigs, reels and ballads.

'You like this stuff?' Goff asked, surprised.

'Would you believe me if I told you I play the accordion? I've won *some prizes for it.'*

Goff shook his head but didn't complain, and the next five miles were punctuated by the sound of lively tunes and mournful songs.

The gunmen were waiting for them at the Red Cow Roundabout.

It was a coordinated attack: two motorbikes swooped in out of nowhere while the convoy was parked at one of the many sets of traffic lights at the busy junction. Seamus was lost in the music, beating a rhythm out on the dashboard, when he noticed a change in the texture of the light. It took him a moment to realise that a motorbike carrying two men, their faces obscured by their helmets, had stopped almost on top of the driver's side of the car, casting a shadow over him and Goff.

This didn't seem strange – there were so many vehicles at this patch of road, it was impossible not to get close. There was a car on his left too, close enough to reach out and touch if the window had been rolled down.

The tune, a jig called 'Out on the Ocean', ended and the DJ began to introduce another. Seamus was about to tell Goff that this was one of his favourites, a reel called 'The Mason's Apron'.

He never got to utter the words, however, because as he opened his mouth to speak, the driver's-side window exploded inwards and the barrel of a handgun was thrust through the gap. Seamus thought he heard Goff shout something, then the fabric of the world was ruptured by the sound of the gun detonating, and his companion's head evaporated in an explosion of red.

Terror made his vision fade, as if his mind shut down, just for a second. Then instinct kicked in, and without even knowing he was doing so, he reached behind and released the door. Suddenly he was tumbling backwards, still blinded – Those are bits of Andy Goff in my eyes, *he thought, the words echoing in the empty space of his consciousness,* those are pieces of that good man *– but then he was up, using the sleeve of his jacket to wipe the gobs of gore from his face, and he was running.* What am I doing? *he thought.* Where am I running to? *No answer came, and the part of him that was watching all this unfold shrank back into the shadows and stayed there.*

And something else took over. And he let it.

Time slowed. Seamus rounded the rear of the car, and there, still parked beside the imploded window with its engine idling, was the bike with its two riders. The one that was riding pillion turned, and Seamus saw the handgun and heard a second report, and something punched him on the shoulder with such force he staggered back a step.

He knew he'd been shot, but it was as if he was seeing all this from a distance, and there was no pain, only motion and momentum – he regained his balance and charged.

The gun fired a third time, but this shot went wide and now he was on top of the bike, and he grabbed a wad of material from the shooter's baggy jacket – he would later remember it was a thick hoody, worn over red tracksuit bottoms – and with a roar dragged him off the bike and flung him to the ground.

'Leggo-of-me-I'll-fuckin'-kill-you!' The voice that came from inside the helmet was hysterical with anger and fear, and Seamus sensed rather than saw the gun swinging towards him. Moving faster than he thought possible, he grabbed it by the barrel, which was so hot it burned him, and twisted, and to his surprise it came away in his grasp.

The prone figure squirmed and tried to regain his footing, but Seamus drove his heel hard into the man's groin and heard a satisfying squeal. Looking up, he saw the bike had started to move, and the driver had a gun in his right hand now. Seamus raised the weapon he was holding using a two-handed grip as he'd been taught – the gun seemed to come up so slowly, as if he was moving through water – but the end of the barrel came to rest in the centre of the biker's body mass, and he squeezed off a shot, hitting the man right between the shoulder blades.

Seamus felt the recoil of the gun and was aware of his wounded shoulder screaming in protest. He saw the flash emit from the muzzle, but there was no sound. No sensation. The world had fallen deadly silent.

The bike swerved and tipped onto its side, spilling the wounded rider onto the asphalt right beside the SUV from the Organised Crime Unit, which was stalled across two lanes, the driver's-side window similarly shattered, its driver slumped across the wheel.

The prison van was nowhere to be seen.

Seamus later learned it had made good its escape when the shooting started. The remaining bike gave chase but peeled off and vanished into a sequence of byroads when two police vehicles arrived on the scene as backup, called by the van's driver.

The whole attack had been a pointless waste of life. The prison transport was constructed from armoured steel, its windows of bullet-proof glass. There was no way such an assault was ever going to succeed.

But Seamus Keneally knew none of this at the time.

He was focused on other things.

As soon as he saw the immediate threat had passed, Seamus gingerly checked Goff for a pulse. He knew it was pointless, but he had to try. Ignoring the gaping hole in the older man's head, he pressed his fingers against the carotid artery.

There was not so much as a trace of a rhythm.

He sat for a moment, not wanting to leave the dead man's side for some reason he could not understand, then shook himself from the torpor and, getting out of the stalled vehicle, handcuffed the man he had pulled from the bike to the car door handle.

The driver of the SUV was similarly beyond help, but his passenger, who had been shot in the chest, was conscious, if barely. Seamus put a compression bandage on the wound and maintained pressure on it while he called for backup. The man, who was bleeding profusely and wide-eyed with fear, drifted in and out of awareness, but Seamus talked to him anyway. Later, he would not be able to remember what he had said.

When an ambulance pulled up to the roundabout fifteen minutes later, Seamus refused to leave the dying man's side. He could not be persuaded until his sarge arrived on the scene.

'You've done all you can, lad,' the sergeant said, taking Seamus gently by the arm. 'Let them tend to you now.'

Seamus Keneally looked at his commanding officer and began to sob.

He refused the commendation when it came, and it was only when he was informed it would remain on his record anyway that he begrudgingly accepted.

As far as Seamus was concerned, he had done nothing to warrant such praise.

Regardless of what his mother said.

CHAPTER NINE

The NBCI took up an entire floor at police HQ, and the bulk of the work was carried out in two long squad rooms that were divided into cubicles and workstations, much of the vacant floor space clogged up by boxes of files and bundles of paperwork. The familiar buzz of muted conversations, phones going off and printers whirring created a pleasant backwash of sound that Jessie found soothing. It was a busy, chaotic space, and she felt right at home, despite herself. It didn't matter what part of the world you were in, she mused: police stations were police stations.

Dawn Wilson was sitting in the main workroom of the National Bureau of Criminal Investigation when they got back, talking to a tiny, freckled girl whose shoulder-length hair was dyed a violent shade of electric blue.

'Jessie, Seamus, I'd like you to meet Terri Kehoe,' Dawn said. 'She's going to be working with you on the O'Dwyer abduction.'

The girl she referred to looked as if she was about to pass out from nervous anxiety. Jessie extended her hand, and for a moment it seemed as if Terri was going to leave her hanging, waiting three uncomfortable beats before gingerly accepting the gesture and returning a half-hearted shake. Seamus didn't give her the chance to delay and simply grabbed her small hand in his much larger one and pumped vigorously.

'Terri is a specialist,' Dawn continued, ignoring the brief moment of discomfort.

'What do you specialise in, Ms Kehoe?' Seamus asked genially.

'I'm… well, I'm a genealogist by profession,' the girl said in a trembling voice. Her accent had similar tones to the young detective's: Jessie reckoned she must be from somewhere to the west of the country too.

'A what now?' Seamus asked, making no effort to hide the confusion he was obviously feeling.

'Terri is an expert in history, Irish ancestral lines and folklore and a bit of a tech wizard,' Dawn said. 'She was instrumental in bringing about the successful conclusion of two cases that would otherwise have remained unsolved in the Sligo/Leitrim region, and looking at the list of names you left in before you and Seamus went to lunch, not to mention the reference to Balor and ancient burial mounds and stone circles and what have you, I thought she would be a useful addition to the team.'

'Have you looked at the twenty-eight names, Terri?' Jessie asked, staring hard at the frightened-looking girl.

'Yes. Yes, I have,' Terri almost whispered.

'What can you do with them that I can't with the standard PULSE database?'

'Um…' Terri said, opening and closing her mouth as if she expected the answer to emerge, although nothing but air seemed to be forthcoming.

'I wouldn't have asked her here if all she could do was punch names into PULSE,' Dawn said, and the sharpness in her voice told Jessie she had aggravated her old friend. 'Terri is linked into countless academic and community-compiled databases, and she is used to approaching problems in ways we're not trained to.'

Jessie shrugged. It all seemed a bit unnecessary, but she wasn't going to refuse the help.

'You have the names then, Ms Kehoe,' she said. 'Let's see what you can do with them.'

'All right,' Terri said meekly.

Jessie turned to the commissioner. 'Can we have a word?'

*

Dawn brought her into the office of the chief superintendent at the end of the corridor. It was a tiny room that had just enough space for a small desk and two chairs.

'What can I do for you?' Dawn asked once they were both seated.

'You keep talking about a team.'

'Yes. You, Seamus and Terri.'

'I said I'd take a look at this, give you my read on what happened. Talk to Morgan.'

'You did for sure.'

'Well, I've done exactly that.'

'I expected no less of you.'

'I'm not sure what else you're expecting though.'

Dawn smiled at her friend. 'You're interviewing the cleaner, aren't you?'

'You know I am. Seamus and I are going to do that this afternoon.'

'Go and do it then. You don't need my permission.'

'Stop pretending to be obtuse, Dawn. What comes after that?'

The commissioner chewed her lower lip and thought for a moment, as if deciding whether or not to show her cards at this stage of the game. Finally, she said, 'I want you to go to Cahirsiveen and see what you can learn on the ground.'

'Why?' Jessie wanted to know. 'Isn't Seamus coordinating things there?'

'He is, but he's a beat cop really. He's good at the procedural stuff, and he knows the people and the geography. He'll be critical when it comes to interviewing suspects, putting the locals at ease. But if this Balor person is real, and we have to assume he is, then I want you at ground zero to pick apart the strands. We have less than a fortnight before that wee girl's time is up. We have to use the time wisely. So far all the work that's been done has yielded nothing. I'm new to this post, Jessie, and I have the minister breathing down my neck. I need your help, and I'm not too proud to admit it.'

Jessie eyed her friend and thought about what was being asked of her. 'And this Terri kid? Is she coming too?'

'Don't underestimate her, Jessie. She doesn't look like much, but I'm tellin' you now, there are people alive today who would be dead if it wasn't for her abilities. Jim Broaders over in Sligo tells me she's a fucking magician when it comes to family records and local history. There is literally nothing she can't find once she's on the scent.'

'She looks as if she's about to burst into tears at any moment. I don't have time to deal with someone who can't cope with pressure. You know as well as I do how tough the work can be.'

'She'll come through. I promise you.'

Jessie sighed deeply and stood up. 'I'll hold you to that,' she said.

She was at the door when she stopped and turned back.

'I owe you, Dawn, but I don't owe you everything there is. I do this, and our debt is paid. Do you hear me?'

'Loud and clear,' the commissioner said.

'All right then,' Jessie said, and left her where she was sitting.

CHAPTER TEN

The cleaner who had smuggled notes to Frederick Morgan in the Central Mental Hospital was a 63-year-old man named Dermot Forrestal. He worked for a company called Hygiene Solutions that were based in Swords, a village to the north of Dublin City, and he had been part of the crew that served the psychiatric facility for fifteen years.

Jessie, seated beside Seamus in Interview Room 3 at police HQ, leafed through the short file on Forrestal. The room was designed to be utilitarian: plain walls that had once been white were now stained and pock-marked from age and the memory of cigarette smoke. A large metal table was bolted to the floor, into the top of which was set an ancient tape cassette recorder that hadn't been used in more than a decade. From the wall, a digital video camera, the current method of recording interviews, gazed down on proceedings with its electric eye.

The cleaner, a diminutive man with a bald pate, his jaw covered in a layer of salt-and-pepper bristles, watched the pair with wide, liquid eyes. He still wore the blue overalls of his trade, the HS insignia of his employer embroidered onto the chest above his heart. The small man sat very still, but the jerky movements of his eyes and the shallow rapidity of his breath told Jessie just how frightened he was.

Jessie was not a cruel person – in fact, she had been drawn to policing by a desire to prevent suffering – but she knew that Forrestal's clear discomfort would make her and Seamus's job easier.

She had been involved in interviews with suspects – hardened criminals or experienced sadists – that had dragged on for hours with little to show for it.

Jessie didn't think this one would take long.

She picked up a remote control from where it sat at her elbow and used it to start the camera.

'This is Jessie Boyle, consultant behaviourist with the National Bureau of Criminal Investigation, and Detective Seamus Keneally, also of the NBCI, interviewing Dermot Forrestal at four fifteen on the afternoon of Friday, the nineteenth of October in Interview Room 3. Let the record show that Mr Forrestal is currently here of his own volition and is helping us with our investigation. Can we get you anything before the interview commences, Mr Forrestal? Water, tea, coffee?'

The little man shook his head. 'No. Thank you.'

'Very well. Let's cut right to the chase, Mr Forrestal. Frederick Morgan alleges that you have, on his behalf, been smuggling notes into the Central Mental Hospital for close to three years. I understand that you have not denied this allegation.'

Forrestal blinked. Swallowed hard.

'I… Yes, I did it.'

He had a small, thin voice. It seemed to be fighting its way out from deep inside him.

'Why?' Seamus asked, his tone betraying none of the friendliness Jessie's had.

Forrestal felt the sting of it, and there was a visible tremor, as if the man's entire body rippled in a wave of fear.

'I can't tell you that.'

'Frederick Morgan is locked up, Mr Forrestal,' Jessie said, her voice gentle, as if she wanted to assure him. 'He can't hurt you. No matter what threats he made or mind games he's played, he can't get to you. We won't let him.'

'I doubt you'll be working in the CMH again anyway,' Seamus said. 'You've mucked that one up for yourself good and proper. The cleaning firm will probably sack you.'

Forrestal looked from Jessie to Seamus and back again.

'Do I need a solicitor?' he asked.

'You haven't been arrested as yet,' Jessie said. 'This is just a conversation.'

'Answer our questions and you can be on your way,' Seamus said.

'But I can't,' he said, his voice rising in pitch; the tone of terror was clearly audible now.

'Can't or won't?' the detective shot back. 'I don't think you want to help us, Mr Forrestal. Did Morgan say he'd pay you? He was… What was he, Jessie? Some kind of banker? I bet he has money stored away somewhere we don't know about. How much did he promise you?'

The cleaner was sitting bolt upright in his chair, sweat beading on his forehead and across the pale dome of his head.

'The thing I have a problem with,' Jessie said mildly, 'is that Dr Kealy tells me you rarely had any contact with Morgan. The patients were always taken to the rec room when you cleaned their rooms, and the bathrooms and the shower block were cleared before your team went in to work. So you had very little opportunity.'

'Did you make it your business to seek him out in your own time, Mr Forrestal?' Seamus interjected. 'Are you one of them lads that's fascinated by murderers and perverts?'

The little man shook his head vigorously, but Jessie ignored him and kept going.

'Here's my guess, and you can tell me if I'm wrong. You generally work days, but according to the roster your employers have provided, you were part of the night cleaning team on three occasions. I know Morgan doesn't sleep much anymore, which isn't unusual for elderly people, so he might have spoken to you as you mopped the corridor outside his room. Was it then he got to you? When you worked the night shift?'

From the sharp intake of breath, Jessie knew she was right.

'Did you bring him the phone too?' Seamus asked.

'I… I had no choice!' he said, and tears were streaming down his face now.

Jessie threw Seamus a rapid glance as if to say, *Okay, we've got him on the ropes – ease back a little.*

'The person… the man… at least, I think it was a man – he told me to do it.'

'Which person, Mr Forrestal?' Jessie asked. 'Did someone approach you?'

'He was on the film!'

'All right, slow down now. You were sent a film? A video?'

'It was on my computer! My wife bought me it for my birthday and… I switched it on one day and the film was just there, playing. He knew my name! He knew where I lived and where my daughter works!'

'What did he look like?' Seamus asked. 'Could you see him?'

'Shadows. He was in shadows. Made of darkness. His voice… it was horrible.'

'Can we see the film, Mr Forrestal? Is it still on your computer?'

'The next day it was gone. Just gone.'

'All right. Just tell us anything you can recall about it.'

'He said he'd kill my wife. That he'd hurt my daughter!'

And then Dermot Forrestal dissolved into uncontrollable sobs, and they knew they wouldn't get any further sense out of him.

CHAPTER ELEVEN

At eight thirty that evening they were back in the same conference room that had started their day, a meeting that seemed to have happened a lifetime ago: Jessie, Seamus Keneally, Dawn Wilson and Dominic O'Dwyer sat in the same seats they had occupied earlier. The latter looked even more exhausted and drawn than he had that morning.

'Where is Ms Kehoe?' the commissioner demanded. 'It would be nice if we could set the ball rolling.'

'Last I saw she was making for the photocopying room, boss,' Seamus said.

'Would you go and get her please, Seamus? I'm not getting any younger.'

As Seamus stood there was a gentle knock on the door, and the errant Terri meekly came inside, carrying a bundle of papers.

'Thanks for taking the time out of your busy schedule to join us, Terri,' Dawn said pointedly. 'I hope we're not keeping you from anything important.'

'I'm sorry,' Terri said, flushing bright red at the remonstration. 'The photocopier got blocked three times. It took me ages to work out how to fix it.'

'Sit down, will you, girl?'

Terri bowed her head and took a chair next to Jessie.

'We've covered a lot of ground today,' Dawn said, 'and I think we've made some progress. I'll begin. Intelligence has been back to us, and they tell me all the individuals Mr O'Dwyer identified as potential threats from the dissident Republican movement have been contacted, and all claim they are not involved. I personally took a call with a commander of the Continuity IRA, and he assures me no move has been sanctioned against either the former Taoiseach or any members of his family, or even his old cabinet members, for that matter.'

'You believe him, boss?' Seamus asked.

'He actually expressed regret,' Dawn said. 'Told me he thought striking at a member of an enemy's family was bad form. Dishonourable.'

'Begging your pardon, boss, but that sounds like shite to me,' Seamus said with passion. 'I've dealt with paramilitaries before, and they'll do what they have to to further the cause. Anyone is fair game.'

'I'm not disagreeing with you, Seamus,' Dawn said, 'and I'm not ruling out the activities of an as-yet-unknown splinter group. We have ears to the ground to see if we can't identify a faction ambitious enough to try something like this.'

'Or skilled enough,' Jessie said. 'We're not talking about sticking a lump of Semtex under a car and rigging it to an alarm clock. The execution of this showed a high level of sophistication.'

'Some of the more aggressive crews have hired in outside operators on occasion,' Seamus said. 'Shooters and contract killers from other parts of the world. Hitmen, basically. Could be one of them.'

Jessie could see the young detective was far more comfortable discussing the crime as a terrorist action than he was a collective of serial killers. It was easier to understand, more straightforward in its rationale.

'That wouldn't explain Morgan's involvement,' she said. 'Frederick Morgan is completely apolitical. He wouldn't lower himself to become an instrument for something as mundane as a group of Republicans.'

Seamus bristled. 'I wouldn't call Republicanism *mundane*. I don't like what the IRA has become in the past twenty years, but—'

'I'm not saying *I* think it's mundane; I'm saying Morgan would see it like that.'

'That's not how it sounded.'

'Well, it's what I meant!'

'Could you two play nicely?' Dawn intervened. 'We're all tired and the day isn't over yet. Jessie, is it possible Morgan might believe he's somehow manipulating a terrorist faction for his own ends? That he's in the driving seat?'

'Maybe, but Morgan isn't a team player.'

'Yet he's carrying messages to you for this Uruz guy?' Dawn said. 'And working with Balor?'

'Not the same thing,' Jessie said. 'It's a subtle distinction, but Frederick Morgan believes he is part of a new breed of human, one that is in the early stages of its evolution. He and people like him, in his reality at least, have achieved a fresh level of consciousness and are privy to truths the rest of us aren't. Which gives them the right to treat we mere mortals as playthings.'

'Morgan told you this?' O'Dwyer asked.

'He spoke about it openly when I interviewed him back in the nineties, and he made reference to it today also, yes. By acting as a messenger for Uruz and allying himself with Balor, he is marking the three of them out as part of the same genus. This new strain of superhuman. By giving me Uruz's message, and pitting me and the NBCI against Balor, he was also acting for himself, as part of that collective.'

'But isn't he supposed to be helping us catch Balor?' Seamus asked, sounding confused.

'No. I believe we are part of a game these three are playing.'

'You're sure the three of them are in this together?' the commissioner asked.

'I am. Morgan, Balor and Uruz have kept in touch using the cleaner, Forrestal, as a messenger service. Balor somehow hacked into his computer and left a video message giving him instructions and threatening his family if he failed to comply.'

'Do the tech boys have Forrestal's hard drive?' Dawn asked.

'They do, but he says the video file vanished the day after he viewed it. I'd guess it was purposely infected by a Trojan virus, something that would make it consume itself within a set amount of time. Tech might find the residue of that, but it won't help us.'

'What orders was he given?'

'A lot of what he said was garbled, because he became so distressed,' Seamus said. 'But it seems he was told to go to a certain part of the Old Dublin City Wall along the quays. There's a portion where archaeologists found a Viking house in 1998.'

'A longhouse, yes,' Terri Kehoe suddenly piped up.

Seamus turned to look at her. 'Is that what it's called?'

She nodded.

'Well, anyway, a patch of the old wall runs by it, just off Eden Quay. It's down an alley, so nice and secluded. The figure in the video told him he would find a loose piece of shale about four feet up, and behind it, a plastic sandwich bag which would contain a note. He was to bring the note to work and leave it under Morgan's pillow when he was cleaning the room.'

'There would be a note left in the same place every two weeks,' Jessie finished. 'Forrestal has been playing messenger boy ever since. Each fortnight for two years and ten months.'

'Is the communication just between Morgan and Balor then?' Dawn wanted to know. 'How does Uruz fit in?'

'I think Balor and Uruz are communicating with one another independently,' Jessie said, 'and probably have been for some time. Which means Balor is the relay between Morgan and Uruz. Balor is the eye of the storm really – everything is spinning around him. From what Morgan told me, he and Balor communicated through Uruz, a serial killer I investigated while I was with the Met. This stopped when Forrestal was co-opted to their service. It meant they could discuss whatever they wished openly.'

'Which leaves us with the question of how Uruz, a predator from the UK, sought out a serial killer we didn't even know existed here in Ireland,' Dawn said.

'The dark web most likely,' Jessie said. 'It's where people with their proclivities gather.'

'You mentioned a game,' O'Dwyer said. 'Please tell me what that means for my daughter.'

'Balor has been working in the shadows for about forty years,' Jessie said. 'If what Morgan told us is true, he is the most successful and prolific serial killer in Irish history. And only a tiny minority know about him.'

'You think he wants recognition?' O'Dwyer asked in horror.

'The women he abducted with his apprentices over the years have all been picked at random,' Jessie said. 'Looking at the list, there is no discernible pattern. They come from the broadest profile of age, appearance, social class, religion and even ethnicity imaginable. There are often huge gaps of time between their abductions, and of the few I looked at, their families could all think of reasons they might have run away. Because of this, Balor has escaped detection completely. But I think he's tired of labouring in the shadows. He wants us to know he's there.'

'He craves battle with a worthy adversary,' O'Dwyer said. 'And it looks as if he has struck you with the gauntlet.'

Jessie didn't respond to that.

'Terri, what did you find on the list of names?' Dawn asked, turning to her.

'Um... yes, I found out a bit actually,' the girl said, passing around her sheafs of paper to everyone.

'The... uh... the first two pages list the names and addresses of the missing women, and the dates they were last seen,' Terri said haltingly. 'As you can see, the disappearances Mr Morgan identified began in 1978, and the timeline brings us right up to two days ago – your daughter's abduction, Mr O'Dwyer. It's a time period of just under forty years. The geographical range goes from as far south as Baltimore, in Cork, to as far north as Belmullet, in County Mayo. If we look at the other axis on the compass, we can see the furthest point west is Dingle, in County Kerry, and the furthest east is Cashel, in Tipperary. This gives us a hunting ground consisting of 273 square miles.'

'That's quite a territory,' Jessie said, almost to herself.

'Jessie… Ms Boyle, that is…'

'Yes?'

'You… um… you said there was no pattern to the women on this list. That their selection was completely random.'

'Yes. It's probably a bit too random, which might be something we can use.'

'No it fucking isn't,' Dawn said. 'And you know it. What are you getting at, Terri?'

'Well, you see, that's the point. The list *isn't* random. There *is* a pattern.'

'No there's not,' Jessie said.

'If you turn to page three in your packs, you'll find a map of the western half of the country, with the abduction sites marked.'

They all found the page. Twenty-eight points had been circled. If there was an internal logic to their placement, Jessie couldn't see it.

'If you turn to page four, you'll see the same locations marked again, but on this page I've also highlighted their proximity to a series of stone circles and burial mounds associated with the Dedad Clan.'

The sites were marked with different-coloured dots and were so close some overlaid the first set.

'Please explain the significance?' O'Dwyer asked.

'The Dedad were a Celtic clan who settled in the West of Ireland approximately four hundred years before the time of Christ. They were an aggressive, warlike people, and expanded their territories as far north as Mayo, possibly even into Sligo, and east as far as Tipperary.'

'I'm seeing a theme developing,' Dawn said.

'Most of the Neolithic traces we have in that part of Ireland come from them – cairns, death mounds, passage tombs, holy sites. All are Dedad remnants.'

'And what does this have to do with the missing women?' Dawn pressed her.

'Every single one of the women on that list lived within a hundred yards of a Dedad site,' Terri said. 'Their homes were in the shadows of a stone circle, a ring fort, a passage grave or a souterrain.'

'You think that's how he's been picking them?' Jessie said, her voice electric with excitement.

'Yes. It's the only thing that makes sense.'

'But Penelope O'Dwyer was taken miles away from where she lived,' Seamus said. 'How does that fit?'

'I… well I thought of that,' Terri replied. 'Mr O'Dwyer, according to your biography on the website of the Department of the Taoiseach, your family home is in Bearna, near Limerick Junction.'

'Yes. The O'Dwyers have farmed there for more than two hundred years.'

'If you turn to page five in your packs, you'll see a map of the O'Dwyer farm,' Terri said. 'I've marked out a field in the top-right quadrant of the map. It contains a series of ring forts and three souterrains. I would go so far as to guess that the site your family have lived on for centuries was once a Dedad settlement.'

'Meaning your daughter fits the victim profile perfectly,' Jessie said.

Terri nodded. 'I'm afraid she does, yes.'

'Are we looking for someone descended from these doodads then?' Seamus asked. 'Is there a register or a database we can check?'

'It's pronounced "daydads",' Terri said. 'You're from Kerry, aren't you?'

'Yes. I grew up right in the centre of Cahirsiveen.'

'I'm from near there too. Sort of. But you see, that means we're *both* descended from the Dedad. They dominated the landscape for almost seven hundred years. Anyone whose family is local has them in their family tree.'

'How can we use this information then?' Dawn asked.

'Whoever did this knows a lot about the Dedad and their history,' Terri said. 'And not just information you can find on Wikipedia. This person has studied them closely.'

'How do you know that?' Jessie asked.

The girl put down her pages and looked at the assembled group. Jessie could see she was beginning to relax, perhaps for the first time since she had arrived in Harcourt Street that afternoon. There was a strength to her voice as she started to speak.

'In 1972, a stone was found buried in a field in Connemara, in County Galway. It was covered in ogham markings, the old runic letters of the Celts. When it was taken to University College Cork, the archaeologists there discovered they couldn't translate it – this was an old dialect, one they hadn't encountered before.'

Every eye in the room was on Terri now.

'It took four years for the writing on that stone to be deciphered, and the full text wasn't published in the journals until 2001. And even then, only in select publications. It told of a line of warriors within the Dedad who became tainted by darkness. Some said a druid who communed with demons bewitched them, others that they were stuck down by a madness brought on by pride and bloodlust. Whatever the reason, a terrible war broke out within the clan. Brother killed brother. Father slew son. Babies were slaughtered where they lay to wipe out the twisted bloodline. A time of great darkness fell over the land.'

'How did it end?' Jessie asked.

'That's the problem,' Terri said. 'The text on the stone is incomplete. The last few lines tell of a fell warrior coming to Ireland from across the sea, Balor of the One Eye, who single-handedly laid waste to entire armies and could only be appeased by the blood of women.'

'Morgan told me Balor was a Celtic version of the Devil,' Jessie said.

'In this story, he's something worse,' Terri said. 'Some believe he was sent to bring about the end of days.'

'But we're still here,' Seamus said. 'So surely the good guys beat him?'

'It would be nice to think so.' Terri smiled sadly. 'Some scholars have tried to complete the story from fragments of other tales. The most widely acknowledged suggests that when the clan leaders realised Balor was unbeatable, they fell back, gathering the wisest among them to try and formulate a plan to depose him. While they did this, the demon established himself as High King. Retiring to a fort somewhere in the Ring of Kerry – the exact location is never named – he drew the fiercest of homicidal warriors to him and nominated the most evil among them as his emissaries.'

'You're saying he attracted prehistoric psychopaths?' Jessie asked, incredulous.

'Those who flocked to him were not ordinary warriors,' Terri said. 'They were all men prone to experiencing *ríastrad*, a ferocious battle frenzy that is said to have warped them physically – they literally turned into monsters when gripped by it and were unable to recognise friend from foe. In these berserker rages, they indulged in the most horrendous and unspeakable violence.'

'So not the nicest of lads then,' Seamus deadpanned.

'Not really, no,' Terri said. 'Because these warriors were so volatile, there could only ever be one in his service at a time. They served him for a number of cycles of the moon and were then released. They say he had three during his reign.'

'It's all sounding remarkably familiar, isn't it?' O'Dwyer said.

'What is perhaps interesting for us is that the old manuscripts refer to these agents of Balor as *printíseach*.'

'Which means?' Dawn asked.

'It's the Irish word for apprentice,' Seamus said.

The room fell silent for a long moment. Terri broke the hush.

'The clans finally appeased Balor by sacrificing one hundred women to him. During the feast, they gave Crom, Balor's current apprentice, ale laced with foxglove root, which caused him to pass into a drugged sleep. Balor, engorged by so much blood, fell into a slumber too and they buried the pair of them alive in a cave beneath Macgillycuddy's Reeks.' Terri was referring to a long mountain range that cut through the Iveragh Peninsula in County Kerry. 'Druids cast spells and enchantments to create an unbreakable seal, one that would hold for the duration of two ages of man.'

'Should still be holding then,' Dawn said.

'The Celts believed an age of man was one thousand years,' Terri said. 'The carbon dating of the stone put it at fourteen hundred years, give or take, making it one of the oldest of its kind. The events it described were said to have occurred in the time of Deda mac Sin, who was King of the Dedad Clan during the first century BC.'

'So the seal has been broken,' Seamus said.

'Theoretically, yes,' Terri agreed.

'Meaning he's come back,' O'Dwyer said, his voice very quiet. 'And he's hungry all over again.'

'You don't actually believe all this, do you?' Jessie asked. 'Demons and druids and monsters and the like?'

'No,' Terri said. 'I don't believe it. But I think *he* does. Which makes him even more dangerous.'

'You said the translation of the writing on the stone wasn't published until 2001,' Jessie said. 'But Balor has been operating since the late seventies.'

'Yes,' Terri said. 'I think the killer is someone who had access to the stone long before the information it held was made public.'

The room fell into silence as they all considered the implication of that statement.

'How many people would have had the opportunity to study the text?' O'Dwyer asked.

'I can't say for certain,' Terri said. 'But probably no more than ten, perhaps twenty academics.'

Jessie looked at Dawn and gave her a nod of resignation.

'Looks like we're going west,' she said.

Detective Chief Inspector
Giles Dunwoody-Taft, late of the
London Metropolitan Police Force

He was just sitting down to his evening glass of port when Jessie Boyle rang, the call coming through on his house phone. His wife, Bessie, answered and he heard her chatting amiably with the young woman both of them thought of as a surrogate niece.

Giles had been Jessie's first commanding officer in the Met, and he'd immediately recognised in her someone with an innate talent for policing coupled with an insight into the darker side of human nature that, in someone on the other side of the criminal divide, might have been terrifying to behold.

She was the only female in the team that year, and while his initial instinct was to go easy on her, Giles soon understood it would make no difference: Jessie Boyle was tougher on herself than he could ever be. She expected nothing less than perfection and drove herself until she came as close as it was possible to get.

She was always the first one into the office – he would arrive at seven thirty to find her already at her desk, files open all around her, several empty coffee cups dotted here and there among the detritus. Similarly, long after everyone else was gone, Jessie would be at her post, sometimes leaving for an hour or so to go to the gym, but always returning.

Back then, he didn't know what drove her. Over the years they worked together he came to learn the pain she carried. But she was guarded, was Jessie Boyle. She didn't trust easily. In the early days of their friendship, Giles felt as if he was trying to tame a skittish wild horse, one that kept bolting every time he came close.

Bessie brought him the phone.

'It's Jessie. She's in Ireland apparently.'

He nodded and took the receiver. 'I hear on the jungle grapevine that you've cut and run,' Giles said. 'Got a better offer back on the ould sod?'

'Hello, Giles,' she said, and he smiled in spite of himself.

When Jessie Boyle loved you, you knew it. He noticed she was unable to hide her emotions from people once she finally opened up to them. She wore her heart on her sleeve, and her affection for her old mentor was evident in every syllable she spoke.

'You might have let me know you were leaving us,' he said. 'I should be hurt.'

'I didn't know I was going until I was at the airport.'

He paused at that.

'I'm sorry about Will, Jess. My heart is broken for you. The best way to treasure his memory, though, is to come back and help them catch the bastard that did for him.'

'Dawn Wilson has asked me to work a case here, Giles. And Uruz might be mixed up in it.'

'Might be?'

'The name has come up. I... I don't know yet. But I'm going to stay and see if I can help.'

Even down the phone line he could sense that stillness that lived in the core of Jessie Boyle. A self-contained field that centred her and helped her work through grief and anger and fear. He had seen her walk into a gunfight just like anyone else might stroll into a supermarket, and many on the force admired her reserve. A part of him, the fatherly part that wanted to take care of her, worried that the cost of maintaining such a balance would prove too great. That it would cause Jessie to emotionally implode one of these days.

'You know where I am if you need help, Jessie. I'm retired, but I still have some influence.'

'I do need something, as it happens.'

'Name it.'

'It's a big ask, Giles.'

'After everything we've been through together, you have a licence for big asks, Jessie Boyle.'

'Will you bring over the MG? I'm driving a tin can of a rental, and it's driving me mad. And… I don't know how long I'm going to be here, Giles. I don't know when I'm coming back.'

Jessie was referring to her orange 1973 MGB GT sports car, the only luxury she allowed herself.

'I can do that.'

'That and my laptop. You still have that set of keys to the apartment, don't you?'

'Of course.'

'If you travel on the ferry via Fishguard I can meet you in Rosslare. I'll leave my rental in the Hertz office there.'

'All right then. I'll come tomorrow.'

'It'll be good to see you.'

He smiled again but sadly, suddenly feeling the loss of her. Knowing, somehow, that she was gone for good this time. That he would be going to Ireland to say goodbye.

'Will you do one thing for me, Jessie?'

'Anything.'

'Be careful, for the love of God. If Uruz really is involved in whatever you're doing over there, then he's tracking you. Which suggests he's coming after you, Jessie.'

'Good,' Jessie Boyle said. 'That's what I'm hoping for.'

PART THREE

Into the West

Eleven days until the eve of Samhain

'We've all got the power to kill in our hands, but most people are afraid to use it. Those who aren't control life itself.'

Richard Ramirez, The Night Stalker

CHAPTER TWELVE

Cahirsiveen was a small town by any definition: according to the 2016 census, it had a population of just 1,041 souls. The River Ferta passed through the town and met the ocean at its marina. As was the case in many Irish towns that evolved organically from Celt to Viking to Norman and onwards, very little urban planning had gone into its construction. A broad throughfare delineated the main street, but eight subsidiaries ran off it to the left and right, opening up into a warren of side streets and alleyways. A bridge crossed the river, leading to a less dense settlement of houses on the other side, and a sports centre that the locals expressed much pride in.

The town sat in the shadow of Bentee Hill, and a short walk up its rolling slopes offered sweeping views of Valentia Island off the Atlantic coast and the town itself. Kerry let you know very quickly that you were in wild country. Many loved this truth, and embraced the feeling of having somehow stepped backwards in time.

Jessie Boyle did not. She found the entire experience deeply unsettling. Cahirsiveen felt different, slower. More thoughtful. It moved through its day with a little more purpose and deliberation than other towns. And it held its secrets close. Jessie sensed this, and she didn't trust it. It was almost as if the town was girding itself, determined not to open itself to her.

But Jessie reminded herself that she could be very determined too.

Driving up Main Street, your satnav would tell you it was called New Street, but the locals never called it anything but Main Street.

Continue past the hair salon and the Spar Express, then take a left down Reenrusheen Road and the route would take you through a housing estate called Woodbrook, beautifully located overlooking the ocean. Just beyond the collection of houses was a building that looked wholly out of place, set in its own grounds atop a low hill with ample space for parking just to the side.

This was The Old Barracks, currently a visitor's centre and museum, but originally built as a station and lodgings for the Royal Irish Constabulary in 1870. With tensions high in the town and a large number of known Fenians abroad, the build had been a hurried one. In the rush – so the story went – the architectural plans were mixed up, and instead of the utilitarian structure meant for the police force in a rural Irish town, Cahirsiveen saw the construction of a building intended for a similar station in Punjab.

The Barracks did look strange: a Disney castle designed for a cartoon set in colonial India, but somehow stuck in the middle of rural Ireland. The locals often referred to the Barracks as 'the Indian Palace' or, less fondly, 'the White Elephant'.

Jessie Boyle looked at the building with thinly veiled distaste as she parked the MG at ten o'clock on a grey Saturday morning and sat for a moment surveying the place that was to be her base of operations for the next few weeks. The Barracks – or two rooms of it at least – were a police station again for the first time in a hundred years.

A fact that did not fill Jessie Boyle with much pleasure.

The drive from Rosslare had taken four and three quarter hours, and while half of that journey was on motorways and dual carriageways, the rest involved navigating some of the narrowest and most ill-kept roads Jessie had ever had the misfortune to encounter. She was glad she'd had her old commander, Giles, bring her MG to her. The car made such treacherous driving almost bearable.

She tried not to think of Will during the journey. Learning that Uruz was part of the Penelope O'Dwyer abduction made it harder for her to ignore the nagging sense of emptiness her partner had left, but she forced herself to listen to music as she drove. The alt country and Americana she favoured brought her comfort, and Jeffrey Foucault and Malcolm Holcombe helped keep her thoughts from travelling to dark places.

The last twenty kilometres felt like she had somehow driven through a time portal and entered an Ireland that had not changed much in at least four decades. People she passed on the road – people she had never laid eyes on before – waved at her as she cruised by.

Jessie had read about this rural custom and was aware she was supposed to find it quaint and hospitable. Now that she'd experienced it for herself, she thought it nice but was still surprised every time it happened.

She stopped for fuel in a little shop just on the Kerry border that had one ancient-looking pump outside. When she went in to pay, the old lady behind the counter spoke to her, and Jessie could not understand a single word she said. She smiled, paid the exact amount and got out as fast as she could. Looking back, Jessie had no idea if the oldster was speaking English or Irish.

And that scared her. How was she supposed to coordinate an investigation if she couldn't communicate with the people she was meant to be interviewing?

Jessie had grown up and gone to college in Dublin, and spent her professional life in London, one of the busiest metropolises in the world. Sitting in this lonely car park in a town in the far west of Ireland, the rolling ocean on one side and a hill dotted with ring forts on the other, she had never felt further from home. She just hoped she could get the case wrapped up and get the hell back to Dublin as soon as was humanly possible.

Knowing there was no point in sitting about feeling sorry for herself, Jessie got out and went looking for Seamus and Terri.

It was time to go to work.

CHAPTER THIRTEEN

The rooms that the trio of investigators would be occupying were in the round tower and up a flight of stairs. When Jessie strolled in, Seamus was already sitting with his feet up on a desk, eating a packet of Tayto cheese and onion crisps and staring at a noticeboard upon which Terri was attaching a series of passport-sized photographs – the twenty-eight women on Morgan's list.

The office contained three desks, upon each of which was a laptop computer, an ancient-looking filing cabinet and a large whiteboard, on which someone – you didn't have to be a detective to work out who – had written the words '*Seamus K anseo*' – 'Seamus K is here'.

'I see you've made yourself at home,' Jessie said, grinning at Seamus, who gave her a vigorous wave.

Terri stopped what she was doing, smiled shyly, then returned to her task.

'Welcome to the Kingdom of Kerry,' Seamus said. 'I'd be happy to be working from my homeplace, only for one thing.'

'You'd prefer to be in Dublin too, huh?' Jessie asked hopefully.

'Jesus, no! I feckin' hate Dublin. What I don't understand is why we have to operate out of a tourist office.'

Unhappiness was writ large across Seamus's youthful features.

'I thought I was being promoted when they moved me to the NBCI. This doesn't feel like a step up.'

'There hasn't been a fully manned police station in Cahirsiveen since 2008,' Terri said. 'The building the police work from in the town two days a week is very small – it only has one office, a single holding cell and broadband with virtually no bandwidth.'

'I take it this location is better equipped for your needs,' Jessie said dryly, taking off her coat and tossing it on a desk opposite the one Seamus was lounging behind.

'For *our* needs,' Terri said. 'The University of Limerick uses these rooms as classrooms for Field Archaeology students when they're on research trips to the Reeks. The commissioner arranged for the Department of Justice to rent them for the month we'll be here.'

'This might be where Penelope O'Dwyer went missing,' Jessie said, 'but if Balor's territory goes from Mayo to the southern-most tip of Cork, wouldn't we be better off in one of the denser population centres? A *city* for example? I bet they have really good broadband in Galway or Cork.'

'Feeling a little out of your comfort zone, Jessie?' Seamus asked, crumpling his crisp bag and tossing it into a waste bin on the other side of the room without even looking where he was aiming. 'Not used to being this far from a Starbucks?'

The detective stood and picked up a hurley, a wooden stick with a flared round end, used in the traditional Irish game of hurling.

'What's with the hurl?' Jessie demanded.

'It helps me to think,' Seamus said. 'I used to play with the Garda team. You not a fan of the sport?'

'I can take it or leave it,' Jessie lied. 'I just don't want you smashing our equipment with a poorly aimed tennis ball is all.'

'Hurlers use a ball called a sliotar,' Seamus said, producing one from the drawer of his desk and balancing it on the end of the hurley. 'You've been away from Ireland too long if you forgot that, Jessie. Anyway, our most important job is finding Penelope and getting her back in one piece. Catching Balor comes a close second.'

'Agreed,' Jessie said. 'But I plan on doing both.'

'No argument here,' Seamus said.

'Okay. Does this place have a coffee machine to match its amazing connectivity?'

'It has a kettle and a cafetière,' Terri said. 'I already checked. I picked up some ground coffee on the way here. There's teabags too. I didn't know what you both drink, so I got Lyons and Barry's.'

'And there's sugar and milk in the fridge,' Seamus said. 'But don't touch the chocolate biscuits. They're mine.'

'I'm promising nothing,' Jessie said. 'Right. Let's have a brew and draw up a plan of action.'

Which is just what they did.

Terri Kehoe

She only had one photograph of her mother.

In it, the woman who had donated half of Terri's DNA looked even younger than Terri's current twenty-five years. She had long dark hair framing a narrow, angular face and was in what looked to be an old-fashioned pub. A young man with a mullet sat on one side and a much older woman with a tight perm was on the other. Terri's mother was laughing, which meant her eyes were closed so Terri couldn't make out what colour they were.

Terri's were green, which was unusual. Maybe she got that from her father.

Whoever he was.

She had never met either of her parents and was beginning to wonder if she ever would.

All Terri's childhood memories were of being in care. When she was thirteen, a therapist informed her that her mother had been 'too vulnerable to raise her' and that the decision to place her in the care of the state had been 'an act of great kindness'.

The fact Terri was meeting with this therapist because another child in the residential unit had tried to stab her in a fight over a bar of chocolate added a layer of irony to that final statement the therapist seemed oblivious to.

Terri had spent most of her childhood waiting for her mother to come and get her and, if she was honest, still woke most mornings hoping today would be the day there was a knock on the door and a dark-haired woman of indeterminate eye colour would be standing there, and all the pain and emptiness would be gone.

It hadn't happened yet. But that didn't mean it wouldn't.

When she was six, social services put her in a foster home with a young couple who informed her, within days of her arrival, that if things worked out, they were going to adopt her. Terri was at first terrified at this news: what if her mother decided to come for her only to find she had been replaced? Finally, though, she decided it would be okay – she could always say she'd been put there by social workers and had no choice. Surely her mother would understand.

Once she decided to go with the idea of getting adopted, a flame of hope kindled inside her and the thought she might have a family became all-consuming. Terri did her very best to be good, doing everything they told her. She was polite, tidied up her toys, ate every scrap of food that was offered, even the stuff she didn't like.

They gave her a lovely bedroom with pink wallpaper that had fairies on it. The couple had a dog, a golden retriever called Scamp. Scamp wagged his tail when he saw Terri coming and licked her face with big, friendly laps. She loved him. He was open and transparent in his affection for her, while her prospective adoptive parents always seemed to be holding something back.

Finally, she found out what it was.

One day they told her they were going to the circus, and she got into the car all excited. Except there was no big top waiting for her at their destination. She knew within ten minutes they were returning to the care home. Neither of them would look at her as they walked to the door. Rosie, the manager of the unit, told Terri that it wasn't anything she had done – the mother didn't think she could have a baby of her own, but then suddenly she'd found she was expecting.

So they didn't need Terri anymore.

Terri wondered why they didn't have enough love for two kids. Eventually she decided she must be too hard to love and they'd given up trying.

Maybe that was why her mother had given her away and never come back for her too.

At that moment, Terri decided she didn't like the world anymore. It was too hard; there was too much unhappiness.

She needed to find somewhere to hide. Somewhere less painful.

She found that place in the past.

It was the teacher who came to the unit who encouraged Terri to fall in love with history.

'If we want to know where we're going, we have to understand where we've been,' he used to say. Terri didn't have a clue where she was going; in fact, she had always assumed she'd remain right there in the residential care unit for the rest of her life. Her teacher asked her to imagine there might one day be a life outside it. And she liked that idea.

The unit was on the Clare–Kerry border, and she became fascinated by the stories of a mythical figure who had, according to the old stories, once lived there: Fionn Mac Cumhaill and his band of warriors, the Fianna. Fionn wasn't just a muscle-bound swordsman. He had tasted the Salmon of Knowledge, a fish that imbued whoever ate it with wisdom, so he was smart too. He could think his way out of trouble, and this made a huge impression on Terri.

She was small, and physically weak, and she didn't consider herself very brave. The bigger kids often picked on her, and she'd been knocked down and beaten up more times than she cared to remember. But Fionn's adventures taught her that you didn't have to be the strongest person in the room to win a fight. Just the cleverest.

One of the bigger kids, a girl named Maggie, decided one day that she wanted Terri to swap beds with her – Terri's room was nearer the bathroom than hers, and caught the sun in the evenings, which made it a less grim location to do homework.

'I'll move my stuff in tonight,' Maggie said, glowering at her. 'You can help me.'

Terri blinked up at the freckled face towering over her. 'Okay, no problem,' she responded, knowing that protesting would only result in violence. 'It's a lovely room all right, and you probably won't mind the mice.'

Maggie narrowed her eyes. 'What mice?'

'See that hole over there?'

There was a small round opening in the skirting board beneath the window. Some workmen had created it six months earlier while removing a pipe when the heating was being improved. Terri pointed at the small dark orifice.

'There's a nest of mice in there,' she lied. 'I don't like them, but I'm sure you'll be fine. They sometimes run across the bed at night. Other than that, you probably won't even notice they're there.'

Maggie decided not to swap rooms after all. Terri thought Fionn would be impressed.

Books became an escape from the misery of her surroundings, and as she learned more about the history of this ancient part of Ireland, she saw the world around her in a different way. The layers of human existence were revealed to her.

A walk in the countryside around the unit brought her to Neolithic cairns. A stroll through the fields unearthed Bronze Age passage graves. The hills behind the unit hid mysterious ring forts. Terri Kehoe could step outside her door and escape into the mists of history.

The problem was, she didn't want to return to the present.

There was nothing there for her.

To everyone's surprise, Terri did well enough in her exams to secure a place in University College Galway, where she completed her bachelor's degree in Irish History in less than two years, and went on to secure a master's in Genealogy and Historical Research. When a series of murders occurred in Sligo, which the police believed might be linked to a dispute over land inheritance, her old college professor suggested Jim Broaders, the investigating detective, consult with Terri, who seemed to have an almost instinctive ability to find obscure threads of information amid the dusty records, whether online or in physical libraries. Terri could see trails and make links others struggled to form.

Terri's research brought a long-simmering feud between two factions of a farming family to light, and she was surprised to be commended by the superintendent for her efforts. Obviously, she was pleased to have helped. And she was proud of what she had achieved on that case.

But it was just a diversion from her real mission.

The history Terri was truly committed to researching was her own.

She was still looking for her mother. And despite all her formidable skills, she had so far drawn a blank in her search.

The woman who had brought her into the world seemed to have vanished.

CHAPTER FOURTEEN

The plan was to start at the beginning: Jessie and Seamus would retrace Penelope O'Dwyer's steps on the night she went missing, then reinterview everyone she'd been in contact with on the days leading up to her abduction, in the hope of finding something that had been overlooked. Terri would research the other women on Morgan's list, to see if they had anything else in common other than living near sites of Celtic settlement.

'I think this is a waste of time, if you don't mind my saying,' Seamus stated tersely as he and Jessie grabbed their coats to head down to the car. 'Shouldn't we treat the work already done as a given and use the new information to build on it?'

'This is still fresh for me though, Seamus,' Jessie said. 'For me to do what I do, I have to construct a sense of who the various players are, and Penelope O'Dwyer is all we have just now. I'm hoping that by learning more about her through all these other people, perhaps I can learn about the person who took her as well.'

Seamus paused at the top of the stairs, looking back. 'That makes no sense to me at all.'

'Every victim tells us something about their attacker. The same goes for abductee and abductor.'

'If you say so,' Seamus said as he loped down the stairs.

'Jesus, are you a petrol head?' he stated when he laid eyes on the MG.

'I suppose I am a little bit,' Jessie said. 'I like vintage cars. They all have a character, a spirit of their own. Modern ones all look like they've been built from the same kit.'

'Never thought of it like that,' Seamus said. 'For me a car is something that gets me from point A to point B.'

'Well, that's another issue we differ on then, isn't it?' Jessie retorted as she unlocked the door to her vehicle.

The detective remained silent during the drive to town, but as they parked just off New Street, he asked, 'Do you think Terri will find out anything useful from Morgan's list?'

Jessie considered before answering. 'Every idea, no matter how compelling, is just a theory until it's been confirmed,' she said. 'Which is what Terri is doing right now – attempting to confirm. In the meantime, we treat this like any other abduction, and assume less… um… *cerebral* motives. If it turns out Morgan's story has legs, we'll all go chasing after it.'

'Less cerebral motives?'

'Human, rather than historical or spiritual,' Jessie clarified.

'Money or sex then?' Seamus offered.

'In my experience, it's usually one or the other.'

'Mine too,' the young detective agreed. 'Gives you a pretty grim view of humanity though, doesn't it?'

Jessie shrugged. 'I'm not ruling out the possibility Penelope O'Dwyer is part of a grand scheme being enacted by a serial killer who thinks he's the reincarnation of the pagan version of Beelzebub, but for now, it doesn't help us to focus on that.'

'I hear you.'

'So we work it from the ground up like any other case, and follow whatever clues present as we come across them. Is that okay with you?'

'It is. I just don't think walking back over the ground I've already trod is going to help. I have some lines of inquiry I'd like to follow up, you know. Theories I formed.'

Jessie tried to force irritation from her voice. Dawn had called her in to use her particular set of abilities to bring this case to a conclusion. Seamus had been working it and had got nowhere. She didn't want to point that out, but she had to assert herself as the lead of the investigation.

Deciding to take the gentle approach, she said, 'And I do want to hear them, Seamus, but for now, could you just bear with me and walk me through her movements on the night she was taken?'

Seamus did as she'd asked.

'She had dinner here,' the young detective said as they stopped on Cahirsiveen's main street opposite a restaurant called The Oak House, a small Italian bistro and wine bar. It was close to midday, and through the windows of the establishment they could see staff busying themselves setting the dining room up for lunch. Shoppers bustled past, oblivious to the dark business the two were conducting.

They knew their days of enjoying such anonymity were numbered – Dawn Wilson had told them she couldn't keep the story out of the papers much longer. Once it broke, their job would become vastly more difficult.

'She was meeting a client named Mervyn Moorehouse,' Seamus said.

Jessie checked the notes she kept on her phone. 'He been interviewed?'

'I spoke to him myself.'

'I'd like to do it again, if you don't mind.'

Seamus bristled immediately. 'I don't, but I'd like to know why.'

'It's not an insult, Seamus. I'm sure your questions were thorough and based solidly around the facts: who, when, why…'

'That's how an interview is supposed to be conducted, isn't it?'

'Police are trained to construct sequences of questions so they build a picture,' Jessie said. 'The idea is to see if that picture changes through inconsistencies in the answers received.'

'Jessie, I'm not a rookie. I know my job.'

'I'm not saying you don't. It's just that I'm trained to do it differently. I'm less about the facts and more about things like body language, tone of voice, patterns of speech, recurring words or themes.'

Seamus snorted and shook his head. 'That's all well and good, but it won't stand up in court,' he said. 'I don't know how they do it in London, but over here, you'd better have a watertight case based around times and locations and physical evidence. You tell a judge the defendant is in front of him because they said the same word three times in a row and scratched their arse while they did it… well, that case will be thrown out right feckin' smart.'

Jessie considered telling Seamus she had successfully brought cases to court long before he'd started shaving. But instead she said, 'Let's walk the route she took on the night she vanished.'

'Right you be,' Seamus said, his voice still sharp.

They crossed the road and stood at the door of the restaurant.

'Moorehouse and Penelope came out of the bistro at approximately ten thirty-five on the night of the fifteenth of October. They spoke for a few minutes, finishing up their conversation, then bid each other goodnight. Moorehouse went south towards Quay Street where he had arranged for his wife to collect him, and Penelope walked west towards her hotel, the Kerry Arms.'

'Lead the way,' Jessie said.

Seamus gave a half-hearted shrug and started to walk.

'CCTV camera there,' he said, as they passed a street lamp. 'But it was out of action.'

'Noted,' Jessie said.

'Another one there.' This time above the window of a phone shop.

'Do you have any theories as to where she might have been taken?' Jessie asked.

'We've checked local areas of waste ground, any abandoned buildings, unused holiday lets – anywhere obvious she might be being held.'

'I meant on the street here,' Jessie said.

'I assume she was either pulled into a car or got into one voluntarily,' Seamus said.

They stopped at a spot where a road intersected the main street.

'Somewhere like this,' Jessie agreed. 'She comes to a stop to let a car go past. She's preparing to step off the pavement, so a little off balance. A good place to snatch her.'

They passed two more junctions just like that one.

'And here's the hotel,' Seamus said.

They paused on the street and gazed across at it – a small country establishment with an old-fashioned brick facade. Olde worlde but welcoming. Safe.

'Let's go in and have a chat with the manager,' Jessie said.

'I already did that.'

'I know.'

And they crossed over, Jessie continuing to ignore the obvious annoyance from her new partner.

CHAPTER FIFTEEN

Derek O'Connor, the hotel manager, was a slim, gently spoken man in his fifties whose hair was dyed a shade of chestnut too dark for his complexion. He was dressed in a grey morning suit, a tailcoat over pinstriped trousers, that looked expensively tailored, and Jessie noted his nails were well manicured and his shoes polished to a high sheen. He brought them into a small office that would have been claustrophobic were it not so impeccably tidy and sat looking pained and uncomfortable.

'I told Detective Keneally all I can remember,' he said. 'I don't have anything to add.'

Seamus sighed audibly at this but didn't say anything. If Jessie hadn't known he was a decorated detective with commendations for bravery, she might have thought he was sulking.

'Ms O'Dwyer has stayed with you before?' she asked.

'Yes. She's been coming here three times a year since 2014.'

'Doe she always take the same room?'

'No. Some guests ask for that but most don't mind as long as they get the type of room they requested. Ms O'Dwyer always chose an executive suite, so we gave her whichever one was available when she rang to book.'

'How long does she stay, on average?'

'Two nights usually.'

'Doe she ever have any visitors?'

'Not that I'm aware of. But then we don't usually pay close attention to that kind of thing.'

Jessie checked her notes.

'CCTV footage of the corridor outside Ms O'Dwyer's room was requested,' she said, 'but you stated that the camera on that floor suffered a malfunction and wasn't working.'

'I told the Gardai that immediately. The company who provide our security were scheduled to come and service the system. It was just that one corridor, so I wasn't overly worried.' He paused, looking uncomfortable. 'Clearly, I should have been more concerned.'

'I'm not here to give you a hard time, Mr O'Connor. We're just trying to get a sense of Ms O'Dwyer's movements while she was here. If she met friends or associates other than her clients, it would be good to know.'

'I can ask my staff. Perhaps one of them noticed someone coming or going.'

'That would be good. How did Ms O'Dwyer usually pay?'

'With a credit card.'

'After her stay or in advance?'

'The room fee was paid in advance. Things like drinks and room service were dealt with when she was checking out.'

'Except she didn't check out this time, did she, Mr O'Connor?'

'No. She did not. She was due to leave the hotel the day after she was abducted.'

'What time did she usually check out?'

The manager straightened his jacket and cleared his throat.

'Checkout is eleven o'clock, but Ms O'Dwyer was often… often a little late. Because she was a regular client, we did our best to accommodate her.'

'How late are we talking, Mr O'Connor?'

The manager looked even more uncomfortable and winced at the question. Jessie didn't alter her physical position, and the tone of her voice did not change either, but in her head something clicked into place. This didn't fit – the Penelope O'Dwyer she and her colleagues had so far learned about was by-the-book and regular in her habits. She was not someone who would consistently miss a checkout time. Which meant this was a point worth exploring in more detail.

'I asked you a question, Mr O'Connor.'

The manager cleared his throat and looked at the floor. 'It was not unusual for her to still be in her room at three o'clock in the afternoon. Her father being who he is and Ms O'Dwyer being someone we know, we didn't make an issue out of it.'

'*Why* was she so late leaving, Mr O'Connor?' Jessie asked.

'I wouldn't like to say.'

'I'd like you to though,' Jessie said.

'It's really not my business.'

'Mr O'Connor, we're investigating a kidnapping. A woman's life might be at risk.'

Resignation passed across the manager's eyes like a cloud. 'Ms O'Dwyer was… I apologise… *is* a drinker. She would often have quite a few bottles of white wine delivered to her room.'

Jessie nodded. She had not suspected this piece of intelligence at all – in fact, everything she had so far learned about Penelope O'Dwyer suggested the young woman was conservative in her habits and lived only to work and serve her clients. That she was a private drinker was something Jessie was genuinely surprised to learn. If the abducted woman had managed to successfully hide this side of her character, Jessie wondered, what else might she be hiding?

'Thank you for being candid, Mr O'Connor.'

The manager nodded but now looked even unhappier than before.

'I believe it was you who noticed Ms O'Dwyer was missing?'

'Yes. When she didn't check out by five in the evening, I sent a cleaner to her room. Obviously, she wasn't there, and her bed hadn't been slept in, but her luggage was all present.'

'Did you try calling her?'

'Of course. But I got one of those messages to say the phone was switched off.'

'How did Ms O'Dwyer seem on the evening she disappeared? Did you see her?'

'I spoke to her that night as she was leaving the hotel to meet Mr Moorehouse.'

'She told you she was meeting him?'

'Cahirsiveen is a small town. Even if she hadn't told me, someone would have seen them having dinner and I would have heard about it sooner or later. But it's no big secret he is a client of hers. I don't believe she was breaching confidentiality by telling me.'

'Of course not. So how did she appear when you saw her?'

'I don't know. Normal. Happy. I wished her a pleasant evening and she smiled and said, "You too, Derek."'

'Did you happen to notice anyone unusual hanging about the hotel during Ms O'Dwyer's last stay, or maybe lingering on the street outside?'

'Detective Keneally already asked me that. The answer is still no. I run a hotel, Ms Boyle. People have coffee in the lobby. Drink at the bar. Have lunch and dinner in the restaurant. There are *always* people here, all kinds of people. Who am I to say if they're unusual?'

'We all draw conclusions, Mr O'Connor,' Jessie said, 'despite our better selves. Cast your mind back. Does anyone stand out to you?'

The slim man paused, making a show of considering the question. 'No. Nothing comes to mind.'

Jessie smiled and nodded at Seamus, who stood briskly.

'Thank you for your time, Mr O'Connor. I'd appreciate it if you asked your staff to think about any guests Ms O'Dwyer might have had.'

'I'll be sure to mention it to them,' the manager said.

Jessie took some business cards from the inside pocket of her long grey coat. 'My contact details.'

O'Connor made that grimace – Jessie suddenly realised it was supposed to be a smile – and took the offering gingerly, as if he might catch something.

CHAPTER SIXTEEN

When they were back outside on the street, Seamus paused, looking conflicted.

'Hang on for a minute, will you?'

Jessie, who had walked ahead a few paces, turned to look at him. 'What's up?'

'Will you just stop and talk to me please?'

Jessie went back to where the young man was standing, shuffling from one foot to another.

'Seamus, we're on the clock.'

'For God's sake, Jessie, I know that!'

'I'm aware you're pissed off with me,' she said, quietly but firmly. 'And I'm sorry about it. But I don't have time to tiptoe around your feelings.'

Seamus rubbed his eyes with the heels of his hands before looking at her squarely. 'I asked him if she had any guests too, you know,' he said, lowering his voice so the passers-by, now a steady flow as lunch hour approached, wouldn't overhear them.

'I figured you would have.'

'The camera being out... that's too much of a coincidence, isn't it?'

Jessie shrugged. 'Sometimes fate can be a bitch,' she said. 'But it is suspicious, yes.'

'I *knew* he was lying when he said he didn't know if she had any guests. I didn't miss that, you know.'

'I never thought you did, Seamus. I know you've followed the correct procedures down to the letter.'

He sighed in irritation and kicked at a piece of gum that was cemented to the pavement. 'I probably didn't push him on it the way you did though.'

'I wouldn't say I pushed him.'

'What would you call it then?'

'I let him know I wasn't going to take his first answer as gospel and gave him some time to think about it.'

He looked up at her for a moment, almost shyly. 'You threw him a bone, you mean.'

'Precisely. There's not exactly a code of confidentiality between hotel staff and their guests, but there is an unspoken rule that what goes on in the rooms stays in the rooms. He thinks he's doing the honourable thing, protecting the reputation of a valued customer. By getting him to talk to his team, I offered him a way to save face – this way he doesn't have to break the veil of implied secrecy; it's one of his chambermaids who's doing it. And he's protecting her by being the one to tell us. Everybody wins. What I was doing wasn't about undermining your work. It was about coming at Mr O'Connor in a slightly different way.'

'This is you using behavioural psychology, isn't it?'

'Yes. Everyone has a moral code. Once you can work out what an individual's code is, it helps you to predict what they'll do in a given situation.'

'I never thought of it like that. I was going to come back in a few days and get heavy with him.'

'Hopefully that won't be necessary now. I have a feeling we'll get a call from Mr O'Connor within twenty-four hours.'

'You reckon?'

'I do. And I suspect he sees a lot of what goes on around the town too. He could be a very valuable asset to us going forward, if we treat him with kid gloves.'

Seamus looked at her again for a moment. For longer this time. 'I hadn't picked up on the late checkout. Never thought to ask.'

'You'd have got there,' Jessie said, putting her hand on his shoulder. 'Probably would have pulled him up on it when you went back.'

'You saw it right away though.'

Jessie knew her partner was trying to tell her he was sorry for his earlier annoyance, and in so doing convey that he admired how she'd handled the interview. He was searching for the words to say she had been right to approach O'Connor, even after he had already done so. And he was struggling to admit she had picked up on things he'd missed.

He was just doing a terrible job of communicating it.

Jessie did her best to ease his discomfort.

'There's been something playing on my mind since our first meeting with Penelope O'Dwyer's father,' she said.

'What?'

'Penelope's friends say they aren't aware of any boyfriends. O'Dwyer claims not to know anything about his daughter's love life too. Don't you think that's odd?'

'I'd say most Irish fathers his age would be the same.'

'He's not most Irish fathers though, Seamus. He used to be the Taoiseach. A man like him *would* know – as a politician, his career depended on information-gathering, and the behaviour of his nearest and dearest was as likely to cause a scandal as anything he did himself. Habits like that stay with you.'

'He's not a politician anymore though,' Seamus offered.

'No, but he is on the boards of half a dozen large companies. Add to that the fact that he has Gardai around him all the time, and contacts all over the country from when he was active in politics – believe me, Seamus, he knows everything Penelope gets up to. The only reason he wouldn't want to talk about that aspect of her life – and I think this might apply in a slightly different way to her friends – is because it's something he'd prefer *we* didn't know.'

Seamus pondered that for a moment. 'You're saying she sleeps around? The friends are being protective of her reputation, and her dad is pretending it isn't happening?'

'I'm saying she has a healthy sex life, probably with more than one partner. Not my business to judge, nor yours, Seamus. She's an adult woman, and as long as it's all consensual, well, good for her. But we're going to need to find out who these partners are so we can exclude them from our inquiries.'

'How'd you know she was a drinker?'

'I didn't. O'Connor seemed uncomfortable when I asked him about the checkout times, so I thought it might be worth digging some more.'

Seamus seemed to relax at that. Jessie saw his whole body loosen, and he grinned, his boyish face lighting up.

'Your instincts are pretty good, Jessie Boyle.'

'I've been doing this work a long time.'

As if prompted by some unspoken agreement, they began to walk back to the car.

'Does her being an alcoholic add anything to our case?' Seamus asked after a few moments of silent contemplation. 'Does it help us?'

'I don't know,' Jessie said. 'Gives someone leverage over her maybe?'

'Maybe she made a serious mistake in her work because she was drunk or hungover,' Seamus suggested. 'That would give a client a good reason to be pissed at her.'

'Possibly,' Jessie said. 'Whatever the implication, it's another piece of information we didn't have yesterday.'

'We're on fire, so we are,' Seamus observed.

'I wouldn't go that far, but we're certainly on the right track. Now let's go and talk to Mr Moorehouse.'

'How about lunch first?'

Jessie sighed. 'Get a sandwich and you can eat it in the car after we do this interview.'

'You don't mind me getting crumbs on your upholstery?'

'I've seen you eat. For some bizarre reason, you never drop so much as a crumb. So knock yourself out.'

'Brilliant. Oh, and in advance, I call shotgun!'

'Seamus, there's only two of us. I'm hardly going to ask you to sit in the back, am I?'

'You have to call it. That's the rule. I forgot to say it earlier.'

'Because you were sulking.'

'I was not!'

'Yes you were.'

'I was quietly enjoying the drive.'

'If you say so.'

'I do. Just like I said that I call shotgun. From now on. No comebacks.'

'This is going to be the longest two weeks of my life,' Jessie sighed ruefully.

She wasn't wrong.

CHAPTER SEVENTEEN

Mervyn Moorehouse was a paunchy man in late middle age with thinning dark hair plastered to his head by some kind of oil or gel. Jessie could smell the pomade from right across the room. It wasn't unpleasant, but Moorehouse's greasy complexion and the way his eyes seemed to linger on her made Jessie dislike the aroma by association.

She and Seamus had been brought into a brightly lit lounge by a woman who looked as if she'd stepped from the pages of a fashion magazine. Moorehouse introduced her as his assistant. Jessie wondered what exactly the woman assisted him with, but the question didn't seem relevant, so she kept it to herself.

The room was decorated with a subtle eye – it spoke of opulence and wealth, but without being overly vulgar or ostentatious. Moorehouse – whose skin was an oaken brown obviously from a bottle and who sported a cashmere cardigan about his shoulders, the sleeves knotted across his chest – did not strike Jessie as someone capable of this kind of interior design.

'How can I help you, detectives?' He smiled, displaying teeth so white they could probably be seen from the International Space Station.

'I'm not a detective, Mr Moorehouse,' Jessie said.

The man's tone changed in an instant from snivelling acquiescence to irritated antagonism. 'Why am I talking to you then?'

The shift in mood was so sudden it caught Jessie off guard. Moorehouse was not what she'd expected. There was a swagger and confidence to him that suggested he had influence far beyond the hills and woods of West Kerry.

'Because I am here at the behest of the Police Commissioner of Ireland,' Jessie deadpanned. 'And because you want to help us find Penelope O'Dwyer.'

'I'm pretty busy, so can we wrap this up rapido, yeah?'

Moorehouse's speech lurched between rapid-fire West of Ireland and an American drawl, so the tempo of his sentences sped up and slowed down depending on the persona he was adopting. Just like his shifts in mood, this seemed designed to keep those around him off balance.

Jessie was determined not to fall for the trick.

'You were the last person to see Ms O'Dwyer before she was abducted,' Jessie said. 'I'd like to know how she seemed during your meeting.'

'Who says I was the last person to see her?' Moorehouse retorted. 'Like, how do ye know that?'

'Let's put it another way. You're the last person *we can be certain* interacted with her before her abduction.'

Moorehouse sniffed and adjusted the drape of the sleeves of his superfluous jumper. 'Is it definite she's been kidnapped?'

'The evidence leads us to believe so, yes.'

'What does that mean? Like, what if she's just run off? Broads like her, they do that sort of thing.'

Broads, Jessie thought. *The guy thinks he's in a 1930s gangster movie.*

'She's been taken, Mr Moorehouse,' Seamus said, and there was an edge to his voice Jessie hadn't heard before. The detective remained sitting in exactly the same position as before, and his facial expression was neutral, but suddenly an energy radiated from him that was unmistakable and fierce.

'So you keep saying,' Moorehouse retorted, a little less full of bluster. 'You don't seem certain at all, but you're still here hassling me.'

'Are you refusing to answer our questions, Mr Moorehouse?' Seamus asked, leaning forward now.

'No.' The businessman, in response, sat back, as if trying to avoid the force of the detective's gaze.

'Good,' Seamus said. 'Can we get down to business then, so Ms Boyle and I can get back out and carry on looking for her?'

Moorehouse eyed the detective gingerly. 'All right, amigos,' he said. 'What do you want to know?'

'You have been a client of Bandon, Ludlow and Murphy for how long?' Jessie asked.

'Ten, twelve years, maybe?'

'Which?' Jessie shot back.

'Let's go down the middle and say eleven.'

'And how long has Penelope O'Dwyer been your contact person with that company?'

'Over three years. Since the start of 2015.'

'How did you find her to work with?'

Moorehouse shrugged. 'I liked her. Before she took on my account, I used to deal with Glen Bandon. He was sixty-four, bald as an egg and always wore tweed. Penny was a nice change.'

'I've noticed people seem to call her Penny rather than Penelope,' Jessie said.

'Yeah. That's what she liked to be called.'

'She told you that?'

Moorehouse paused for a moment, thinking, before saying, 'She did. When we met. "Call me Penny," she said. I remember distinctly.'

'What exactly did Ms O'Dwyer do for you?'

'Managed my stock portfolio.'

'What does that involve?'

'Keeping an eye on my investments. Informing me if there are major peaks and troughs in their value. Taking charge of selling and buying if that needs to be done. Looking out for new fiscal opportunities... the usual stuff.'

'How often were the two of you in contact?'

'By phone and email, I'd say twice a month. We met three times a year. Four that first year. I wanted to establish where her skills lay.'

'You didn't trust the judgement of her employers?'

Moorehouse laughed – a loud, almost vulgar guffaw. 'Penny was in her late twenties, but she looked like she was just out of school. I wasn't going to trust her to handle investments worth millions of euro without getting a handle on her abilities.'

'And after your initial meetings, you were satisfied she was up to the task?'

'I was.'

'How did she win you over?'

'Penny was a tough kid. I know I can be an asshole. To be successful in my line of work, you have to be. I like a drink and I can be fuckin' ruthless when it comes to my finances. She took all of that in her stride. Wasn't fazed by it. If I let a roar out of me, she roared back.'

'What exactly is your line of work?' Jessie asked.

'I buy and sell stuff.'

Jessie raised an eyebrow. 'What kind of *stuff*?'

Moorehouse smiled. It wasn't a good look for him. Fat as his jowls were, he still managed to appear cadaverous. 'This and that.'

'I'm going to need you to be more specific, Mr Moorehouse,' Jessie said.

'Why?'

'Because it makes perfect sense that the work Penelope O'Dwyer was engaged in could be linked to her disappearance.'

'If that's so – and I'm not sayin' it ain't – you won't find any bodies buried in my back garden.'

'Where should we look then?' Jessie asked.

Moorehouse considered that for a moment. 'Penny worked with people with their fingers in pies a lot nastier than the ones I occasionally dip mine into. Lads whose business interests are less… well, let's just say less *mainstream*.'

'You're losing me, Mr Moorehouse,' Jessie said. 'Are you suggesting Penelope was involved with dangerous people?'

Moorehouse made a wobbling gesture with his hand: *comme ci comme ça.*

'I don't like to tell tales. That ain't the type of guy I am.'

'Well, you've started now,' Seamus said tersely. 'You might as well finish the feckin' story.'

Moorehouse crossed his legs and gazed at the two investigators, obviously pleased with himself. Jessie knew he thought he had steered their attention away from his own dealings. She decided to let him continue thinking that for the time being.

'Penny didn't just meet me when she came to Cahirsiveen,' the rotund man said. 'And I'm not talking about her… well, her recreational meetings. Y'know what I'm sayin'?'

So Moorehouse knows about Penelope O'Dwyer's dalliances, Jessie thought.

'Were you part of those recreations, Mr Moorehouse?'

Something changed in the man's eyes. There was a flash of fury. It was just there for a moment, but for that instant, Jessie was sure Mervyn Moorehouse wanted to kill her.

'I was not,' he said through clenched teeth.

'Really?'

'Really.'

'According to Bandon, Ludlow and Murphy, you are the only client Ms O'Dwyer has in the area,' Seamus said.

Jessie didn't know whether or not he'd seen that burst of emotion, but she was starting to learn that her partner didn't miss much.

'Let's just say,' Moorehouse said, making a flourish with his hand like a magician reaching the climax of his act, 'that I am the only client for *Bandon, Ludlow and Murphy* in the area. Penny may have been running a side project of her own.'

Jessie looked fixedly at Moorehouse. 'Penelope O'Dwyer had a client she was seeing off the books?'

Moorehouse nodded. 'She had a few, in fact. Ran her own private practice alongside the work she did for Bandon and the boys.'

'Ms O'Dwyer told you this?' Jessie asked.

'That she did. I would not be inclined to break her trust, only for the fact that Penny – my business associate and, dare I say it, friend – is in trouble.'

'How civic-minded of you,' Jessie said.

'Who else did she meet?' Seamus asked.

'Youse didn't hear it from me, all right?'

'We won't mention your name unless we have to,' Jessie said.

'Why would you have to?'

'The court system can be a funny thing,' Jessie said. 'They like to know where information came from, the names of witnesses, precise details of chains of evidence – tedious, I know, but what can I say?'

'The day before she met me, Penny had lunch with Ultain Cloney,' Moorehouse said.

Jessie looked at Seamus. 'Does that name mean anything to you?'

'It does,' her partner said. 'He's a gangster. A very bad man.'

'If you're planning on paying Ultain a visit, be warned,' Moorehouse said jovially. 'He's likely to be far less welcoming than me.'

'And probably less charming too,' Seamus said without a hint of irony.

Moorehouse didn't argue the point.

CHAPTER EIGHTEEN

The rest of that first day in Cahirsiveen and all of the second day involved painful hours of desk work broken by trips out to rein-terview locals who had interacted with Penelope O'Dwyer during the two days before she went missing. While these individuals had all been questioned before, Jessie insisted they be revisited, as she wanted to ensure nothing had been missed.

So she and Seamus met the girl who worked at the local newsagent, where Penelope had bought a copy of the *Financial Times*. They spoke to an acned youth at the local off-licence, where the missing woman had bought a bottle of gin and some limes. They spent an hour with an elderly lady who worked in Chic Lady boutique – Penelope's credit-card receipts showed she had spent €150 there on the day she went missing. The elderly proprietor informed them – throwing uncomfortable looks at Seamus, who was doing his best to outdo her in the discomfort stakes – that Penelope had purchased two sets of lingerie there.

This left them none the wiser, except they now knew Penelope O'Dwyer drank gin as well as wine, and that whoever she was having sex with was being treated to some classy underwear during the event.

Which didn't really help.

The only person on their list who was playing hard to get was Ultain Cloney, the businessman Penelope O'Dwyer had met the day before she was abducted. When Jessie had called, the man who answered the phone had informed her that his employer was in Belfast for a couple of days on business, but that he would be happy to talk to them when he returned. Jessie assured him this was a matter of some urgency, but the assistant only reiterated that Cloney would be back in a couple of days.

Jessie asked for Cloney's mobile phone number, and the man on the other end of the phone obliged, but it rang out each time she called. There wasn't much Jessie could do but wait. And she was nothing if not patient.

If only the clock weren't ticking. They now had ten days.

*

Terri continued trawling through Morgan's list. While they now knew why the women had been picked, Jessie told her that serial killers require access to their victims. History showed predators tended to stalk them, familiarise themselves with their movements, and victims were usually people their killers encountered through work or casual association – passing them in the park every day or eating in the same café.

By the end of day two, Terri had found circumstantial links between three of the women – they had all worked part-time jobs at a famine museum in Cobh, in County Cork, during the summer months when the place would have had lots of visitors. Jessie pointed out that while this was interesting, the periods of employment were years apart: the first of the women to work there had been in 1983, the second in 1994 and third in 2000.

'It's worth following up on,' Jessie told her, 'and I know how deep you've had to dig to find it, but we've still a long way to go.'

Terri knew she was right. But she was just getting warmed up; she sensed she was close to finding the key to the puzzle. She just had to keep looking.

*

The morning of day three was devoted to Jessie and Seamus giving Penelope O'Dwyer's phone records, emails and social media another run-through to see if they might get some hint at her romantic entanglements. Jessie loathed social media, and found the entire process gruelling, but she tried not to show her team the irritation she was feeling. It was labour-intensive, tedious work for all of them, but after three hours it yielded seven names.

'Right, so Penelope had the numbers for these five people in her phone,' Seamus said. He was perched on the edge of his desk, hurley in hand, bouncing the sliotar up and down on the bas without dropping it. Jessie marvelled at the fact that it seemed to be a completely unconscious action. 'Of those five, three are businessmen, two of them pretty high-profile.'

'Probably just business acquaintances,' Jessie said. 'We'll interview them, see what kind of dealings they had with her.'

'Sure thing,' Seamus said, putting down the hurley and turning his laptop so she could see the screen. 'This is interesting though. Penelope was in regular contact with these two *only* on Instagram – she direct messaged them almost daily while she was here.'

'Why wasn't this picked up on before?' Jessie wanted to know. 'Haven't her messages been checked already?'

'She has her Insta set to private,' Terri piped up. 'It could take months for Instagram to unlock it for us.'

'How are we in her account then?'

'I hacked it,' Terri said briskly.

'Oh,' Jessie said. 'Thanks, I think.'

'I know it's an invasion of privacy, but I figured it was to save her life, so was probably for the best.'

'We'll need to go the official route with the company if we want to use it in court, but for now let's just see where it leads us,' Jessie said. 'I don't do social media, so you who are in the know: why would someone only communicate via direct message on Instagram?'

'It leaves less of a trail maybe?' Seamus offered. 'You can delete the messages with one tap of your finger, and it's not like with a phone provider, where they're still kept on file.'

'Not strictly true,' Terri piped up from across the room. 'They can still be retrieved, but it's difficult.'

'Could you do it?' Jessie asked the younger girl.

'If I needed to,' Terri said, her fingers still clattering across the keys as she worked, her eyes never leaving the screen.

'Good to know,' Jessie said. 'The two she only chats with on Instagram – who are they?'

'One of them is a chap who calls himself Alistair Burns,' Seamus replied. 'His entire life is laid out online between his Twitter, Facebook and Instagram accounts: he's forty-two, an accountant, married with one child. He likes cycling and craft beer. And growing beards apparently. He's a hipster cliché, apart from the accountancy.'

'He's from Cahirsiveen?'

'According to Google he lives half a mile outside of town on the Cork side,' Seamus said. 'There's photos of his home and garden all over his Instagram feed.'

'What were he and Penelope talking about?'

'Um… it's a bit racy, Jessie.'

'So she was having an affair with this man?'

'They were sexting, at any rate,' Seamus said, sounding a bit uncomfortable with the subject matter.

'Doesn't mean they met up,' Terri cut in again (Seamus seemed relieved to have the spotlight removed from him for a moment). 'Lots of people have relationships that remain exclusively online these days. It's like… a whole new way of connecting with someone. And if they weren't planning on meeting, Instagram is the perfect medium.'

'I'll keep that in mind,' Jessie said. 'What about the other Insta-relationship?'

'Well, here comes the mystery,' Seamus said, regaining some of his swagger. 'This account belongs to someone who only calls themselves Reek, and the profile picture is a Photoshopped image of one of Macgillycuddy's Reeks, with this fella's face superimposed on it.'

Jessie peered at the photograph. 'Why does he look familiar?'

'It's a still from the TV show *Game of Thrones*. That's the actor Alfie Allen.'

'Who plays a character who is given the name Reek after being tortured unspeakably while being held hostage,' Terri piped up.

'What are we supposed to make of that? I assume it's safe to say Penelope was not having an affair with an American actor.'

'He's English,' Terri interjected.

'You know what I mean,' Jessie sighed.

'Well, there was that quote from the video that was sent to her dad,' Seamus said, 'the one from the fantasy book.'

'"Each grain is a heartbeat closer to the end. When the last one falls, so does my blade,"' Terri said. 'A line from the fantasy author Joseph Jack Stephens.'

'And here we have another fantasy reference,' Jessie mused. '*Game of Thrones* is a bit pedestrian though, isn't it? This Stephens guy is more obscure.'

'I still think it's worth looking into,' Seamus said. 'I don't like coincidence.'

'Me either,' Jessie agreed. 'And what did Penelope and Reek message one another?'

'There are only three exchanges,' Seamus said. 'We have to assume the others were dumped.'

'Are these racy?'

'No. They're all about setting up a meeting.'

'For when?'

'For the night Penelope O'Dwyer disappeared. She was to meet Reek after she finished with Moorehouse.'

'Where?'

'Well, that's also quite interesting,' Seamus said. 'She was to be picked up outside her hotel.'

'Meaning she may well have made that meeting, and we wouldn't know about it,' Jessie said.

'Exactly.'

'Which leaves us with the burning question,' Terri said, her fingers still tapping a staccato rhythm, 'who is Mr Reek?'

CHAPTER NINETEEN

Jessie and Seamus were getting into the MG when they heard someone calling them and looked up to see Derek O'Connor, the manager of the Kerry Arms, jogging towards them up the driveway from the road.

'You were right,' Seamus said. 'He came to us after all.'

'Took longer than I thought though,' Jessie agreed.

'I'm glad I caught you,' O'Connor said, out of breath. 'I've spoken to my staff, and I have some information for you of the kind you requested.'

'You mean which men were visiting Penelope O'Dwyer's room?' Jessie asked.

'Or women,' Seamus said. 'These days, it's everyone for themselves.'

'Well... well, yes. That,' O'Connor said, flustered.

'Sit in and I'll give you a lift back to the hotel,' Jessie said. 'Seamus and I are going into town anyway.'

'Oh. Well thank you very much.'

'I call shotgun!' Seamus barked immediately.

O'Connor looked at him in confusion.

'You have to call it,' the detective said, lifting up the passenger seat so the hotel manager could get in the back.

'You've been chatting with your staff,' Jessie said as she pulled out onto the road for town.

'Yes. I apologise that it took a couple of days. I was waiting for some of the cleaners to come back on shift.'

'And what did you learn from them?'

'Greta, one of our chambermaids, witnessed a gentleman arriving at Ms O'Dwyer's room the first night of her most recent stay with us.'

'I see,' Jessie said. 'And did Greta recognise this gentleman?'

'She did, yes.'

'I assume you came over to divulge the name of this gentleman,' Jessie prompted, 'or you wouldn't have come.'

'It was Joshua Harding,' O'Connor blurted. 'She was visited by Joshua Harding.'

'You know this man?'

'I do. His offices are only a few doors up from the hotel.'

'He runs Harding and Associates,' Seamus said. 'An accountancy firm.'

'Accountancy?' Jessie asked. 'That has a familiar ring to it.'

'Yes,' Seamus said. 'Alistair Burns, that other chap we want to talk to – Joshua Harding is his boss.'

'Makes for a shorter trip I suppose,' Jessie said.

*

Terri had started to collate all the information she could on the missing women.

She began with details like age, hair colour, occupation, sexual orientation, marital status, children, last known location, ethnicity, religion and so on. It took hours to complete her chart, and when it was done, she was tired and had a headache from lack of caffeine.

Gazing up at her completed work, she knew that the answer to the puzzle of what connected these disparate lives was on that patchwork of information before her. The answer always lay in the data – Terri had learned that a long time ago. The evidence wanted to tell her how Balor had come into contact with these tragic people.

She went into the kitchen and made herself a cappuccino, mixing a store-bought sachet with a strong blend of black coffee she brewed in the cafetière. Drink in hand, she wandered back into the office, pulled her chair up so it was right below the whiteboard, sat down and continued working.

She ran a check on all the abducted women's criminal records and affiliations. Seven of them had what could only be described as frivolous offences to their names – speeding fines or parking violations – and one, Belinda Grogan, had been arrested three times for shoplifting. All the others were clean.

So that avenue of inquiry drew a blank too.

It had to be something else.

As Terri sipped her drink, her attention went back to the link she had made to the famine museum in Cork. Three of the women had worked there. It wasn't much, but it was still all she had to go on. Picking up her iPad, Terri googled the museum. The website told her the endeavour was a joint project run by Cork Urban District Council, the Department of Tourism and Heritage and University College Cork.

Is there something in that?

She sat back down at her desk and punched each of the victims' names into Google, first alongside Cork UDC. This was a total loss except for the three names she already had. She repeated the process for the Tourism and Heritage department and got the same result.

Third time lucky, she told herself, and tried UCC.

And this time, she hit paydirt.

Twenty-two of the twenty-eight had direct links to the university – some had worked there briefly, as cleaners or administrators or nurses in the health centre; even more had done evening courses there or had engaged in distance learning; one woman had given a guest lecture on the arts programme. Of the six Terri did not find immediate connections for, five yielded their links to the university after half an hour of digging, and the last girl, she finally learned, worked at a chip shop just across the road from one of the entrances.

Terri had it.

Which meant that Balor was linked to UCC as well. To the university that had excavated the stone that recounted his story.

Terri sat back for a moment. She had a contact in UCC, an archaeologist named Miskella whom she corresponded with occasionally on more obscure points of historical interest. Perhaps he might have some useful information, and if he didn't, he would certainly know someone who would.

Terri picked up her phone and looked up the number for John Miskella, PhD.

CHAPTER TWENTY

Alistair Burns was tall and built like a tennis player. He wore a suit that fitted his lean frame perfectly, and his dark beard was thick, but sculpted into one of those square shapes all the hipsters seemed to favour. When he smiled, his teeth were so white Jessie wondered if they glowed in the dark.

They sat in the accountant's artfully decorated office. Above his desk he had a painting of a golden eagle, its wings scissored upwards as if it were about to go into a death dive.

'Yeah, me and Penny were screwing,' he said as soon as Jessie mentioned the missing woman's Instagram account.

'How long had you and she been having a relationship?'

'About a year. We'd meet up when she was in town. It was casual. Fun. Which was how we both liked it.'

'You're wearing a wedding ring,' Seamus observed.

'It's not against the law to play away from home.' The accountant laughed. 'If it was, you two would be extremely overworked.'

'I was wondering if your wife knows about your casual fun,' Seamus said.

'You think my missus is a kidnapper? That's rich. I mean to say, that's fuckin' *rich*. You should meet her. Five foot nothing in heels and maybe seven stone soaking wet. Penny would have broken her in half if she'd tried to confront her. Jesus – do your homework, guys.'

'Where were you on the night Penny was taken?' Jessie cut in.

'Here. A client is being audited. Diane, my assistant, was here too, and Josh was in the office until well after midnight. You can ask any of them. There's cameras in the file room too, and I was in and out of there a lot. So I think you can cross me off your list of suspects. How d'ya like that, Mulder and Scully?'

'Was Ms O'Dwyer meeting anyone else for... for casual connections?' Jessie asked.

'I don't fuckin' know. Probably. What do I care?'

'Thank you for your time,' Jessie said, and Seamus knew her well enough by now to hear the edge behind her words. *She hates this guy*, he thought.

'Is Mr Harding in the office at the moment?' Jessie asked.

'He's meeting a client over at the Lord Dunsany – a pub right across the road. He uses it quite a bit because he likes a large whiskey about this time. And about that time too. About every fucking time, if you want the truth of it.'

Jessie nodded, stood and they left.

'I still don't know if I like Penny,' Jessie said to Seamus as they left the offices. 'But if I was starting to, knowing she's slept with that asshole kind of lowers her in my estimation.'

'Amen to that,' her partner said.

Penelope O'Dwyer

She grew up knowing she was a politician's daughter.

At its most basic and fundamental, she understood that what she did impacted on her father's standing in the community, so it was important she do well at school and play the right sports for the best local teams and not raise her head above the parapet in a manner that might cause anything other than positive comment.

When he achieved the status of Taoiseach, it seemed to Penny as if she was being handed a life sentence, and as young as she was, she knew instinctively that she was going to have to, symbolically at least, break free. By the time she got to college, she'd been shackled to her father's legacy for far too long, and if she was to take the path she had laid out for herself, considerations of his needs had to be secondary.

A life in politics – Dominic O'Dwyer consistently referred to it as 'public service', which Penny thought was nonsense, because her father never did anything but service his own ego – meant constantly being aware of how one was perceived. The esteem of the public must always be checked. Voter opinion was the yardstick by which your success was measured, after all.

By the time she was nineteen, Penny did not care what anyone thought of her – not on a personal level anyway. She knew she was seen by her peers as smart. They understood she was ambitious. And they knew she was self-contained and took bullshit from no one.

Whether or not they liked her, well, that was inconsequential to Penelope O'Dwyer.

She truly did not give a damn.

And she found that freeing.

Her love affair with alcohol began during her college years.

She worked hard, participating actively in lectures, asking lots of questions and really testing the skills of her lecturers, as well as pushing her own command of the topic that now consumed the bulk of her attention. When not in class she was in the library, and when not there she was in the flat her parents had bought for her near the campus, working on projects and assignments, writing and rewriting until her work was of a standard she could be proud of.

She found that by the time she was finished with her studies and should have been lying down to sleep for the night, her mind wouldn't still. She would toss and turn for hours before sleep finally claimed her, and would then be tired and sluggish the next morning. Which just would not do.

Alcohol helped her to switch off.

It started as a few glasses of wine while she watched a couple episodes of The Wire, *but it soon became an entire bottle most evenings, and on a Friday and Saturday night that would increase to two, or even three.*

She wondered idly if she might be an alcoholic and decided it didn't matter. As long as she continued to perform to a high standard, such labels were just that: labels and therefore meaningless.

And regardless of how much she drank, her work was exceptional.

Dr Gerry Forde, PhD, the head of the economics department during her time at university, was so impressed by an assignment she wrote on the Keynesian model of aggregate demand that he encouraged her to forward it for publication. She did, not really expecting it to be accepted for peer review, but to her surprise and delight it was. It came out in the International Journal of Economic Studies, *and Penny was immediately acclaimed as a fresh new voice in a field she was not even qualified in yet.*

Dr Forde went out with Penny and her classmates to celebrate.

She didn't know why she decided she was going to have sex with him, but she determined by ten that evening that she was going to have him before the night was out. He made no secret out of the fact he was married – she'd been in his office and seen photos of his kids on his desk – but Penny somehow understood that would not be a barrier. And that was not meant as a moral judgement – far from it. She liked Dr Forde well enough. He was in his forties, and wasn't bad-looking per se. He wasn't even one of those lecturers who was always trying to hit on the students. He was, in fact, always polite and respectful.

Maybe she just wanted the challenge.

A bit like with her assignment getting published, it came as a surprise when she succeeded.

It wasn't romantic and it wasn't pretty: at the end of an alleyway in Dublin's city centre, her back pressed against a concrete wall and the smell of bins hanging in the late-night air, him grunting like a wild animal as he told her again and again how they shouldn't be doing this, but he wanted her, oh how he wanted her.

The experience wasn't like anything you'd see in a movie, that was for sure.

But it was, to Penny, exponentially better.

It was honest.

She'd wanted him. He'd wanted her. And afterwards they'd both walked back down that alleyway completely satisfied with what had transpired between them. She lost no respect for him, and she was relieved that, even though they did not have sex again, things never got weird between her and Dr Forde.

She liked him for that.

She got the job with Bandon, Ludlow and Murphy one year after she finished her master's. She'd spent a year clerking at the Central Bank first for a pittance, but being so close to the nursery in which money was weaned gave her a certain sense of perspective, and she made important contacts in those twelve months.

She also learned something crucial: money is aspirational.

Vast quantities could be moved at the click of a mouse, figures that could change the well-being of entire populations of people. Similarly, currencies could be devalued on a whim and markets shattered because a certain industrialist was caught in bed with a rent boy. This seemed absurd to her, but it taught her that this thing she had come to revere was actually deeply sensitive and needed to be treated with tenderness and care.

Money was subject to mood swings and tantrums if it was not cosseted.

She met a group of friends at the Central Bank who may have looked like bespectacled nerds, but she had never met people who worked so hard. And they played harder still.

By the time she moved to Bandon, Ludlow and Murphy, Penny had developed a taste for artisan gins and good cocaine. And she was ready to end her period of training and take on the role she had wanted from the moment that handsome man had told her about it in the Dáil bar ten years earlier.

The first jobs she was given were menial, taking charge of what she knew were lower-tier clients with stock and investment portfolios that offered few challenges. Initially she played it safe, advising them to put their money into high-security, low-yield funds that would protect their savings and pay out steady dividends over the medium to long term.

That was never going to set the world on fire though, and she quickly became bored.

After three months of this, she asked to have a meeting with Arthur Ludlow, one of the named partners.

'I want to be challenged,' she said. 'I didn't come here to help middle-aged shopkeepers sort out their pensions.'

Ludlow was a waspish-looking creature whose suit had an almost Victorian cut to it. He peered at her over wire-framed glasses and said, 'How challenged do you want to be, Ms O'Dwyer?'

'I've got a master's in finance and a year at the Central Bank behind me,' she said. 'I want to learn exactly what this business is all about. I'm not looking for special treatment – give me something that will require lots of work and let me prove myself.'

Ludlow thought for a moment before opening a filing cabinet and handing her a folder.

'This is the file for the McGonagle family,' he said. 'Freddie McGonagle is as shrewd an operator as you will meet, but he is also deeply corrupt and utterly ruthless.'

'What do you want me to do?' Penny asked.

'Make him happy while ensuring that nothing shady will ever blow back on this company.'

Penny nodded. 'I'll see what I can do,' she said.

She worked the McGonagle account for the next three years. She was given other tasks to do, but it was always clear the McGs – as she came to know them – were her main clients.

It took her one week to realise they were involved in just about every kind of unscrupulous business practice imaginable, from insider trading to offering bribes to planners and politicians. They had loans from banks they had not serviced in decades, but the family had such influence, the bankers were too afraid to force the issue. Vast fortunes earned from every kind of criminality were held in numbered accounts in Switzerland and the Cayman Islands.

Penny approached Freddie, the patriarch of the family – he had three sons, each more dim-witted than the next, who were given a modicum of responsibility but were effectively useless for anything other than wearing tuxedoes at parties and voting the way they were told to at board meetings – one afternoon after she'd been working for him for a fortnight.

Freddie was sixty-five but could have passed for eighty. Three stone overweight and with a round, bald, purple-hued face, he resembled a slug in human form.

'I need to tell you something,' she said once she was seated opposite him in the dusty office he used in the mansion that was the McGonagle homestead.

'What?' he croaked.

Years of cigar smoking made every word the man uttered sound like it was passing through a bucket of gravel.

'I've spent a couple of weeks looking at your finances, and I have to tell you, your money is not working for you.'

He peered at her through tiny eyes. 'I'm rich,' he said. 'Which would seem to suggest my money is doing fine, thank you very much.'

'I can make you richer,' she said.

'How?'

'Right now, the bulk of your money is hidden in unnamed accounts because you're afraid to use it in case you bring the authorities down upon yourself. So you live off the percentage of your income that is... kosher. Legitimate.'

He sat there, silent except for the wheezing of his breath.

'Your son Broderick owns a nightclub in Tallaght. We could use it to make your money more... socially acceptable.'

'You're talking about laundering it for me.'

'Yes. It's a simple procedure. I bet I could teach your sons how to do it. It wouldn't be hard.'

'And?'

'And you could start enjoying it. I could even invest it for you in some thoroughly legitimate funds. You'd never have to hide your wealth again.'

Freddie eyed her with curiosity. 'You can do this?' he asked.

'I can. On one condition.'

'I'm listening.'

'We do this off the books of Bandon, Ludlow and Murphy. This is an arrangement between you and me. For this, you and I would draw up a fresh contract of business. Is that acceptable?'

Freddie told her it was.

And together, they got rich.

It was to be the first such arrangement of many for Penny.

CHAPTER TWENTY-ONE

The Lord Dunsany was dark and cool in the early afternoon, all stained wood and paintings of racehorses. A portrait of the writer after whom the pub was named hung over the bar, looking sallow and austere. Joshua Harding – probably in his early seventies with a well-groomed head of white hair and a neatly manicured moustache – was just finishing with his client when they entered.

'I was very sorry to hear about Penny. She is an amazing young woman. And I've known her since she was a child. Her father and I are friends. We went to NUI Galway together, you know.'

'You visited her in the Kerry Arms,' Jessie said.

'I try to see her each time she comes to town. I'm very fond of her.'

'You went to her hotel room though, Mr Harding. That seems unusually, well, unusually intimate. I would have expected you to meet her in the bar.'

The older man shrugged and had some of his drink. Jessie, however, was not about to relent.

'What is the nature of your relationship with Ms O'Dwyer?'

'I suppose I am something of a mentor. I've given her some hints and tips on trading. Put her in touch with the right people. Passed some deals her way.'

'Did you employ her?'

'I wouldn't say she worked for me, in that she wasn't paid, but she helped me out on a charitable donation my company made last year.'

'Did this go through Bandon, Ludlow and Murphy?' Seamus asked.

'No. They would have taken a commission. I wanted every cent to go to the cause, and Penny said she'd channel it in such a way no governments or other traders would take a slice. And she didn't want anything to do it. It was a favour to me.'

'So it was an off-the-books deal?' Jessie said.

'If you like.'

'Do you know about any other off-the-book deals Penny was involved in?'

'Why would I know about that?'

'Any information you could offer us would be helpful.'

Harding gazed at Jessie. She got the impression he was used to people wilting under that stare. Not her though. She held his eyes, and he eventually turned away.

'If I were you, I would speak to Mervyn Moorehouse. He and Penny are… I would say they are friends.'

'Friends like her and Alistair Burns?'

Harding laughed – a dry, bitter sound. 'No. I would not say Penny is friends with Al.'

'How would you characterise her relationship with him then?'

Harding pondered that for a moment. 'It is one of mutual, intimate loathing.'

Jessie didn't know what to say to that, so instead asked, 'Were you sleeping with Penelope, Mr Harding?'

The accountant picked up his glass and drained its contents. 'Al called to let me know you were coming,' he said, 'so you already know where I was on the night Penny was taken.'

'We do,' Jessie said. 'My question still stands. Were you in a sexual relationship with Penelope O'Dwyer?'

Harding smiled. 'What difference would it make if I were?'

Jessie nodded. 'Thank you for your time, Mr Harding. We know where to find you if we have any more questions. Oh, and we'll need those recordings from the cameras in your offices – just to confirm you and Mr Burns were where you claim to have been on the night in question.'

'I'll have them sent to your office,' Harding said.

'That's very decent of you,' Jessie said and left him sitting there with his empty glass.

'He was so sleeping with her, wasn't he?' Seamus asked quietly as they walked out.

'He so was,' Jessie agreed.

PART FOUR

Elsewhere on the Field...

'I was born with the Devil in me. I could not help the fact that I was a murderer, no more than a poet can help the inspiration to sing. When I was born, the evil one stood as sponsor over my bed, and he has been with me ever since.'

H. H. Holmes

CHAPTER TWENTY-TWO

As much as he admired Jessie and wanted to better understand her way of working, Seamus still believed good old-fashioned police work was the key to breaking a case.

There were too many gaps in the case at present, and while Jessie seemed to feel these spaces could be filled by a better comprehension of the motivations and unconscious drives of the participants, Seamus was of the opinion that physical evidence would tell them far more.

After their interview with Harding, Jessie got stuck into her profiles, and Seamus went back to the Kerry Arms and spoke to Murphy, the security man, whom he knew from school. He brought along some takeout coffee and a couple of salad rolls from the deli. Murphy was a slow, ponderous man who had always wanted to be a cop but was never going to pass the physical: he was four stone overweight and couldn't run a hundred yards without having to sit down.

But for all that, he was honest and well-meaning, and Seamus had always liked him.

They sat together in the renovated broom cupboard that held the CCTV cameras, and where Murphy spent most of his days.

'There's no footage for the last time Penelope O'Dwyer stayed here,' Seamus said to his friend.

'No. The camera was broken. I told Mr O'Connor about it weeks ago, but he didn't want to spend the money gettin' it fixed.

He said the company was meant to be comin' to do a service soon enough, and they'd mend it then.'

'Yeah, he said that when I talked to him,' Seamus concurred.

'It's a real pity,' Murphy said around a mouthful of his roll. 'Might help you find that lady.'

'You liked her?'

'She was really pretty. And she was nice to me. Always said hello when she saw me. Lots of the guests don't, you know? Some don't even look at me when they walk past.'

'That's mean,' Seamus agreed. 'Murph, do you have the tapes for the last time Penelope stayed? Like, a few months back.'

The obese man stopped with his coffee cup perched on his lower lip.

'When was that exactly?'

'It was June. June third to June sixth.'

'I'll see if that's still on the computer. The videos get wiped automatically.'

'I'd really appreciate it if you had a look for me, Murph. It would be a big help.'

'I'll look right now.'

Murphy used his forefinger to punch the keys as he entered the dates Seamus had just indicated.

'You're lucky, Seamus. Those are the last days we still have!'

'Brilliant. Can we have a look? See if anyone called to see her?'

'Yeah, we can do that.'

Over the next hour, Seamus and his old school-friend watched Penelope O'Dwyer arrive at the room and let herself in. They watched her come and go a few times. Food and several bottles of wine were delivered. Alistair Burns called twice. Joshua Harding once. And on the last day of her stay, she had another caller, who stayed in her room for four hours. Seamus noted she didn't check out of the hotel until after six that evening.

The final visitor, who'd spent so long in her company, was Mervyn Moorehouse.

*

Jessie was staying in a guest house a five-minute walk from the White Elephant but only went there to sleep. And sleep did not come easily most nights. She would lie on her back staring at the ceiling, missing Will so much it was almost a physical pain. She often thought of their last meal together – he wasn't exactly a great cook, but two nights before he vanished he'd spent four hours cooking a three-course extravaganza that featured all of her favourites: French onion soup to start, roast lamb for the main and tiramisu for dessert. That it was actually edible (the lamb was a little overdone, but it would have been finicky to mention it) had amazed her, and they'd spent the entire evening laughing and talking about everything other than policing. It had been a wonderful night. A memory to be treasured.

Sleep would eventually claim her through outright exhaustion, but she rarely felt rested. Yet at least in those brief hours she did not dream, and for a while her mind was stilled.

Her waking hours were spent working, and their rooms in the tourist office became her home.

Jessie was consumed with drawing up a profile of Penelope O'Dwyer, and so far the girl was eluding her. The client list that Bandon, Ludlow and Murphy had provided was mundane to say the least and suggested the financial advisor was a moderate, by-the-book operator with no inclination to take risks.

Yet the picture Jessie was forming from their investigation suggested otherwise. Penelope was a drinker. She had a colourful sex life. She seemed unafraid to use her father's influence to her advantage. Wouldn't someone like that have pushed the envelope at work by then, attempted to claw their way up the ranks?

Yet Penelope had been at the firm for five years and remained squarely at entry level.

This baffled Jessie.

She turned her attention to Alistair Burns. As Seamus had indicated, on the surface, his life was writ large across social media: a perfect house, a beautiful wife, a healthy, beaming child. He posted photos of himself cycling in Macgillycuddy's Reeks, canoeing off the coast in Connemara, hiking trails in the Ring of Kerry, sinking frothy pints of craft ale with his hipster friends. A cursory web search brought up articles about him giving talks for the Chamber of Commerce, organising outdoor pursuits for the Christian Youth. Jessie finally asked Terri to have a crack at him, and within ten minutes, the girl presented Jessie with pages from various dating and hook-up groups.

'He's a player,' Terri said before going back to her desk. 'My guess is Penelope is too, but if she's on those sites, she hides it better. I haven't been able to find her profile yet.'

'Will you keep looking?' Jessie asked.

'I have a few different pieces of software running searches,' Terri said as she went back to her desk. 'If she's on there, I'll find her.'

Joshua Harding offered a different set of challenges.

In Kerry, he was considered something close to royalty. The charitable donations he had mentioned were given several times a year to a number of organisations, all of which were devoted to finding homes for orphaned or abandoned children. Harding's firm gave their services gratis to more than a dozen charities, and Harding and his wife had fostered and adopted thirty children over the years, many of whom had publicly spoken about how the Harding family had changed their lives for the better.

The old man was also a political animal, contributing generously and without any sense of partisan loyalty. Dominic O'Dwyer had benefitted from his generosity on numerous occasions, but so had the other side when it looked like they were destined to take the seat of power. Joshua Harding seemed unconcerned by either scruples or conviction. He sided with the winner while supporting the underdog.

Which made him impossible to pin down.

Terri tried to track down Harding's presence on dating websites to no avail.

'Sorry. No hits,' was all she had to say.

Jessie could find not a whiff of scandal relating to him or his family either. If he was engaged in a sexual relationship with Penelope, it seemed to Jessie as if this was the only extramarital affair he had pursued. Which, in Jessie's opinion, didn't make him much better than Alistair Burns. Just less energetic.

After hours of digging, the only red flag Jessie stumbled across was triggered by Mervyn Moorehouse, the man Penelope had met the night she vanished. While he was, on the surface, a legitimate businessman, Moorehouse had been in trouble with Revenue on countless occasions, had been sued by competitors for industrial espionage and had been fined three times for insider trading.

Jessie also found a photograph of Moorehouse at a party with a man named Vladislav Constatin, a Polish millionaire with links to the Russian mafia.

Moorehouse, it seemed, was crooked.

It was four in the morning when she found that photo. Terri was sleeping at her desk, her head resting on her hands, snoring gently.

Jessie stood up, stretched and, walking over to the unconscious genealogist, took her jacket off the back of her chair and wrapped it around her shoulders. Then she walked to the window and watched the first rays of the sun spreading across the sky.

She was about to push her chair back and get some sleep herself when her phone buzzed with the arrival of a text message. It was from a number she didn't know.

Time is ticking and the hour draws nigh. I am watching your progress with interest. I promise you, Penelope O'Dwyer will experience a far harder end than I gifted your dear Will. I hope you will be there to share it with her.

Jessie had been in contact with the tech squad at the London Met regarding these messages, but they had informed her there was nothing they could do about them. They came from different numbers each time, and though Jessie had changed her number repeatedly, it made no difference. The taunts kept coming.

Uruz was watching her. The problem she had was that, in her previous dealing with him, he had appeared to be a lone wolf. Now he was working alongside others, though in exactly what capacity she wasn't sure. Was he just egging Balor on? Was his involvement with Morgan simply about sharing stories and appreciating one another's evil pasts? Or was it more than that?

Sleep did not find Jessie Boyle that night at all.

CHAPTER TWENTY-THREE

There was a blue Ford Focus parked outside the White Elephant the following lunchtime when Jessie and Seamus returned from interviewing a teenaged girl who claimed to have seen Penny on the night she was abducted. The interview turned out to be a colossal waste of time, as the person the teenager described seeing looked as different to Penelope O'Dwyer as Seamus did.

'I know it's frustrating,' Jessie was saying to a seething Seamus as they pulled into the car park. 'But it was a lead and we had to follow it up. We were able to rule it out very quickly, and now we move on to the next task.'

A handsome woman who looked to be in her mid-to-late sixties got out of the Ford to meet them. Jessie noted her partner was grinning from ear to ear as he exited the MG.

'Mammy! I told you I'd see you at home this evening!' he said, his voice betraying mild embarrassment as the woman embraced her son.

'You forgot to bring your lunch. I brought you some sandwiches.'

Sure enough, Seamus's mother had a lunch box under her arm.

'I got something earlier,' he told her, looking a bit sheepish.

'Sure, you can have a few at the three o'clock slump,' the woman said, squeezing his arm. 'And you can share some with your friends. Who is this now? Introduce me.'

Jessie extended her hand. She was a little bemused at her partner's mother coming to bring him his lunch, like a schoolkid who'd left it behind because he'd got out of bed late. But then, it also fit some of the ideas she was forming about Seamus. And it didn't make her like him any less.

'I'm Jessie Boyle, Mrs Keneally.'

'I'm Kathleen. But people call me Katie.'

'Well it's very nice to meet you, Katie.'

Seamus's mother was perhaps five feet in height, maybe even a little smaller. She had a pleasant face with laughter lines around the mouth, and her hair was a natural grey that actually complemented her eyes, which were a dark shade of blue. She was dressed in jeans, a green cord jacket and an open-necked mannish shirt, her feet clad in work boots. Jessie sensed an energy and strength about her that was quite powerful. Seamus had a similar aura, and Jessie suddenly realised she found it slightly comforting. She liked Katie Keneally immediately.

'I hope Seamus has been looking after you,' the older woman said.

'He has been the perfect host.'

'I want to invite you and your other friend, the history girl, to dinner this evening. To welcome you to the town.'

'That's very kind of you, but I really don't want to intrude,' Jessie said. 'And we do have a lot of work to get done and a rather pressing deadline…'

'Jessie, I won't take no for an answer,' Katie said. 'You'll hurt my feelings, and that's the end of it.'

'You might as well stop arguing,' Seamus said. 'My mother won't be swayed once she sets her mind to something. You have to eat, Jessie. You might as well do it at our house.'

'Well, in that case, thank you very much.' Jessie laughed. 'I'd be delighted.'

'Is the other girl around? So I can ask her too?'

'Terri is away at the moment. I'll give her a buzz, but I'm pretty sure she won't be back tonight,' Seamus said.

'I'll be putting out the food at six,' Katie Keneally informed them as she got back into the Focus. 'So don't be late now.'

And then she was gone, waving out the window as she sped down the drive towards the road, probably a little too fast.

'So that's your mother,' Jessie said.

'It is.'

'Can she cook?'

'Oh, yeah. You'll be glad you came.'

CHAPTER TWENTY-FOUR

Seamus opened the lunch box his mother had brought. Jessie, who hadn't had a morsel since breakfast, accepted when he offered her a sandwich – they were chicken salad on fresh home-baked bread, and utterly delicious.

'Tell me about Ultain Cloney,' she said, referring to the man Penny had met the day before she'd vanished. 'He gets back from his trip to Belfast this evening, so I thought we might pay him a visit tomorrow morning.'

'He's a gangster,' Seamus told her around mouthfuls. 'Runs most of the crime in these parts. Has done for years.'

'When you say he runs most of the crime, what are we talking about?'

'Same as what you'd have in any city, just over a wider area,' Seamus said. 'Drugs. Prostitution to suit every taste. Gun running. Illegally produced fuel for agricultural machinery. Gambling. Money lending. You name it, he's into it.'

'Where's his base of operations?'

'He owns half a dozen pubs and a few betting offices that he uses as a show of respectability, but you won't ever find him in any of them. Cloney is a recluse. His family has an old farm out in the middle of Cois Donn bog. He's there most of the time with a small army of soldiers for protection. If we want to speak to him, we'll have to go there.'

'Have you met him before?'

'Once. When I was a trainee. I was posted in Limerick for a month, and the lad I was shadowing and I were called to a shooting in Ballinacurra Weston. By the time we got there, it was all over. This mid-terrace house had been shot to smithereens – they'd used some kind of semi-automatic weapons – and everyone inside was dead. That was a tactic the gangs were using back then. A car or a motorbike would pull up outside your house and the driver and passengers would just open fire indiscriminately. The guy they were trying to kill was shot to tatters, but so was his girlfriend and their wee baby. A two-year-old. Fucking sick, if you pardon my French.'

Jessie waved it off.

'There were five patrol cars securing the scene, and we were cordoning off the area. The usual bunch of spectators had gathered to see the bodies taken out. As a rookie, I was on crowd control, keeping them all back, when I noticed this older guy, who seemed to be on his own. He was wearing a long, black coat, a broad-brimmed hat low on his head, and when I got close to him, he smelled of pipe tobacco and diesel oil. I asked him to move back, and he turned to look at me, and I swear to God, Jessie, I felt as if someone had walked over my grave.'

'I've met people like that,' Jessie said. 'You just know they're… well, that they're not like the rest of us.'

'I kind of froze, and he says to me: "Do you think this was God's punishment on a bad man, Guard?" I opened and shut my mouth, and no words came out. He smiled at me, and I nearly pissed myself. "They must have done something very wicked to meet such a reckoning," he says, and then my sergeant was at my shoulder, and Cloney disappeared into the throng. It was Sarge who told me who he was. "If he's come out of hiding, we know who was behind the shooting," Sarge said. Seems the man who lived in that house had been acting as a spy for Cloney in the ranks of one of the Limerick gangs, but he'd been playing both sides off against each other.'

'Probably not a good idea,' Jessie said.

'No. He got off lightly though, all things considered. Cloney is famous for being a sadist. Most people who cross him are taken to that farm in the bog, which is miles from anywhere. No one can hear you scream. Cloney brags about how long he can keep a man alive while he "questions" him.'

Their eyes met. A voice somewhere at the back of Jessie's mind reminded her of the cost of dealing with men like that. Of the loss and the pain and the grief such encounters could levy. But she ignored the fear she felt, pushed it deep down and remembered she had a job to do.

'Might be our guy,' she said, nothing of what had just gone through her mind showing in her voice. 'A criminal with a long history of violence, ideal premises to hold victims and very probably someone in his crew with the tech know-how to hack street cameras.'

Jessie felt a sudden surge of real fear for Penelope. If Cloney had her, she was in very serious danger. She wondered how a man like Cloney might have got in contact with Uruz and suddenly understood that what she thought she knew about her old foe was starting to seem flimsy at best. Jessie knew she would have to do something about that – and soon.

'And Penelope O'Dwyer was already on his radar,' Seamus agreed. 'The fact she was working for him though, Jessie – I mean, this is as bad a man as you could hope to meet. What the hell else was she into?'

'That's what we're going to have to find out,' Jessie said. 'If we're to stand any chance of finding her alive.'

'Which means tomorrow, we're going to Cois Donn,' Seamus said, picking up his hurley and sliotar. 'It's a good thing you're coming to dinner then.'

'Why so?'

'Might be your last meal. At least it'll be a good one.'

'Brilliant,' Jessie said. 'Just brilliant.'

CHAPTER TWENTY-FIVE

As Jessie and Seamus were tucking into their sandwiches, Terri was arriving at UCC, where the aisles of the library were full of students quietly browsing. There was a gentle hum of whispered conversation and the occasional whirr of wheels as a librarian passed by with a trolley laden with returned volumes. These were all sounds Terri loved – libraries were her happy place.

Yet something about the object Terri had come to see caused her unease. It shouldn't have: Balor's Stone was just a chunk of rock with marks hacked into it, after all. But a menace the display case was unable to contain seemed to radiate from the object in waves.

The ogham stone was approximately six feet in height and three in width and was standing at a slight recline on a plinth made of wood and marble inside a wide glass box. A laminated card on a pole to the left of the display contained a sanitised version of the story Terri had shared with the investigative team, and also gave a brief explanation of how the stone had been found, and how it fit into Celtic tradition.

Terri barely read the card, as she already knew that 360 ogham stones had been found in Ireland, with another forty discovered in the British Isles, clearly the work of ancient Irish explorers.

A display card told Terri that Ogham was an alphabet designed for purely practical purposes, in that it lent itself perfectly to being carved into stone with a hammer and chisel. Letters are constructed using one to five lines, with a crossed notch added to signify vowels. So the letter 'n', called 'nin' in ogham, is represented by IIIII, while 'ne' is represented by H̶H̶H̶.

Most ogham stones apparently featured a single line of text running up the edge of the stone, across the top, and down the edge on the other side. This artefact in its glass case, however, was unique in that virtually every inch of its four planes was covered in dense etchings. Whoever had carved it – and it appeared to have all been done by the same prehistoric scribe – had been determined to lay out their story for posterity. Terri marvelled that, the story on this stone being incomplete, there must have been a second that accompanied it. They would have made an impressive sight while they stood erect in the earth, a warning to all who could read them of the dangers of pride and bloodlust, and of the horror that had come to Ireland from across the sea.

'You've found our treasure then?'

Terri turned to face a bespectacled man wearing a black sports jacket over a *Star Wars* T-shirt and jeans. He had a friendly, open face that sported probably four days' worth of beard. Terri put him somewhere in his fifties. His short hair was shot through with grey, his stubble the same. There was a warmth and humour to the man she found immediately attractive.

'Dr Miskella?' she asked cautiously.

'The same. And you must be Ms Kehoe.'

'Terri, please.'

'Then I insist you call me John.'

As Terri shook the man's hand, she realised he wasn't much taller than her, a fact that put her at ease.

'You're interested in Balor then?' Miskella asked.

'Well, as I said when we chatted on the phone, I'm actually here to inquire about the researchers who worked on the stone when it was first unearthed,' Terri said. 'I'd like a list of everyone who was involved before 1978.'

'And you're still consulting with the police?'

Terri held out her identification card, which she wore on a lanyard about her neck.

'Guilty as charged,' she said, blushing in spite of herself.

'And correct me if I'm wrong – you're an historian?' Dr Miskella asked. 'Forgive me, but I've always been curious about how that works. I spend my time digging up clay pots and translating monastic manuscripts. You chase murderers. I'm fascinated. How does an historian end up working with the Garda Síochána?'

Miskella was using the police force's full title in the Irish language, meaning 'Guardians of the Peace'.

'Well, as you know from our previous correspondence, I consult on cases where historical research is necessary. It's not much different than what any other historian does really.'

'But you help them catch crooks and murderers?'

Terri shrugged. 'I do whatever I'm asked to do. Sometimes it's a murder case, sometimes it's no more than tracing the movements of a person of interest. It's all just research really.'

Miskella grinned. 'Well I'm very impressed.'

'Do you have those names, John?'

'I can get the department administrator to print you out a list,' Miskella said. 'If that's all you've come for, it's been a bit of a wasted journey. You could have got them with a phone call or an email.'

'I was hoping I might ask you a few questions about the finding of the stone? The excavation that discovered it?'

'Of course.' The academic smiled. 'Have you had lunch yet?'

'No.'

'Well then please allow me to treat you. The food in the staff canteen is serviceable, if a little uninspiring. Are you prepared to risk it?'

Terri nodded, a bit unsure of how to answer.

'Then walk this way,' Miskella said.

They were still talking three hours later.

CHAPTER TWENTY-SIX

'It was Dr Henry Quilt who found it first,' Miskella said.

They were in the long, high-ceilinged room that housed the staff dining hall. Old photographs of former academics hung on the walls, and a radio station playing classical music was piped through speakers at a volume that did not intrude on conversation.

Terri had a mixed salad, her dining companion lasagne and chips. Terri secretly thought the pasta dish looked appetising but was too nervous to eat. She had learned long ago how easy it was to pretend to eat a salad – she just moved the leaves and chopped vegetables around the plate, and no one really noticed. Few people experienced food envy when it came to a salad, so no one was surprised when most of it was left on the plate. Or in Terri's case, all of it.

'Is Dr Quilt still alive?' she asked, spearing a bunch of lettuce leaves with her fork and holding it aloft for a few moments, as if about to take a bite.

'He died in early 2016.'

'I'm sorry to hear that. Did you know him?'

'He taught me field archaeology during my first semester here. Awful lecturer, but he had a passion for it, I'll give him that. Couldn't keep on topic though to save his life. He'd come in with the intention of giving us a presentation on different types of soil strata, and we'd distract him by asking about his experiences uncovering a Norman castle in Waterford. It didn't take much to get him off topic.'

'Did he ever talk about Balor's Stone?'

'All the time. He was a bit obsessed by it. Quilt was convinced the stone indicated an extinction-level event in Celtic civilisation of that era.'

Terri pushed her plate of leaves aside. She'd played with them enough so that Miskella would think she'd eaten her fill.

'What did he mean by that?'

'All cultures have their myths about an event that brings about, for want of a better term, a hard reset for that particular epoch. If you look at the Old Testament, there's the Great Flood, you know, where Noah builds the ark and takes his family and two of each animal on board. The waters rise and wipe out most of humanity, and when they recede, Noah and his children and their cargo repopulate.'

'Of course,' Terri said. 'Ancient Greece had a similar story, didn't it? The sinking of Atlantis…'

'Yes. You'll find stories like it all over the world in almost every tradition. Except for the Celts. Their legends don't speak of a flood per se. What they do tell of, though, is Balor, who came from the ocean and brought a time of great darkness and evil.'

'Dr Quilt wasn't looking for an ogham stone when he embarked upon the dig in Clare, was he?' Terri asked. 'What brought him to that field at that time?'

'A calf got its hoof stuck in a hole in the field. When the farmer came to pull it out, he looked in the hole with a view to filling it in and saw what seemed to be shards of something inside. The farmer – a man called O'Fiagh – called the local Garda, who called the priest, who, as luck would have it, had studied archaeology in college and realised what he was looking at when he arrived on the scene. He called the university.'

'And they sent Dr Quilt,' Terri said, almost to herself.

'He travelled to the site with a couple of research assistants,' Miskella went on. 'Old Quilt knew as soon as he saw the field that it contained a burial mound – any archaeologist worth their salt would have discerned the slight rise in the centre of the pasture, and that was where the cow had come a cropper. He began to excavate, and on the first day they uncovered some old pottery.'

'Celtic, I presume?' Terri asked.

'Yes. Right below these they found the stone,' Miskella said, 'then things began to get *really* strange.'

Balor

He was two beings in one.

It was a truth he never shared with his apprentices, and the other killers he communed with – Uruz and Morgan and the others – were completely unaware of this uncomfortable reality. It was a condition he hoped to rectify before circumstances reached their climax, but he was no longer certain he could force the other out.

And maybe it wasn't important he did.

Because his task was almost done. He just had one final act to complete.

Balor had planned it carefully, lured the woman to him with consummate skill. For the ritual to work, she had to come to him as a willing participant, so he offered her something she wanted. Something shiny only he could provide.

In the end, the meeting was suggested by her, and he had only to propose a night when the moon was in its correct alignment and the stars were laid out in the sky in just the right pattern.

And she took the bait. It was almost too easy. He was a little disappointed actually, because he relished the chase, the hunt. In this instance though, he was prepared to forfeit that thrill, because this woman was exactly what he needed. She had some qualities that were essential if the magic were to be manifested: she was a princess and heir to an empire. She had lived with power, and it coursed through her.

That power would now be his.

It was a simple matter to draw her into the car, and once that was complete, the rite was begun.

This closing action was complex and wrought a deep magic. It required the sacrifice of the daughter of a king on the eve of Samhain, the Festival of the Dead, a rite performed while Balor also vanquished a hero sent to thwart him. Those two aspects of the human character – the hero and the maiden – needed to be eradicated to complete the cycle.

The maiden was currently locked in his dungeon, guarded by his apprentice, and the hero was already embarking on her quest.

All Balor had to do was sit back and wait.

The time of darkness was almost upon him.

The Dance of the Dead was about to begin.

CHAPTER TWENTY-SEVEN

'I think Quilt knew the moment he brushed the earth off the surface of the stone that this was a unique find,' Miskella said. 'The pattern of the markings, the age of the stone, the blanket coverage of the glyphs, the dialect itself – this was something truly special. A once-in-a-lifetime discovery. He knew they'd be writing about it for years to come.'

'He didn't immediately identify the writing as ogham?'

'No. Ogham is read vertically – in this case the scribe etched out sets of parallel lines running from the bottom of the stone to the top, across the summit and down the other side. Without having properly cleaned the stone down, Old Quilt assumed he was dealing with something Mesopotamian or even Egyptian. When he realised the stone was actually Irish in origin, he understood he had something even more remarkable. And then the university sent a larger team.'

'I've noticed in the articles I've read that Dr Quilt is not listed as chief excavator.'

'No, although he felt he should have been. Quilt was an expert in late Celtic civilisation and had studied Dedad sites for two decades. He would have been in his late forties in 1972, so hardly a rank amateur, but he was outranked by Professor Richard Dunbeg, who swooped in and took over from the second week onwards.'

'That must have annoyed Dr Quilt,' Terri observed.

'Oh, it did. The Balor dig saw the beginning of an academic rivalry between those two men that continued to fester right up until Quilt died in 2016.'

'How did that rivalry manifest itself?'

'You've been around academics, haven't you, Terri?'

'Yes. Quite a bit actually.'

'Then you'll know,' Miskella said, grinning, 'that academic rivalry is all about figurative back-stabbing and escalating attempts to ruin each other's legacies, often through the writing of bitchy articles to debunk whichever theory the other is expounding that week.'

'Professor Dunbeg doesn't seem to have done much of note after analysing the stone.'

Miskella gave her a rueful look. 'There's a story there,' he said, 'but you're jumping ahead and ruining my carefully constructed narrative.'

Terri found herself laughing, despite herself. 'All right then,' she said. 'Things became strange during the dig?'

'Yes.'

'Strange in what way?'

'The standard practice when an artefact like Balor's Stone is found is to take it to a research lab for the purpose of study, after which it is placed in a museum. But by the time Dunbeg had coordinated the stone's complete excavation, the team, and a small contingent from the local community, were at loggerheads over what was to be done with it.'

Terri shook her head. 'I don't understand.'

'Professor Dunbeg, probably with some encouragement from the farmer, O'Fiagh, decided the stone should be left onsite. He wanted to set it back in the earth, in that same field, to be left as some kind of monument. Several of the other academics claimed they agreed with him, and he found even more support among members of the local historical society. It got quite heated. There were demonstrations and stand-offs. The police had to be called to facilitate the stone's removal to UCC.'

'I know some digs do attract negative attention from heritage and environmental groups,' Terri said.

'Yes, but I've never heard, before or since, of a protest that involved members of the archaeological team.' Miskella laughed.

'Well… no,' Terri said, laughing along with him.

'Dunbeg faced disciplinary proceedings when he arrived back on campus. Claimed he had experienced some kind of temporary insanity. I will say it wasn't like him. He was a relatively young man – only in his late twenties – but he had a tendency to steer clear of confrontation.'

'Isn't twenty-odd extremely young to achieve a professorship?'

'Absurdly so. But Dunbeg was a savant. He had very poor people skills, according to the stories, and would come in to work wearing odd shoes and mismatched suits. Sometimes he didn't turn up at all – I don't think he paid attention to mundane concepts like the days of the week. But he had an encyclopaedic knowledge of ancient history. He was quite brilliant.'

'Was that the end of the difficulties?'

Miskella thought for a moment before saying, 'That piece of rock… I've never seen an item generate such feeling.' He paused, taking a sip of water. 'Perhaps it would be fairer to say that *Balor* generates passion rather than the stone itself.'

'Balor?'

'Yes. As we've already discussed, Quilt believed the story on the stone was rooted in historical fact and tried to explain it by finding real-world, mostly plausible explanations for what might have happened – Balor was a Roman mercenary backed by a highly skilled attack force being a case in point.'

'A common enough historical methodology,' Terri said.

'Yes. There were others though – Dunbeg chief among them – who believed the story on the stone should be taken literally. I'm told Dunbeg submitted a paper for presentation at the conference for the Irish Celtic Society outlining these beliefs. It was rejected of course.'

'You mean he believed Balor was really a demonic entity who lived on the blood of maidens?'

'In a nutshell, yes. All this was hushed up by the board of the university, but there are whispers Dunbeg experienced violent outbursts. Attacked a female colleague, according to the rumours, although I don't know the details.'

'Another cover-up?' Terri asked.

'This was the 1970s,' Miskella said. '"Me Too" was not yet a thing. Suffice it to say, Dunbeg began to identify with Balor more and more as he researched the stone and its mythology.'

'And he had supporters, this Professor Dunbeg?'

'He did. One junior lecturer in particular. Coogan or something.'

'Coogan? Like the comedian?'

'Yes. I didn't have much to do with him. He and Dunbeg had a notion they could find the cave where Balor was supposed to be buried, and they more or less moved into the mountain country in Kerry for six months while they searched. Dunbeg was summoned back to the department – he still had teaching responsibilities and he was supervising PhD students. But Coogan stayed out there. Which is how he got his nickname. They used to called him the Fella Who Lives in the Reeks. It eventually got shortened to Reek.'

Terri froze. 'You're sure of that? They called him Reek?'

'Yes. I'm certain.'

'What happened to Professor Dunbeg?'

'He left academic practice in 1985, I think.'

'Is he still alive?'

'I have no idea.'

'And this Coogan or Reek or whatever his name is?'

'Again, I'm not certain, but the admin office will know more. Shall we go and ask them?'

'Please,' Terri said.

She could feel her heart quickening. If the Reek from Penelope's Instagram was genuinely linked to Balor's Stone, then Morgan had been telling the truth. Knowing she was looking at a lead that could fundamentally influence how they pursued the case, Terri followed Miskella from the dining room.

'Do you mind terribly if I smoke as we walk?' he asked. 'It's a filthy habit, I know.'

'Not at all. I quite like the smell of tobacco smoke, to be honest.'

He laughed at that. 'You won't like the ones I smoke – I picked up a taste for Woodbines when I was a young fellow. You know, the old-fashioned, unfiltered cigarettes?'

'Well, you are an archaeologist.' Terri smiled. 'So old-fashioned is going to be your thing, I suppose. Do you mind if I follow you in a moment? I just need to ring my team.'

'Of course. The history office is clearly signposted – just follow the path.'

Terri watched him disappear among the crowd of students and then pulled her phone from her pocket and called the White Elephant, filling Jessie in on the fact that she had found an academic named Reek who had a direct link to Balor's Stone. Jessie congratulated her and told her to keep digging.

Which of course she said she would. Then she ran to catch up with her guide, whom she was beginning to like very much. And the feeling seemed to be mutual, because by the time Terri and Miskella were finished in the history department, he had asked her if she would like to have a drink with him that night.

And, to her great surprise, despite their age difference and her natural reticence towards social encounters, she said she would.

CHAPTER TWENTY-EIGHT

Terri had only brought one change of clothes with her to Cork, so she didn't have many options for her date – should she even think of it in those terms? – with John Miskella. But she mixed and matched and eventually settled on a floral skirt over black tights, coupled with a rust-coloured silk shirt. She put her leather jacket over the ensemble and then checked herself in the mirror of her room at the B & B. She had spent almost an hour teasing her hair this way and that, but Terri's hair never did much other than sit there, no matter what product she put in it or which way she brushed or combed.

Her freckles were another feature that rankled her. She'd spent her childhood hoping she would simply grow out of them, but as she approached, then entered, her twenties, she understood that wasn't going to happen and had been forced to accept that the collection of brown splotches were going to be a part of her physical make-up for good. Applying a little foundation helped, but she could still see them peeping through.

She hoped John wouldn't mind.

He had asked her out, after all. That must mean he found her at least a little bit interesting, didn't it? Maybe not physically attractive, but at least someone he enjoyed talking to. And even if he had only made the offer because he was bored or lonely, there was always the chance she'd learn more about Richard Dunbeg and the story of the stone. And now that Terri knew about Reek, she was excited to learn as much as she could.

That was why she was in Cork in the first place, after all.

They had arranged to meet in a pub off Patrick Street. Terri hated arriving to pubs alone. She always felt ill at ease, social anxiety pressing down on her like a physical weight. The bar was busy, a traditional music band made up of bearded musicians with lots of greying hair clattering away in the corner. For a moment she looked about and couldn't see John. Panic gripped, and she was sure she'd been stood up: it seemed he'd been making fun of her after all, luring her to this place for the purpose of humiliation, another in a long line of people who didn't want her. Just as she was about to leave though, she spotted him, waving at her through the crowd. Relief cascaded and she waved back and hurried over.

The rest of the night was magic.

When they'd talked in the university earlier, Terri had guided the conversation, as she was effectively questioning him about the case, but tonight he took charge, and within moments she was completely relaxed – all sense of worry and concern evaporated.

Funny things students had written in their exams over the years, reasons why Cork should really be Ireland's capital city, unusual rural colloquialisms he'd encountered on his travels: there wasn't a single lull or uncomfortable silence, and Terri found herself marvelling at how confident he was and how at ease he made her feel. Never much of a drinker, she found herself having a couple more gin and tonics than she would usually consume, and as closing time approached, John asked her if he could walk her back to her accommodation.

'Please don't think I'm being unchivalrous,' he said when she seemed uncertain. 'I really do just want to be sure you've got back safely. There is no ulterior motive.'

And to Terri's surprise, that disappointed her.

The B & B was a short taxi drive away. She sat in the back, next to him, feeling the radiant warmth of him beside her in the darkness, not quite touching, but near enough that she could smell his cologne, which was masculine but still just a little sweet, a little flirtatious. It was intoxicating.

When the cab pulled up to the kerb, she turned to him and, without giving herself a chance to back out, said, 'Would you like to come up?'

He looked into her eyes, as if searching for doubt, then smiled, a warm, jovial grin, full of good humour and merriment.

'Yes. I'd like that very much indeed.'

It had been more than a year since Terri had been with anyone. John seemed to sense that, and when she closed and locked the door behind them, he took her gently in his arms and just held her for several minutes, and it was exactly what she needed. When he felt her hold on him tighten as she was moved by the need for him, he lifted her face to his and kissed her, and the rest was like a dream.

Afterwards they lay entwined in each other on the bed, and he traced the pattern of scars on her inner thigh with his forefinger.

'I'm sorry,' she said.

'What for?'

'Those. I know they're ugly.'

He continued to run his finger along the topography she had etched into herself. 'You did this? You cut yourself?'

'Yes.'

'When you were younger?'

She didn't want to lie to him. 'Not that much younger than I am now. Sometimes it's the only thing that helps. When everything else is out of control... I can do this and it's... it's my choice.'

'You feel your life spins out of control?'

'Yes. I... I never knew my parents. I grew up in care.'

His finger paused in its journey.

'Everyone has their burdens to carry. You shouldn't be ashamed of these. They're just a mark of where you've been.'

For a moment she searched his face, wondering if he was making fun of her, but all she saw was openness and honesty there.

'We do what we have to do to cope,' he said. 'There's no shame in it, Terri.'

She held him tightly then.

It felt like coming home.

CHAPTER TWENTY-NINE

Katie Keneally lived in a two-up two-down house on Fisher's Row, a narrow street that ran towards the waterfront off New Street, right in the centre of Cahirsiveen. Jessie found the place without any trouble.

Seamus opened the door at her knock, dressed in a Kerry Gaelic football T-shirt and baggy jeans, his hair wet from the shower.

'Welcome to my humble abode,' he said, taking from her the bottle of Sauvignon Blanc she'd bought on the way before giving her a quick hug, which to Jessie's surprise didn't feel as awkward as she might have expected.

'Bring Jessie through to the living room, Seamus,' Katie called from inside. 'And get her a drink before she dies of thirst.'

'Hello, Katie,' Jessie shouted past Seamus's shoulder. 'Something smells good!'

'Your own mother has you well trained,' Katie said. 'Now, you are the guest of honour, so please take a seat and we'll have you fed in a few moments.'

Seamus showed her to a tiny living room, where a table had been set by the window. A small suite of furniture was at the other end, beside a door leading to a well-appointed kitchen, where Katie was busy plating up.

'Do you want a glass of what you've brought, or can I offer you something stronger?' Seamus asked Jessie as he indicated an armchair for her to sit.

'Do you have any whiskey?'

'A woman after my own heart. Scotch or Irish?'

'Surprise me.'

He came back with a glass of Famous Grouse for each of them.

'*Sláinte*,' he said, offering her the traditional Irish toast that means 'to your health'.

'Right back at you, partner,' she said. 'We lead, others follow, so let's not fuck it up.'

Seamus laughed. 'I don't know that one.'

'It's a toast we used to use at the Met.'

'I like it.'

'*Tá an dinnéar réidh*,' Katie said as she came bustling in, carrying a tray so laden with plates Jessie marvelled she could carry it at all.

'That means dinner is ready,' Seamus said.

'I did know that,' Jessie said. 'But even if I didn't, I think I could have worked it out from the context.'

'When we're alone, Mammy and me, we speak only Irish to one another,' Seamus explained as they got up and went to the table. 'When we have guests, we use English—'

'But sometimes we forget, and a *cúpla focal* – a couple of words – slip out,' Katie cut in. 'Now stop yapping, the pair of you, and dig in!'

The meal was a simple roast dinner with all the trimmings: beef cooked to just the right degree of pinkness, crisp potatoes that had been roasted with rosemary-infused goose fat, carrots and green beans that were still al dente, Yorkshire puddings with a gorgeous crust, but still perfectly fluffy inside, and gravy made from the meat juices that sang in savoury notes on the tongue. Jessie hadn't had a meal like it in several years and found herself gorging. Seamus, as was his custom, cleaned his plate in a matter of minutes then went and got seconds. Katie appeared to eat little but watched the two younger people consume her work with pride.

'Have you had enough to eat, Jessie, pet?' she asked when Jessie sat back, replete.

'I think I might burst,' was the response.

'You've no room for dessert then?'

'Katie, I don't think I could!'

'Why don't you let the main course settle – the evening's still young, as they say. Seamus, get Jessie another drink and we'll retire to the lounge. We can have some cake in a bit.'

'Retiring to the lounge' meant returning to the armchairs and couch at the other end of the room.

'Seamus, will you play us a tune?' Katie asked when they were all seated.

'You play an instrument?' Jessie asked in wonder.

'I do, but I don't think now is the time,' Seamus said, giving his mother the first less-than-loving look Jessie had seen him use.

'You head off on your adventures to Dublin and I barely get to see you and I haven't heard you play a tune in months. I am your mother and therefore it is my right to show you and your skills off to your new friends!' Katie said vehemently. 'Now, your melodeon is in its case under the stairs. Go, and be quick about it!'

As he went, looking chastened, Katie winked at Jessie.

'He's actually very good – he's won all kinds of medals at fleadhs all over the country, and he was in a céilí band when he was at school. I wanted him to be on the Garda Band, but sure, he doesn't play the right instrument for that. They only take brass and percussion.'

Seamus returned, looking a little flustered, carrying a two-row button accordion.

'Now play something nice,' Katie said. 'What about "Cape Clear"? That's my favourite.'

Her son sat down, arranged the accordion straps about his shoulders, closed his eyes and began to play.

Jessie didn't know much about traditional Irish music. Growing up in Dublin, she was familiar with the usual well-known ballads and street songs all Irish children are taught in school, but she had never really been exposed to the great tradition of Irish folk music. Cape Clear, an island off the coast of West Cork, had always been a home to poets and musicians. The tune Seamus was playing dated back to the early nineteenth century and was said to be a lament for a sailor leaving his love behind. It was lilting, plaintive and beautiful, and Jessie found herself watching the young detective as he played. His face was completely serene, as if he was meditating, and she was interested to see that he teased the notes from the squeeze box while barely moving the bellows in and out at all – his control of the instrument was absolute. Seamus's long fingers danced across the buttons as if independent of him, and the melody filled the room, sweet and gentle yet full of soul and yearning.

Jessie had developed a picture in her head of who Seamus Keneally was: brash, boisterous, a little immature. That he could create such soulful and sensitive music suggested depths she had not assumed he possessed.

And the music spoke to her.

Somehow, the images it conjured for Jessie were of William Briggs, the man she loved, who Uruz had taken from her so cruelly. Despite herself, tears welled in her eyes. She saw that Katie was watching her. The older woman reached over and gently placed her hand on hers.

'That's all right, child,' she whispered. 'Music will do that to you, if you let it.'

When the tune came to its end, Jessie felt as if she had been on a journey to somewhere she hadn't known existed. Seamus remained as he was, fingers on the keys, eyes closed for just a moment, before stirring as if from sleep and opening one eye playfully.

'Wow, Seamus,' Jessie said, putting down her glass to applaud and wiping her eyes hurriedly. 'I didn't think you had it in you!'

'Oh,' he said, putting the accordion on the carpet at his feet. 'I'm full of surprises.'

It wasn't to be the last surprise of the evening either.

CHAPTER THIRTY

They sipped their drinks and talked about everything and nothing. Seamus played a couple more tunes, jigs and reels, full of wild, violent flurries of notes that almost made Jessie feel light-headed. Somewhere around nine o'clock, Katie went to the kitchen and returned with a pot of coffee, cups and a beautifully made Victoria sponge.

'Now you'll have a small slice of this, Jessie, because I made it in your honour.'

'Katie, you've discovered my Kryptonite,' Jessie admitted. 'I can't refuse cake.'

'Well, that makes me even more fond of you, my girl. I don't think anyone who turns their nose up when offered a slice of cake should be trusted.'

It was expertly made, so light it almost melted in the mouth.

'You're a talented woman,' Jessie said, slightly drunk by now. 'I bake when time allows me, but this leaves my best efforts in the rear-view mirror.'

'I could give you the recipe, but the best way for you to learn would be for us to bake it together,' Katie said, picking at a tiny sliver of her creation. 'I don't offer that to many now – I'm quite particular who I bake with. Isn't that right, Seamus?'

Seamus, who was on his third slice, nodded. 'If Katie Keneally lets you into her kitchen, then you know she's taken you to her heart,' he said.

'Then I'm honoured,' Jessie said, and she meant it.

Forty-five minutes later, Katie informed them she was going to bed.

'Jessie, you're welcome to sleep here tonight. I have the spare room made up for you.'

'That's very kind of you,' Jessie said. 'I'm sure I can get a taxi though.'

'Well, you might and you mightn't, but either way, there's a bed here should you need it. Now I'll bid you both goodnight.'

As her steps echoed on the stairs, Jessie said, 'Your mum is pretty cool, Seamus.'

'I know that, but thanks anyway.'

'I love the fact you're so close. I... I never had that with my mam.'

Seamus got up and refilled her glass before sitting on the chair beside her, which his mother had just vacated, leaving the bottle so it could be easily reached by each of them.

'My dad died when I was thirteen,' he said. 'He was a fisherman, and he was my hero, but one day, he didn't come home – lost at sea during a storm. So it was just me and Mam. Now, she never told me I had to step up and be the man of the house – that's not her way. If anything, she took on more of the responsibilities to try and protect me. She had to be a mam and a dad, like. But I tried. I did my best to be there for her too. We've both been there for each other ever since.'

Jessie smiled in sympathy. 'My dad died when I was eight,' she said. 'Cancer.'

'I'm sorry,' Seamus said gently.

'Oh, it took him fast. He was this big, strong man one moment – he played football for Dublin when he was younger – and the next he was just a collection of bones and skin. He and my mum, they were crazy about one another. She never really got over it when he died. Maybe she was fragile to begin with, I don't know. But she never came back from it.'

'Some people don't,' Seamus offered. 'My mam has never been with another man since Dad passed. None I know of anyway.'

'Oh, mine was,' Jessie said ruefully. 'A complete asshole, in fact.'

'Oh. Right. That's not great, is it?' Seamus said, clearly unsure how to respond.

'No. Not great at all,' Jessie said.

'Is he... is he still with your mam? The asshole?'

Jessie sighed and swallowed what was in her glass in a single gulp. 'No. He... well he left. Good riddance.'

They were quiet for a time, each in their private thoughts. After a while, Seamus said, 'Come here. I have to tell you – it took me a little while to get into your groove, but I like the way you work. You're a really good cop, Jessie. For someone who isn't a cop, if you get what I mean.'

'Thanks, Seamus. You're not so bad yourself.'

'No, listen to me. You've got some skills. I can see that. I... I just hope I can learn from you, okay?'

Jessie grinned and patted him on the arm. 'We'll learn from one another, Seamus. We're partners, yeah?'

He took her hand and held it. 'I'm glad you came this evening. Good to have a chance to get to know one another outside of work, isn't it?'

'I'm glad too. It's been a great night. Thank you.'

They were very close on the two chairs, their faces only inches apart. She suddenly noticed he had brown eyes that had green and purple flecks, and that his cheekbones were strong and well formed, and that he had the lightest of stubble on his chin. He was watching her closely, and she could see he was absorbing her too, recording the symmetry of her face. Expectation hung between them for a long, quizzical moment. Neither of them moved, then Seamus squeezed her hand gently, almost in a question. He was still holding her eyes with his.

What am I doing? she thought. *An hour ago, I was crying over Will, now I'm mooning over Seamus? Fucking pathetic. Snap out of it, Jessie!*

'I think I should go,' Jessie said, almost in a whisper.

'I don't want you to,' Seamus said, still holding her hand, which she suddenly realised she hadn't drawn back.

'Yes, but I should,' Jessie said.

As she watched, the younger man seemed to shake himself – although he didn't physically move – and whatever it was that had them in its grasp dissipated. Seamus gently let her go and stood.

'I'll call you a cab, shall I?'

'That would be good, Seamus.'

'Right then. I'll get my phone.'

He left her, and she sat back on the chair, closing her eyes, thanking whichever gods were listening that she'd had the good sense not to give in to that temptation.

She'd been trying not to think about Will, forcing herself to push all the grief and anger and self-recrimination aside until this job was done. She'd always been good at that: compartmentalising her life so the bits that hurt were put somewhere safe until she was able to deal with them.

Of course, that meant they sometimes didn't get dealt with at all. And now, as she sat in the taxi back to her B & B, she allowed herself to think of him.

In the beginning, she and Will had had a purely physical attraction. Perhaps that was why she had given in to it. The Met didn't specifically have a rule against work partners being in relationships, but it was actively frowned upon, so when she'd first realised she liked William Briggs, she'd forced herself to ignore it. He was tall, not exactly muscle-bound but broad and powerful. When she was around him, she knew she was safe, that he would be able to deal with whatever they encountered. Being Will's partner had made her feel indomitable, as if there was nothing the two of them couldn't achieve so long as they were together.

If only she had been there when Uruz had come for him, Jessie believed things would have played out differently. If only.

Will was a few years older than her, a former Royal Marine whose father had been constable in a small village in Scotland. Briggs still had a slight Scottish burr, even though he'd been London-based for more than two decades when she'd met him. It had made him even more attractive to her, though she never told him so. There was so much she never told him.

She remembered the first time they made love. That afternoon Will had led an assault on a house where five women were being held captive by a trafficking gang, the culmination of an operation that had taken five months of intense investigation. This gang were animals, bringing girls as young as five years old into the city for the sex industry, selling them at auction like livestock.

The extraction was messy, the strike team drawing heavy fire: Casper, one of Will's officers, was hit with an armour-piercing round that punctured his flak jacket, and he almost died. By the time they got to the room where the girls were being held, the gang leader had already started executing them. Despite all their efforts, they saved only two.

When Will emerged, the last man to exit the building, carrying the body of a fifteen-year-old girl in his arms, Jessie found herself weeping.

It was the custom to have a few drinks after an operation was concluded, but no one felt much like celebrating. She found Will in the squad room at eleven thirty that night, still poring over the files, searching for anything they might have overlooked.

'They could have other safe houses,' he told her urgently. 'We can't let this be the end. We owe it to those girls we failed today.'

She sat beside him, put her arms around him and let him cry.

And somewhere amid the tears, she kissed him.

They ended up back in his apartment, and it was passionate and frantic, and when it was finished they just lay, looking at one another, smiling.

'This has to be a one-time thing,' she told Will.

'I agree with you completely,' he said, before kissing her again.

They saw one another every night for the next six months. He told her he loved her after three of those months had passed. She responded that she cared for him, knowing he was disappointed, but she'd never been good with that word. Life had taught her that words were cheap – it was how you acted that mattered.

Now, she just hoped that, in his final moments, when the suffering became too much and his beautiful, strident heart had given out, he knew she had loved him too. That she had shown him what he meant to her. It was all she had left to hold on to.

Seamus Keneally reminded her of Will more than she wanted to admit – the swagger, the confidence, the intelligence.

Yet he was almost two decades her junior, and he still had so much to learn. The moment they had shared was, for her, brought on by the feelings his music had stirred, the memory of Will. And the need to feel some kind of physical closeness.

It had only been a few weeks, yet she desperately missed being touched.

But it had been a mistake. She knew that. Jessie just hoped it wouldn't make things difficult with Seamus. She liked him. In fact, she thought this was a professional partnership that could work. Hopefully, he would see that too.

As Jessie drifted off to sleep, she wondered where Penny was and hoped she would be able to do for her what she had been unable to do for Will: save her from an awful death.

CHAPTER THIRTY-ONE

Dawn Wilson was in her office at ten o'clock in the evening on the fourth day Jessie and her team were in Kerry.

Dawn worked from a gated complex in the Phoenix Park, which contained the laboratories for Forensic Science Ireland, a parade ground, barracks and stables for the Garda Mounted Unit, as well as rooms for both the Garda Band and the Officers' Club. Dawn knew every single person who worked there by name, and no one could get in or out of the area without her having signed off on their presence – permission had to be given for any individual to pass through security.

So it came as something of a surprise when two men she did not know walked into her office without knocking. One of the pair closed the door quietly before joining his comrade before the commissioner's large burnished-oak desk.

'Come on in, boys, don't mind me,' Dawn said, sitting back and taking a draught of tea from the Black Canary mug one of her staff had given her as a birthday gift the previous year.

Both visitors were tall, well over six feet in height, and while the one on the left looked to be carrying a little more weight than his companion, both seemed to be in excellent shape. The commissioner judged them to be bodybuilders, individuals whose size was intended to intimidate. The fact they were dressed in black from head to foot and the bulge of a weapon showed beneath the jacket of the larger one suggested she was the person they were supposed to be intimidating.

The brazenness of it all impressed her though: to march into the head office of the nation's police force and accost the highest-ranking officer of that force took some gumption, that was for sure.

'We're here to offer you assistance,' the bigger one said.

He spoke without an accent and looked to be in his early thirties. His face was plain and unremarkable, and Dawn noted he had blonde hair.

'How precisely are you going to do that?'

'By giving you an incentive.'

Dawn raised an eyebrow. 'Well, now I'm fascinated.'

'Our employer would take it as a personal favour should you find Penelope O'Dwyer with all due haste,' Blondie said, 'and he would like her found alive. If you do this, he is prepared to furnish you with information relating to a large drugs operation. One you have been trying to quash since your promotion.'

Dawn looked at the other guy, whose skin was pocked with acne, his ginger hair receding to a widow's peak.

'Could you tell me how your employer knows Ms O'Dwyer is missing? It's not been in the papers.'

'People talk,' Blondie said. 'News travels.'

Dawn had to accept the truth in what the man had said: the media blackout wouldn't last much longer. She made a mental note to hold a press conference the following day. Best to get out in front of it.

'Does your friend talk?' she queried.

'Only when he needs to.'

The commissioner nodded. 'Like that, is it?'

'It is.'

'Okay, let's try something else. Who's your employer?'

Blondie smiled and shook his head. Ginger just looked at his boots.

'If you're so devoted to my finding Ms O'Dwyer, do you have any information that might help me locate her?'

'If my employer knew that, he would have brought her back himself.'

'He's a man of action, your employer, is he?' Dawn asked, standing up and placing her mug on a coaster on her desk before flexing her arms and rolling her head to loosen the muscles. 'I admire that in a person. What's Penelope O'Dwyer got that your employer needs so badly?'

Blondie shook his head again. 'The only thing I'm authorised to tell you is that Ms O'Dwyer drew the attention of very bad men upon herself,' he said. 'She was not discreet. That may be a place to start looking.'

'What the fuck do you mean by "not discreet"? I mean, seriously, lads. That's all you've got for me? I'm none the wiser. If this is helping, I'd hate to see you trying to encumber the investigation.'

Blondie held out his hands as if to show her they were empty. 'That's all I can tell you.'

The commissioner came around to sit on the front of her desk. 'Maybe you'll remember more when we bring you down to the interview room for some closer questioning.'

Blondie laughed at that and pulled open his jacket to reveal the butt of a handgun. 'And who is going to take us down, Commissioner Wilson?'

'That would be me,' Dawn said, and standing up sharply, she kicked Blondie directly in the testicles before, without missing a beat, punching Ginger in the throat with a single, vicious blow.

Both men dropped without a sound, though Ginger did make a slight rasping noise as he lay on the floor, clutching his compressed windpipe.

'Now that didn't go very well for ye, did it, boys?' the commissioner asked, looking down at the prone men and tutting sadly.

Opening her office door, she shouted, 'Can I get some fucking security in here please, or am I in the goddam building alone?'

Blondie needed to be taken away in a wheelchair.

That fact didn't make him any more inclined to talk.

CHAPTER THIRTY-TWO

It was five in the morning before Dawn got home to her two-bedroom house in Clonsilla, by which time she was bone-tired and angry.

Both of the intruders were on the PULSE system, although each had multiple aliases and histories of working for many different criminal organisations. Dawn suspected they had been contracted to approach her for that very reason – it would be impossible to trace them back to whoever had sent them. To the commissioner's relief, the security detail on the gate were both alive and well, if oblivious to the fact there were interlopers in the Garda complex.

After some urgent reconnaissance, it was revealed that a hole had been cut in the fence to the rear of the barracks using an angle grinder, through which the duo had made their entrance. Someone had hacked into the security cameras, planting a loop that was fed to the monitors and giving the impression that all was well.

Of course, both men revealed nothing whatsoever under questioning. The Gardai could hold them for twenty-four hours without proffering charges and Dawn knew she could stretch it out another twenty-four if she thought it would do any good, but she suspected such an extension would serve no purpose. All they could book them for was trespass, destruction of property and carrying an unlicensed firearm. That Blondie had threatened her with said firearm would be her word against his, and a good lawyer could rip that to shreds. After all, who had been physically injured in the affray?

She couldn't even get the thugs on attempting to interfere with an investigation, as they claimed they were there to help. The two leg-breakers might serve a few months in a low-security prison for being in her office without permission and for having guns about their persons, but that was all.

The commissioner was in a foul mood indeed when she finally sat on the end of her bed after a day that felt as if it had lasted three months. Her home was decorated in a spartan style – interior designers might have called it 'minimalist', but Dawn just preferred to keep things simple. She was rarely home for more than a few hours, so all she needed was a bed to fall into and a cupboard to store some clothes. The house was devoid of pictures or ornaments of any kind, and still had the same beige paint on the walls that had been put there by the builders. Dawn had a mortgage on the place, but this was more out of a vague sense that a person should own their own home by the time they hit their forties. She felt no love for the place. It was just somewhere to lie down between shifts.

Her mobile phone rang as she was pulling off her boots: it was a number she didn't recognise. Sighing deeply, she answered.

'This better be critically important.'

'Commissioner Wilson,' said a voice she thought she knew.

'Yeah. Who is it?'

'Frederick Morgan at your service.'

Dawn froze. 'What the fuck do you want, Morgan?'

She might have asked how he'd managed to secure another phone while being on total lockdown in a secure psychiatric facility. She would certainly have liked to know how he had her number. Another perfectly valid question would have been why he was sabotaging himself by ringing that number. But she kept these queries to herself. She reasoned that if he was breaking cover again, it had to be for a good reason.

'To tell you that circumstances in the West are changing rapidly. There are pieces in play on the board which Balor did not expect. They are… muddying the waters.'

'These pieces wouldn't happen to be linked to a criminal fraternity, would they?'

Morgan laughed merrily. 'I take it they have reached out to you then?'

'Morgan, I'm tired and pissed off and I have to be back at work in four hours, so if you have something to say, say it.'

'One of the criminal factions your team in Kerry may already have crossed swords with has links to Balor.'

'What do you mean by links?'

'Balor worked with one of their enforcers.'

'Why would you tell me this?'

'Time is ticking for you. It's also ticking for me.'

Dawn lay back on the soft mattress of her bed, knowing she would not be spending any time in its tender embrace now.

'Give me a name, Morgan. If you want to make a deal, give me something I can properly fucking use.'

The line went silent for a moment as the serial killer considered what Dawn had just said.

'The person you seek walks between two worlds,' he said finally. 'Most believe he is thoroughly respectable and completely trustworthy. But dig a little – peep just below the surface – and you'll see what lies beneath.'

'A name, Morgan.'

'Alas, that is all I know, Commissioner.'

'Then we do not have a deal.'

'I will give a more detailed account to Jessie Boyle. Tell her I require another visit.'

There was another long silence before Frederick Morgan hung up. Dawn immediately called the Central Mental Hospital to inform them Morgan's cell needed to be searched again and every staff member he was in contact with questioned. Then she showered quickly, changed her clothes and went back to Garda HQ.

Dawn Wilson

It was a simple plan. Foolproof – or at least that was how it had seemed to her and Jessie all those years ago.

Jessie told her he went to a particular pub in Ringsend every Friday. He would, inevitably, get drunk and stagger home close to midnight. The expectation was that a plate of ham sandwiches would be waiting for him, and either Jessie or her mother would make a pot of tea the moment he came in, so it would be freshly brewed while he consumed them.

If the sandwiches were not cut just to his liking, or the tea was too strong or too weak or too hot or too cold, violence would ensue. Jessie told Dawn that she and her mother had tried every variable in the preparation of such an uncomplicated meal, but more often than not a beating was their reward.

'I've taken to insisting she goes to bed before he comes in,' Jessie said. 'I'd prefer to take the hiding than know she's enduring it.'

Dawn nodded. She knew about such things all too well.

'You're sure you want to do this?' she asked.

Jessie nodded. 'I have to. Sooner or later, he'll kill one of us.'

'Or both of you,' Dawn corrected her.

'Maybe,' Jessie agreed.

So the plan was set.

That Friday night, Dawn met Jessie in Ringsend, and by eleven thirty they were in an alleyway he would have to pass on his way home. Dawn noted her friend never called her stepfather anything other than 'him' or 'he'. Jessie's mother was Beatrice – Dawn thought it a pretty name. But she didn't know what the man terrorising Jessie and Beatrice was called.

She supposed it didn't matter. These bastards were all the same in the end.

He staggered past the mouth of the alley at a quarter to midnight. Dawn only caught a glimpse as he went past, a shambolic figure that seemed more like a scarecrow than a person in the darkness. Jessie looked Dawn in the eye, and she could see fear in her friend's face but also anger.

'I'm right here,' Dawn said.

Jessie nodded and stepped onto the pavement.

'Hey!' Dawn heard her shout.

Jessie was thinner in those days. Her height made her seem even skinnier than she actually was, and she wore her hair long, usually tied back in a ponytail, which added to her streamlined shape. Even in the darkness though, Dawn thought her friend looked strong and strident and, terrified as she must be, Jessie exuded confidence.

'Wha' the fuck d'you wan'?' a voice slurred.

Dawn had to concentrate to make out the words. He was deeply intoxicated.

'To tell you that if you ever lay a finger on me or my mother again, I'll put you in the hospital,' Jessie said, her voice unwavering. 'She's not here now; it's just you and me. So if you want to test my ability to make good on the threat, now's your chance.'

Drunken laughter followed. Dawn held her breath, waiting for what was coming.

'You don't got the balls, missy,' the voice said. 'Now fuck off home and make me my supper before I hurt ya really bad.'

Jessie didn't budge. Nor did she say anything for a long, painful moment. Silence boomed about the night-time street for so long Dawn worried the tall girl had frozen in panic. But finally she said, 'No one is making you any fucking sandwiches tonight, you evil bollix.'

Barely had the words been uttered when Dawn heard a guttural roar, and to her surprise something dark and ragged crashed into Jessie, knocking her off her feet.

How does someone so pissed move so quickly? *Dawn thought, but then she was moving too, running to her friend's aid.*

What happened next seemed to occur in slow motion.

Dawn came out of the alley and turned left. They were on a narrow row of houses, and there was only one street lamp about fifteen yards away, so the figures struggling on the ground were wreathed in shadow. It took Dawn a moment to see that Jessie was flat on her back on the pavement. Sitting atop her was a heavyset man with a completely bald head, dressed in what appeared to be a blue-and-pink shell suit. As Dawn watched, he drew back his fist and brought it down with crushing force on her friend's head – once, then twice. Each blow made a popping sound in the late-night air.

'I'll teach you a fuckin' lesson, missy,' he slurred. 'You won' talk to me like that again in a fuckin' hurry.'

Dawn didn't waste a second. In two steps she was behind the drunkard and had him in a chokehold. The Students' Union held self-defence classes for students, and Dawn Wilson was a regular attendee. Jessie's stepfather made a gagging sound as she cut off his air supply and dragged him backwards off her friend.

The fallen girl was up in a second, and with a shout that vocalised years of pent-up frustration, she lunged at the man who had abused her and drove her fist into his nose with furious force.

Dawn knew from the sharp crunching of bone that Jessie had done damage. The man in her grasp sagged against her, stunned, and sensing an advantage – and pumped full of adrenaline – Jessie hit him again.

It was this second blow that did it.

Dawn felt something change in the man she was holding – something tenuous and inexplicable but crucial, nonetheless. She didn't know it at the time, but Jessie had struck her stepfather's nasal bone with such force she had pushed it back into his brain, killing him instantly.

What she did know was that in that second, the figure in her arms seemed to double in weight, and she had no choice but to drop him to the pavement, where he lay in a crumpled heap. Dawn had somehow sensed what had happened, but Jessie drove her boot into her stepfather's gut for good measure before sinking to the ground herself in tears.

PART FIVE

Criminal Connections

Seven days until the eve of Samhain

'The criminal is a creative artist; detectives are just critics.'

Hannu Rajaniemi

CHAPTER THIRTY-THREE

Jessie was woken at five thirty by her phone ringing, her pounding head a reminder of the Scotch she'd consumed the night before.

'Sorry to wake you so early,' Dawn Wilson's voice said. 'But I've just heard from our mutual friend Frederick Morgan.'

She filled Jessie in on her visit from the two thugs and the brief conversation she'd had with the incarcerated killer.

'We're going to visit Ultain Cloney later today,' Jessie said. 'In terms of suspects, I'd say he's a good one. If I get so much as a sniff of anything, I'll be looking for a warrant to turn his farm upside down. Just so you know.'

'He doesn't fit the bill according to what Morgan said though,' Dawn mused. 'The person he referred to "walks between two worlds" apparently: the general public believe he's a good person. No one, even within the criminal underworld, thinks Ultain Cloney is anything other than a dangerous psychopath.'

Jessie lay on her back, staring at the ceiling.

Morgan again. Playing games and trying to be a puppetmaster from his room in the Central Mental Hospital. Jessie was not going to be toyed with. She was sick of evil men taunting her.

'I'm not inclined to go hightailing it across the country every time Morgan clicks his fingers.'

'Has anything he's given you borne fruit yet?'

'Terri is away digging into it. She's reporting back later today. As of right now, I'm more inclined to think the criminal connection is a better lead.'

'The boyos that called on me claimed they wanted her found. Which leads me to believe their boss doesn't know where she is any better than we do.'

'Just because one crew want her found doesn't mean another don't have her. If she's been helping gangs to launder money or hide their earnings in offshore accounts, she may well have key codes or passwords to access any amount of cash. And there's nothing a warring gang likes better than to pick the pocket of a rival.'

'She's been missing for more than a week,' Dawn said. 'If that's why she's been taken, she's already dead. A wee girl like that will have given them everything she knows right away.'

'Moorehouse said she's tough,' Jessie said. 'She may hold out longer than you think. And if she's smart, she'll know she's only worth keeping alive as long as she has information they want.'

'You've more confidence in her than I do,' Dawn said.

'The picture I'm forming isn't of a helpless little girl,' Jessie retorted. 'I think there's more to Penelope O'Dwyer.'

'All right. Keep me posted, won't you? I've got all kinds of people breathing down my neck on this one.'

'I know. And I will.'

'Good. Well, daylight's burning. Go and wake up the Boy Wonder.'

'Can I shower and get some coffee first?'

'Jesus, Jessie – you're back a wet weekend and already you're making demands!'

'You know I'm worth it.'

'You'd better be. Now go and find Penelope O'Dwyer please. There's seven days left before the hammer drops.'

CHAPTER THIRTY-FOUR

Seamus looked as if he hadn't slept much when Jessie picked him up two hours later. His mother waved at her from the front door before going back inside hurriedly.

'Take the Tralee Road,' he said. 'I'll let you know when to turn off.'

She nodded and pulled away from the kerb.

'Want to talk about last night?' she asked when five minutes of uncomfortable silence had passed.

'Not really.'

'If things are going to be weird, I think we should. We're about to pay a visit to some very bad people. I don't need you beating yourself up over a silly mistake we *both* made, or nearly made anyway, when you should be completely focused on watching my back.'

Seamus sniffed and said nothing, gazing out the window at the fields scrolling past.

'Seamus, I will throw you out of this car if you don't answer me.'

He looked at her, and she could see he was desperately embarrassed.

'I don't know what came over me,' he said. 'I'm sorry, Jessie.'

'Oh, for heaven's sake, you've nothing to be sorry for!'

'I don't normally drink so much. I think maybe it was that.'

'Are you saying you only found me attractive because you were drunk?'

'Um... yes... no... I don't know!'

She laughed, and then he laughed, and the bubble of embarrassment and discomfort burst.

'Let's write it off as a moment of temporary insanity and put it behind us, okay?' Jessie said.

'Agreed.'

'I dread to think what your mother would have said if she'd walked in on us canoodling on the couch anyway. I reckon she'd have thrown me out and withdrawn her offer of a baking tutorial.'

'Oh, for definite,' Seamus said. 'No one is ever good enough for me as far as Mammy is concerned.'

Jessie drove on for a few more minutes. Seamus whistled a jig through his teeth.

'The cheek of her,' Jessie said suddenly.

'What?' Seamus asked, puzzled.

'Your mother could do a hell of a lot worse than me for a daughter-in-law, you know.'

Seamus gazed at her for a second, and then the two of them disintegrated into guffaws again. Though somehow, Jessie suspected, Katie Keneally knew something had happened after she'd gone to bed. Her demeanour that morning suggested as much.

Deciding there was no point in dwelling on it, however, Jessie turned her thoughts to the business at hand. Which was just as well. It was to be a challenging morning.

CHAPTER THIRTY-FIVE

Cois Donn peat bog – the name meant 'beside the Brown' – stretched over fifteen square kilometres east of Tralee.

Ultain Cloney's homestead could only be reached via a meandering, narrow road through the bog. The farm was right in the centre of the wetlands, and as Jessie navigated the winding concourse, she could see no signs that anyone had dug up the peat for drying and using for burning, as was usual in Ireland. The only purpose Cois Donn had was as a defence. If bogs are left untended, large sections become impassable, and Seamus confirmed the area was full of sinkholes and deep, treacherous pools.

'One road in, one road out,' Jessie observed.

'Just the way Cloney likes it,' Seamus agreed. 'He'll have known we were here the moment the car hit the laneway. I'm told he has wires laid across it every five hundred yards that trip alarms in the house. He'll have a welcome ready.'

'Good old-fashioned Irish hospitality,' Jessie said.

Five minutes later they passed a camera mounted on a metal pole in the verge.

'Now he's got a good look at us,' Seamus pointed out.

The road finally began to broaden, and then they came to a wall made of what looked to be breeze blocks, and in the centre of this a solid, black metal gate.

'Now this *doesn't* look so welcoming,' Jessie said.

'There's only one thing for it,' Seamus stated.

'Which is?'

'We knock.'

Getting out, he strode to the barrier and, using his closed fist, pounded on it – once, twice, three times. Then he waited. No response.

'This is the police here, to see Mr Ultain Cloney,' he shouted. 'Please open up so we can have a chat.'

No response to that either.

'If at first you don't succeed,' Seamus said, and he pounded again, this time continuing to thump the metal of the partition until it was obvious he was hurting himself from the force of the blows.

Jessie waved for him to come back to the car.

'They know we're out here,' she said. 'They're just hoping we'll get bored and go away. So we need to show them we're more stubborn than they are.'

'How are we going to do that?'

'With the power of music,' Jessie said.

Taking out her phone, she synched it with the stereo system in the car.

'Have you ever heard of a band called the Bottle Rockets?' she asked Seamus.

'Can't say I have.'

'Well, you're about to become acquainted.'

She hit play on the music player on her handset, then turned the volume on the car stereo as loud as it could go. For a moment, there was just a dull hiss, then, so loud it made Seamus jump and a meadow pipit explode from the cover of some bracken to their left, the sound of a chord sequence playing on a swampy-sounding electric guitar cut through the air. Seconds later drums and bass kicked in.

'I kind of like it!' Seamus shouted at Jessie over the din.

'I do too!' she bellowed back. 'But that's not the point. This is our way of telling Mr Cloney that we aren't going anywhere in a hurry.'

The vocalist, a man with an American country drawl, started to sing about getting a tow from a guy named Joe, and how it cost him sixty dollars. Jessie pushed her seat back.

'Might as well get comfortable!' she shouted.

'How exactly do I relax with that noise?'

'That's sort of the point!'

*

Seamus got out of the car again, walked a little way back up the road and sat down. The music was still deafening, but it hurt his head less at this slight remove.

An hour later, he was still sitting there, and he was already tired of the Bottle Rockets.

CHAPTER THIRTY-SIX

The gate slowly swung open two hours later, and a thin man wearing a black suit that was cut too short at the legs came out and stood, looking at Jessie through the windscreen. She waved and turned the volume down very slightly. Seamus, who was leaning against the passenger side of the car, praying to be afflicted by temporary deafness, walked around to the front of the vehicle.

'Mr Cloney would like to know what you want,' the emaciated man said in a reedy voice.

It was impossible to put an age on Cloney's doorman – he could have been thirty or sixty. But that wasn't the only thing disconcerting about him. His skin had a leprous quality – it was so red it appeared inflamed, and large swatches were flaky and peeling. The shoulders and lapels of the ill-fitting suit were dusted with large pieces of dandruff. The man's hair, which was plastered across his head in a greasy comb-over, was off-white in colour and hung in strands, almost to the small of his back. What was most chilling, though, were the eyes that peered from the ruined face: they were a pale blue and showed neither compassion nor mercy. They were the eyes of a predator.

Jessie got out of the car and went to stand beside Seamus, killing the music as she walked. Her partner heaved an audible sigh of relief.

'We're from the National Bureau of Criminal Investigation,' she said, holding out her ID, an action Seamus mirrored. 'We'd like to talk to Mr Cloney about a matter we're investigating.'

The gatekeeper remained completely motionless. Only his eyes were active, moving with slow purpose from Jessie to her partner and back again.

'Mr Cloney is indisposed.'

'That's okay,' Jessie said. 'We can wait until he's free. I have lots more music on my phone.'

Without taking her eyes off the peeling man before them, she hit play again, and the Bottle Rockets surged into sonic life, this time declaring that trains are diesel-powered and feel no pain. Seamus flinched just slightly – Jessie probably wouldn't have noticed it if he hadn't been right beside her. The doorman, to her satisfaction, took a step backwards.

'All right,' he said. Jessie discerned the word more from lip-reading than anything else, his voice lost amid the guitars and pounding bass.

She hit pause.

'Has Mr Cloney suddenly become available?' she asked.

'You have fifteen minutes.'

'I could come back with a warrant and an army of uniformed officers,' Jessie said, all good fellowship gone from her voice. 'If I do, we'll take as long as we damn please. So maybe you and your boss should think about that.'

If the strange soldier was fazed by Jessie's change in manner, he showed no sign of it.

'Please follow me,' he said. 'Your vehicle will be quite safe where it is.'

Seamus threw Jessie a look, but she just shrugged and followed the gatekeeper into Cloney's compound.

CHAPTER THIRTY-SEVEN

Terri was in Cork's City Bus Station in Parnell Place, sitting at a table in the café, waiting for her transport back to Cahirsiveen. On her laptop, she scrolled through the transcripts of police interviews relating to the disappearances of the last ten women on Morgan's list.

Terri was still looking for connections, clues, similarities, anything that might link the women to the man Miskella had called Reek.

She wasn't sure if she'd found a link or not, but one detail popped up in several of the testimonies of the friends and family of the women who had vanished: a man described either as 'homeless', 'ragged' or 'dishevelled' had been seen either hanging around their places of work or close to where they lived. Terri wondered if this might be him – Reek stalking his victims before abducting them.

This detail didn't appear in all the accounts, and the description of the individual differed widely in each of the files where it did appear, but Terri thought it might be worth following up.

She added it to her list and put a large asterisk beside the file name.

Terri believed there was no such thing as an irrelevant piece of information. If it didn't prove useful now, it might later.

CHAPTER THIRTY-EIGHT

The Cloney farm was made up of a collection of single-storey buildings, all clustered – apparently without thought or design – around an old-style farmhouse, the whole ensemble surrounded by a wide cobbled yard, about which the high wall had been constructed. Two of the outhouses Jessie saw as they followed the peeling man, contained machinery; their doors were open and she could see tractors and quad bikes inside. All the others – she counted eight of them altogether – were closed and padlocked. What – or who – was inside was anyone's guess.

Here and there about the yard were surly-looking men, pausing in whatever job they were doing to watch as the trio approached.

'I didn't catch your name,' Jessie said to their guide.

'I don't think I offered it.'

'That's not very friendly.'

'We're not friends.'

'Well, now I'm offended.'

They reached the farmhouse's front door, upon which their anonymous companion knocked smartly. It was opened by a short, fat man in blue overalls, who looked at Jessie and Seamus disbelievingly.

'They were not to be dissuaded,' the peeling man said.

Overalls shrugged and stood aside, and they were in.

A long, ill-lit hallway led to an old-fashioned kitchen that was dominated by a long wooden table, at which were sitting three men, one of whom Jessie knew immediately was Ultain Cloney.

He was exactly as Seamus had described: an older yet still powerful man swathed in a long black coat, a crumpled fedora on his head. The other two at the table were younger – one bald, dressed in a leather jacket over an AC/DC T-shirt, the other long-haired, clad in a lumberjack shirt and ripped jeans.

Jessie was only vaguely aware of the other two though. Cloney's presence filled the space. He projected a magnetism and charisma that reminded her of Frederick Morgan; less subtle and baser, but terrifying nonetheless.

'I don't know what you want,' the gangster said, his voice a bass-baritone. 'But whatever it is, you have ruined my morning. So speak quickly and then get the fuck out of my house.'

'They're Gardai, Mr Cloney,' the peeling soldier said.

'I don't care if they're magical elves from the North Pole,' Cloney rumbled. 'They're here because I allow it. They can be gone just as quick.'

'My name is Jessie Boyle,' Jessie interrupted, 'and this is Detective Seamus Keneally.'

'State your business and then *get out*,' Cloney seethed.

'Penelope O'Dwyer,' Jessie said.

Cloney's face grew even more surly. 'What makes you think I know anyone by that name?'

'We have reason to believe you do.'

'What reason might that be? Who has been talking to you about my private business?'

'Do you know her, Mr Cloney?'

'Am I under arrest?' The question was spat at her.

'You are not under arrest, Mr Cloney. This is just a courtesy call.'

'There is nothing courteous about you, madam. If I'm not under arrest, I am not obligated to answer a single question of yours. Do you think I don't know my rights?'

'Mr Cloney, we can go away and get a warrant, and we can come back and take your property apart a brick at a time,' Seamus said. 'And while we're doing that, we can most certainly arrest you for obstruction, and bring you to the station and hold you for questioning for up to forty-eight hours if we feel the situation calls for it.'

'But we don't want to do that,' Jessie added, giving her partner a look that told him to dial down the aggression. 'Wouldn't it be easier to resolve this here?'

Cloney was eyeing the young detective now. 'Do I know you, boy?'

'No, sir, you do not.'

'Yes, I do. I can't place you just now, but it'll come to me.'

'Mr Cloney, I am asking you to assist us in our inquiries,' Jessie tried again. 'Have you had any business dealings with a woman called Penelope O'Dwyer?'

'Are you here because I've committed a crime?' Cloney asked, and Jessie sensed the peeling man moving to stand in the doorway, barring their route of egress.

'We have no reason to believe that at present,' she said, hoping Cloney wouldn't notice her checking the room for other exits. To her dismay, she saw there were none.

'I didn't think so.' The pitch of Cloney's voice was rising, the words coming out with sharper rapidity. 'Do you possess any evidence that I have a connection with this O'Dwyer girl? Other than a story some rat or other has whispered in your ear?'

'I would simply like to know what your relationship with her was,' Jessie said, remaining calm in the face of the man's building rage.

'And I am declining to answer you! If you want to run off and come back with a piece of paper that says you can poke around in my home, away with you. You won't find it so easy to get in next time, I'll tell you that.'

'To be clear, Mr Cloney, are you refusing to answer our questions?' Seamus said.

'I am!' Cloney said, his voice a hoarse roar now. 'I do not recognise your authority here! I have done nothing wrong, and you arrive on my property and try to harass me! I am a working man, minding my own business on my legally owned land. You have no right to interfere with me or my employees.'

'If you would just talk to us for a few moments, we could be on our way,' Jessie said. 'All we want to do is eliminate you from our investigation.'

'Eliminate me, is it?' Cloney said, sitting forward in his chair, where he had been slouching up to this point. 'You'd like to *eliminate* me?'

'I think you are being wilfully obstinate, Mr Cloney,' Jessie said, nodding at Seamus that it was time to leave. 'If you are not prepared to speak civilly, you leave us no choice but to—'

'I did not give you permission to go,' the gangster said. His voice was calm but deathly cold.

Jessie and Seamus froze, and in that instant it all went to hell.

As Cloney shouted his annoyance, the skinhead in the leather jacket stood sharply, knocking his chair over, and suddenly he was holding a gun and pointing it at Seamus. His companion in the lumberjack shirt lunged at Jessie, a hunting knife appearing in his hand as if by magic. From the corner of her eye, Jessie saw the peeling man produce a Glock 17 from inside his dandruff-peppered suit. In the midst of this chaos, Cloney started laughing.

Jessie was afraid. There was no point in telling herself anything other than the truth – she and Seamus were trapped in what amounted to a compound in the middle of a bog, miles from anywhere, and three gangsters with weapons were attacking them while a fourth man with a reputation for casual sadism looked on in delight. The fear coursed through her like an electric current, but she had long learned to see that pulse of anxiety as her friend. It sharpened her reflexes, aided clarity of thought, made her see with more accuracy.

As Lumberjack charged, Jessie did the one thing she knew he did not expect her to: she stepped *in* to the attack, angling her long body around the blade and bringing both hands down on his extended wrist. She gripped tightly before using the man's own momentum against him, twisting the knife-arm to the left sharply and causing the elbow joint to turn in a direction it was never meant to go. The sharp *crack* of the bones snapping filled the kitchen, followed by a solid thump as Lumberjack continued his trajectory and crashed bodily into the wall. He staggered back, dazed, his broken arm hanging limp and useless, before sitting down hard on the floor. The knife fell from his grip and skittered across the stone tiles, coming to rest at Jessie's feet. She scooped it up in time to see that Baldy was now lying flat on his back, blood pouring from his nose as Seamus stood over him. The Heckler & Koch pistol the detective had just confiscated from the fallen man was in his left hand and trained on Cloney, while his own police-issue SIG Sauer P226 was in his right and pointing at their peeling guide, who in turn was holding a Glock 17 in a two-handed grip.

'Looks like we have a good old-fashioned Mexican stand-off,' Cloney rumbled.

The gangster appeared completely relaxed, and where before there was rage, now he seemed happy and relaxed. It was as if the immediate threat of violence had soothed him.

'This isn't a stand-off,' Seamus said, his arms completely steady and his voice firm and in control. 'If your ugly bastard of an associate moves, I will put a bullet in you. End of story.'

'Benson, I am ordering you to shoot the woman in the fucking ovaries,' Cloney said.

Without pausing, Seamus shot the no-longer-anonymous Benson in the shoulder, the force of the shot at such short range knocking him backwards out the door and into the hallway beyond.

'I was about to add that I could just as easily put a bullet in him, but you just made my point for me,' Seamus said. 'Now stand up, Mr Cloney. You're going to walk us out of here.'

Cloney shook his head and chuckled throatily. 'You're never getting out alive. You know that, don't you?'

Jessie heard scuffling and saw the fat man who had let them in helping the injured Benson to his feet.

'Come anywhere near this room and I will shoot your boss in the head,' Seamus warned.

He tossed the H&K to Jessie. 'Tell me you know how to shoot.'

'Of course I do. What's the plan?'

'We use him as a shield to get the hell out of here.'

'What I admire about that is its simplicity.'

'Strategy was never my strong suit. Come on.'

He grabbed Cloney by the collar and hauled him upright.

'Don't think for a moment I won't kill you if I have to to get us out,' he hissed at the gangster.

'Do you think that scares me, boy? I stopped caring about whether I live or die a long time ago.'

'Things did not have to go this way,' Jessie said, jabbing the barrel of her gun into Cloney's back to urge him forward. 'All we wanted was to ask you about Penelope O'Dwyer. A conversation is all we were looking for. Anything that might help us find her.'

Cloney gave her a startled look, but she didn't have time to absorb it. They started to move slowly back down the hall. The fat man peered out of a doorway to their left.

'If I see so much as a nose, I will shoot it off,' Seamus called out.

'So, she is really missing then?' Cloney said suddenly to Jessie.

'What?'

Jessie was keeping watch on their rear. Benson and his portly friend were standing in the corridor now, barring their way back. Blood had coloured the front of the wounded man's shirt crimson, though his grip on the gun was unwavering.

'Penny,' Cloney went on conversationally. 'You're telling me she's missing?'

They were at the front door now.

Suddenly he's all talk, Jessie thought. *He's trying to distract us.*

'You open it,' Seamus said, getting a firm grip on the back of Cloney's coat.

The gangster turned the handle and pushed the front door wide. Twelve men, each gripping a firearm of one kind or another, some of which looked like antiques, were arrayed in a semicircle before the house.

'No one needs to get hurt,' Seamus called out. 'Keep well back, let us past, and we'll let your boss go once we're out the gate.'

'Do you think we're not going to come after you?' Benson said from behind them, his voice heavy with anger and pain. 'You think *I'm* going to let this slide?'

'Start walking,' Jessie said, and they started to move, one painful step at a time, towards the metal gates.

'I liked Penny,' Cloney said as they passed through the gauntlet of his men, who immediately closed ranks again and followed. 'Smart girl. Sassy. Reminded me of her father. I mean, I hate politicians, but he has some class, doesn't he, her dad?'

Jessie was walking backwards, keeping one hand on Seamus's coat tails, the other holding the gun on the men behind. She felt a little giddy, as if she'd had too much coffee.

'What did she do for you, Mr Cloney?'

'I employed her in an advisory capacity,' the gangster said. 'I'm a businessman. There's no crime in having an advisor, is there?'

'That depends on what she advised you to do,' Jessie said.

The gate seemed an impossibly long way away. Each step they executed, the twelve following– who had now been joined by Benson and his chubby friend – took one to keep pace. It was like a fatal dance. Jessie felt sweat trickle down the small of her back. Her arms ached from holding the gun and maintaining her grip on Seamus.

'She helped make my money work better for me,' Cloney said.

'Meaning she laundered it.'

'I didn't say that.'

'You didn't have to.'

They were five yards from the gate now. Jessie chanced a look and could make out cracks in the paint. Patches of rust.

'I've tried ringing her a few times. She's still not come back, and I never got a reply,' Cloney went on.

'When did you try calling her?'

'Does it matter? The phone wasn't answered.'

'When did you first hear she was gone?'

'A little over a week ago, but I didn't believe it. To be honest, it would be good to have her back. She's been a great help to me.'

'Are you serious?' Jessie asked in disbelief.

'Deadly serious. I thought her being gone was just a rumour. I wondered… well, let's just say I thought she'd been pulled in by some of your people. The Criminal Assets Bureau or the forensic accounting unit. Not that she's ever done anything to deserve it, I hasten to add, but you know how vigorous those departments can be.'

'You thought we were here to question you about your business dealings,' Jessie said, and suddenly it all made sense. 'Maybe to confiscate some of your books.'

'I did if I'm honest. It's why I came on so strong.'

'I hate to interrupt, but could you please unlock the gate?' Seamus said, annoyed.

Cloney produced a set of keys from one of the pockets of his voluminous coat.

'Stand down, lads,' he called back to the phalanx of men. 'I want to talk to our visitors before they go.'

His crew looked uncertain, glancing at one another and then back at Cloney in disbelief.

'Go on back to the house now,' he called. 'I'm okay. What could be safer than being in the company of two representatives of the Garda Síochána?'

Sheepishly the men began to scuffle back the way they'd come. Cloney unlocked the gate and pushed it open, stepping onto the lane with Jessie and Seamus.

'What do you want to know?' Cloney said when they were outside.

'Who do you think might have her?' Jessie said. 'If she helped you launder cash or hide funds, do you have rivals who might want to compromise you by abducting her? Maybe forcing her to help them access your money?'

'Oh, there's one or two,' Cloney admitted.

'Names might help us.'

'I'm not a fucking snitch.'

'We can't look for her if we don't know where to look,' Jessie said. 'You'd be helping yourself too.'

Cloney pondered that. 'My main rival, in this part of Ireland anyway, is Charlie Doherty.'

'He's associated with one of the Limerick mobs,' Seamus, who was still watching the gate, said.

'You said there were two possibilities,' Jessie pressed.

'There is a development happening locally that a number of operators are involved in. A large hotel and leisure centre that is effectively going to be a front for money laundering.'

Jessie glanced at Seamus.

'And Penny was doing the books on this project?'

'She was. And it is a project that offers her an insight into a lot of secrets held by many dangerous men. Secrets they might not want her to be able to share.'

'Who's the lead on the development?' Seamus asked.

'Like I said, I'm not a snitch.'

'Developing a hotel isn't a crime,' Jessie said. 'You're not informing on anyone.'

Cloney chewed on that for a moment and finally said, 'Mervyn Moorehouse is coordinating the whole thing.'

Jessie nodded. There was Moorehouse's name. The man who had sent her and Seamus out here, into a situation that could so easily have got them both killed, and who, it seemed, was more involved in criminality than he had suggested when she had last spoken to him. Jessie decided there and then to make it her mission to look much more closely at Mervyn Moorehouse's affairs.

'There's one more thing before you go,' Cloney said suddenly. Jessie paused. 'I'm listening.'

'For a long time, there's been someone operating very much under the radar locally. Only does a couple of jobs a year. But they're always big, and they have regularly overlapped with mine.'

'How do you mean "overlapped"?'

Cloney looked out across the bog, as if the answers to life's problems might be found amid its green expanse.

'Six months ago, a car containing items of value that one of my boys was transporting to a client was hit. The lad's body was never found, and the... the items were taken.'

'That kind of thing has happened before?'

'And not just to me – other operators have been hit too. Normally I'd retaliate, but it's hard to do that when I don't know who to strike against. They seem to know the country, whoever they are, I'll give them that.'

'How do you mean?'

'We used to use back roads, country lanes and that, to transport merchandise. We particularly liked to use one that went right through the Reeks. That's where the fucker would hit us. We changed the route, used a different one through the mountains, but we still got hit. Finally, we stopped using that and found other avenues, but it made life very difficult for us for a while.'

'Do you have any suspicions as to who it might be?'

'Some of the lads think it's a legitimate businessman who gets a thrill out of playing Robin Hood. Only the profits don't seem to find their way to the poor and needy.'

'It sounds like they're doing a lot more than playing, whoever they are.'

Cloney shrugged. 'I thought it might be worth mentioning.'

Jessie thought for a moment, then asked, 'Has your money been tampered with yet?'

'Not that I'm aware of. But I haven't checked this morning.'

'If it has been, could you let me know?' Jessie asked, giving him her card. 'And if you could also pass on any other information that comes to mind about this... *shadow operator*, I'd be grateful.'

'I'll be in touch.'

'Goodbye till then,' Jessie said.

Cloney doffed his fedora, revealing a full head of grey hair, nodded at Seamus and went back into his lair, pulling the gate shut behind him.

'What the hell just happened?' Seamus asked, sitting down heavily on the bonnet of the car.

'I think we just made a new friend,' Jessie said.

CHAPTER THIRTY-NINE

Later that afternoon Jessie, Seamus and Terri met in their office in the White Elephant and shared what they had learned. They each sat at their respective desks, Seamus with his feet up on his, his tie askew and his hurley stick resting across his lap; Jessie with her long legs stretched out in front of her, her hands behind her head; Terri straight-backed, her arms folded across her narrow chest.

'So here's where we're at,' Jessie said. 'We can now say for certain that Penelope O'Dwyer, while officially working for Bandon, Ludlow and Murphy, was also running a sideline advising organised criminals, either on the best way to launder their money or how to hide it in numbered accounts in the Cayman Islands or wherever. The commissioner has been approached by representatives from one gang, stating they want her back because she's so valuable to them, and Cloney expressed something similar.'

'Which means she's bloody good at her job,' Seamus added. 'Making her a very attractive target. The gangs hereabouts have been in free fall since the Limerick wars of the noughties. There has never been a proper realignment of power, so they're still taking potshots at one another, lobbying for territory and influence.'

'If Penelope, or Penny, as she seems to have been called by everyone, was a part of that scene, we have to think a mobster is a good fit,' Jessie said. 'I'm inclined to channel our resources into this line of investigation. Cloney mentioned a hotel development in which a number of local criminal operators are coming together to try to create a front for money laundering.'

'A project Mervyn Moorehouse is running,' Seamus added. 'Now if he was facilitating that build, and he knew she was already actively involved in the process of washing dirty money, it makes sense to me he'd want to try and exert some influence over her.'

'All right, explain your thinking to me,' Jessie said.

'Moorehouse is not a major player locally, but he clearly has an ego and I reckon he wants to grow. Penny knows how to access the funds of every single gangster she helps to manage their finances. Which actually makes her the most powerful person on the scene when you think about it.'

'We have Moorehouse visiting Penny's room too, don't we?' Terri said.

'We do,' Seamus agreed. 'But she was also sleeping with a few other guys. So his sexual liaison with her wasn't getting him the control he wanted.'

'So you think he abducted her to torture the information out of her?'

'Why not?' Seamus asked.

'Him sending that video makes no sense then,' Jessie said.

'If he wants to achieve some good old-fashioned notoriety, what better way to do it?' Seamus shot back. 'You get gangsters going toe to toe with the police all the time, just to increase their street cred. Like the General puncturing the tyres of all the police cars that were surveilling the housing estate where he lived.'

'You think he's ultimately planning on letting the criminal fraternity know it was him who did it?' Jessie said, mulling this over.

'I'm going to tell you, I like him for this,' Seamus said. 'A lot of these gangsters are basically psychos. I think Moorehouse is our man.'

'Maybe,' Jessie said. 'The only problem is that I can't fit the whole Balor element in with him. He's just not that... intellectual. Cultured. He's vulgar, if anything. And he doesn't seem to have any connection to UCC.'

'Yes he does,' Terri said.

Jessie and Seamus both gazed solemnly at their colleague.

'Would you care to enlighten us on that?' Jessie asked.

'Mr Moorehouse owns a construction business that built the most recent extension to the Boole Library,' Terri said. 'Which is where Balor's Stone is currently housed.'

'Well, that is compelling,' Jessie said, almost to herself.

'What about Reek?' Terri asked. 'I think that's key to all of this. It has to be.'

'I'm starting to think the demonism element is a cover to throw us off the scent,' Jessie said. 'These crimes are really about something much more simple. Even accepting this Reek character is part of it all somehow, that truth remains.'

'And what is that simple truth?' Seamus queried. 'What do you think we're looking at here?'

'Money and power. Isn't that what these things are always about?'

'They do tend to be,' Seamus agreed.

'Of course, Uruz being involved adds a whole other level of difficulty to everything,' Jessie said.

'Do you have any thoughts on that?' Seamus asked. 'What do you know about him? Why is he messing about in this?'

'The problem is, I know so very little about him,' Jessie said. 'University students were being abducted and murdered on a small campus just outside Islington. All the evidence seemed to point to a sociology lecturer – we even found underwear from one of the missing girls in his rubbish bin. When his DNA was found at the scene of one of the murders, we arrested him.'

'It wasn't him though,' Seamus said.

'No. The man we took in was, certainly, a sex pest, but he wasn't a killer. Uruz, it turned out, was someone I had not even considered.'

'He'd not been in the frame at all?' Terri asked.

'The day after we arrested the lecturer, a porter at the university failed to show up for work. Later that day, my partner, William Briggs, disappeared. His body was found in the Thames three days later. When we investigated the porter, it turned out all his papers were forgeries. The address he'd given Human Resources was for an abandoned warehouse in an industrial estate. He was a ghost. He *is* a ghost.'

'So him being in this doesn't really help us?' Seamus asked.

'I don't know yet,' Jessie said. 'He was someone completely below the radar. Maybe that's the case here too. So keeping that front and centre, what have you got for us, Terri?'

'I've been looking through the list of people who had access to the stone and its text pre-1978,' Terri said. 'Most of the academics don't raise flags at all – ten of them have passed away, three are still alive but too incapacitated to be a risk to anyone, and three aren't in the country anymore. Two of the academics who worked on the stone, though, became obsessed with the idea of Balor as a religious figure. And at least one of those exhibited violent tendencies – I've looked into their work history, but a lot of this stuff is anecdotal; the university covered it up to avoid scandal.'

'So what do you now know about these boffins, Terri?' Seamus asked.

'Professor Richard Dunbeg, who was the lead excavator on the initial dig, and his research assistant, Damian Coogan. Dunbeg resigned from his post at UCC in 1985 after sexually assaulting a woman who worked in the canteen. I couldn't get much information on it, but one of the lecturers in the history department I spoke to certainly thinks she wasn't the first. The professor became very disturbed after the Balor dig.'

'Where did he go after leaving the university?' Seamus asked.

'I'm sorry to say he went off-grid. I found one reference to him giving a talk to an historical society in Brittany in 1992, but after that, the trail goes cold. I'll keep looking though. I have some ideas.'

'The other one?' Jessie asked. 'Coogan?'

'He drew a lot of attention in the mid-to-late 1980s with a series of articles he wrote claiming he had found Balor's resting place – a cave system in the mountains considered so treacherous even spelunkers were afraid of it. He'd moved into a camp in the foothills of the Reeks at that stage, became completely obsessed with Balor and his creed. Coogan claimed that, despite the danger and with barely any equipment, he'd explored whole sections of the caves and found ogham markings in there proving he was correct, that the old god was interred down there in the dark.'

'I'm sensing a "but" coming,' Jessie said.

'Damian Coogan disappeared in 1987. A colleague from the university went to visit him at his camp, as he hadn't been heard from in weeks. The place was deserted, and his crude caving equipment was gone. The verdict, after a short investigation, was that a tunnel collapsed while he was underground, trapping him down there. A rescue team found a sizable rockfall six hundred metres down the first tunnel when they went to see if they could find him.'

'Did they ever recover his body?' Jessie asked.

'No,' Terri said, 'the caverns were too unstable. The system has been declared a no-go area.'

'That crosses Damian Coogan off the list then,' Jessie said.

'Except for the fact of his nickname,' Terri said. 'They called him Reek, after the place he was so devoted to. That's surely too much of a coincidence for us to just ignore.'

'Didn't Cloney say the vigilante who preys on him and the other gangs likes to use the Reeks as a hijack point?' Seamus said, thinking aloud. 'As if he knows those wild places like the back of his hand?'

'I don't know, Seamus – it's too wild an idea,' Jessie said, shaking her head.

'This whole thing is wild, Jessie. It might be worth exploring.'

'I don't like it. We're running out of time, Seamus. I don't think we can waste what little we have left chasing a dead man.'

'You don't think—' Terri asked.

'That maybe Damian Coogan survived the rockslide and has been in hiding ever since?' Jessie said. 'And is somehow now waging a private vendetta against the local mob? No. I don't think it's plausible. I mean, he wouldn't be on Instagram for a start, would he?'

'It's a theory,' Seamus said. 'I'm not saying it's a good one.'

'It's wafer-thin, Seamus,' Jessie said. 'Drop it. What else have we got?'

'There were reports of a man who appeared to be homeless hanging around some of the missing women on Morgan's list,' Terri said.

'Do the descriptions match?' Seamus asked. 'Ireland doesn't exactly have a shortage of homeless people, sadly. And what else can they do except hang around on the street?'

'They just reference the person as being homeless, or scruffy-looking. The word "ragged" was used a few times. I think one person described him as "wild-looking".'

'I think that's worth following up,' Seamus said. 'What do you reckon, Jessie?'

'We're so stuck for time,' Jessie said, 'I don't want to waste a moment of it chasing after what is most likely several totally unconnected homeless people.'

'I don't need to spend long on it,' Terri suggested. 'Shouldn't we be checking every lead?'

Jessie eyed her team-mates, turning the information over in her head.

'Okay,' she said. 'If we put that together with the Instagram messages, it does give us a reason of sorts to examine Coogan in more detail. What was the tone of the Instagram messages? They were all business, weren't they?'

'Purely functional in nature,' Seamus agreed. 'Just setting up a meeting.'

'And we don't know what the meeting was about, or what the nature of that business was?'

'No. It looked as if the previous messages were deleted.'

'Terri, can you try and retrieve them?' Jessie asked. 'And would it be possible to find out who that Reek profile belongs to?'

'I can see if I can track down the IP address,' Terri said. 'It might not tell us anything, but I'll give it a try. Should I also see if I can trace Professor Dunbeg?'

'Yes. What age would he be now?'

'Seventy-four. Old, I know, but he could still be fit and able.'

'Agreed. Will you keep digging, Terri?'

'Of course I will.'

Terri's phone beeped and buzzed.

'Do you want to get that?' Jessie asked.

Terri gave it a quick look, blushed and set it aside. 'No, thank you. It's personal.'

Jessie stood, stretched and gazed out the window for a moment.

'There are three things going in our favour,' she said. 'First off, I think Penelope O'Dwyer is a much tougher cookie than anyone gave her credit for. She's smart, and she's used to dealing with bad people, criminals. Cloney and Moorehouse both like her; they claim she's able to hold her own. We have to think those instincts will keep her alive. We're also dealing with a small community here. I don't believe someone could have been abducting women, or running an organised crime enterprise, or maybe even both, for decades without a few people picking up on it. Someone out there knows who has taken Penny. We just need to work out who.'

'I don't see how that second one works in our favour, but I'm probably not that smart,' Seamus snorted.

'You said there were three things?' Terri said.

'I did.'

'So what's number three?'

'We don't need to find Balor at all,' Jessie said. 'Even if he does exist, which I'm far from sure about, he's not important to getting Penny back. If we accept the Balor theory, the person we should be looking for is the apprentice. Morgan says he's someone who walks in two worlds, so we could well be looking at some of the local gangsters who try to present a veneer of respectability, or even some of Penny's business associates who like to play a little harder than they'd want the general populace of the town to know. Remember, it's the apprentice who has her. And if we follow that train of logic, he's probably less experienced than Balor. Greener. Probably more impulsive. Which gives us a real advantage.'

'How?' Seamus asked.

'He'll be much easier to draw out,' Jessie said. 'And I think I know how.'

'It would be good to find Balor too though,' Seamus said. 'If we don't, we're just going to be back here in six months' time trying to find the next girl he takes. We need to begin crossing suspects off the list.'

'Agreed,' Jessie said.

'So what do you want to do about that?'

Jessie sighed deeply. 'I know what *you* want to do,' she said.

'Just say the word, Jessie.'

She shook her head in resignation.

'All right, Seamus,' Jessie said. 'Make the arrangements to bring in Mervyn Moorehouse.'

*

The message on Terri's phone was from John. It read:

> *I can't stop thinking about you. Can we skip the respectable waiting period and just arrange another date now?*

As soon as their team meeting was over, Terri texted back:

Of course we can! I'm busy tonight, but I could arrange something for tomorrow?

She put the phone down beside her laptop as she awaited his response and began to read through an article from a Fortean history website about Balor.

The author of the piece also put forward the notion that Balor had styled himself 'King Under the Mountain', seeking to establish a kingdom within Macgillycuddy's Reeks, utilising a network of caves there as a defensive bulwark that could easily be held against intruders with a relatively small force.

This sent Terri looking for information on the Reeks.

She already knew from her schooling that they were Ireland's highest mountain range and contained the country's three peaks over 1,000 metres in height. Near the centre of the range lay Carrauntoohil, Ireland's highest mountain at 1,038.6 metres. Popular with hillwalkers and mountaineers, the Reeks were home to a number of celebrated hiking routes, most notably the twenty-six-kilometre Reeks Ridge.

Terri was about to print off the notes she had collated when her eyes were drawn to a news item from three years earlier: 'Hiker Goes Missing Near Devil's Ladder'. She clicked into the piece. The Devil's Ladder was once a popular ascent route for those hardy enough to climb Carrauntoohil. It consisted of a narrow mountain pathway that had become unstable over time and was now only used by more experienced climbers. An English walker, attempting the 'three peak challenge' – which involved scaling each of the sub-thousand-metre peaks within a single twenty-four-hour period – had vanished, having last been seen leaving Cronin's Yard, the starting point for the Devil's Ladder, at eight in the morning.

Terri googled 'missing' and 'reeks' and discovered that since 1975, ten people had vanished while traversing routes in the mountainous region. She sat back and thought about that. Ten people over forty-three years wasn't exactly an epidemic. But when you added it to everything else…

On a hiking forum, she found a strand relating to the disappearances.

There are places in the Reeks you just don't go one user, hikerboy12 wrote. *The Devil's Ladder gives me the creeps. Steer well clear.*

This sentiment seemed to elicit widespread agreement.

Three hours had passed before she realised John Miskella hadn't responded to her text.

PART SIX

In the Deep Woods

Six days until the eve of Samhain

'She fell down on her bended knees, for mercy she did cry
"Oh Willy dear, don't kill me here, I'm unprepared to die"
She never spoke another word, I only beat her more
Until the ground around me within her blood did flow'

'Knoxville Girl', Traditional murder ballad

CHAPTER FORTY

Dawn Wilson held a press conference the following morning, announcing that Penelope O'Dwyer, daughter of former Irish Taoiseach Dominic O'Dwyer, had been kidnapped. She gave the date and time the young woman had disappeared, discussed the route she would have walked and appealed to the public to come forward with any information they might have. Her address to the cameras lasted all of four minutes before she passed the baton to Penny's father.

Jessie's team were watching events unfold via video-streaming on the Garda website from the White Elephant. They knew that Dominic O'Dwyer's statement was what the press conference was really all about.

'I wish to speak to the man who has taken my little girl,' he said to the camera, speaking with the authority and articulacy of a born orator. 'You have reached out to me already, so I am confident you are open to a dialogue. I know you are working alone, and that you must be frightened and angry at the world. You have probably been hurt at some point in your life, possibly let down by those you trusted. Maybe your parents didn't love you as they should, or your school or the church abused your faith in them. If that is so, then I'm sorry, and I want to assure you that I am not an oath-breaker.'

O'Dwyer leaned forward, as if he was looking down the camera lens and right into the soul of the person who had taken his daughter.

'You told me you want money for the return of my child,' he lied. 'You say you need one million euro before three weeks has passed. I wish to tell you that is a small price for me to pay. You can have it – you can have it now, if you wish. Money is of little consequence to me in exchange for someone I love. I can see that you struggle to understand that, and it makes me pity you even more.'

O'Dwyer's voice rose in timbre as he reached the end of his address.

'My daughter's name is Penelope, but she likes to be called Penny. She adores cookie-dough ice cream, watching reruns of *Murder, She Wrote* and walking her dog in the park. When she was a little girl, her favourite toy was a teddy bear named Oscar. She is oh so clever, hilariously funny, and she is the only person on this planet I would gladly give my life for.'

He paused, his eyes never leaving the camera.

'You are holding a remarkable person, sir. A strong, beautiful soul. I don't expect you to grasp that, but it is a fact. I have your money. Please return Penny to me unharmed.'

A flurry of questions followed, but neither Jessie, Seamus nor Terri needed to listen to them. The gauntlet had been thrown down. They just hoped it would be enough.

Dawn Wilson

She remembered standing over Jessie's dead stepfather and how remarkably, unnaturally calm she had been.

'I'm calling 999,' she said.

Jessie didn't answer. Comprehension of what she had done was sinking in, and Dawn was worried her friend was going into shock.

'You can't call anyone,' Jessie said.

'I have to, Jess. It's going to be fucking horrible, but you won't get in trouble. It was an accident. I'll swear to the fact you were defending yourself.'

'It's not the police I'm worried about.'

Dawn, who had been about to run to the nearest payphone, stopped dead in her tracks.

'What are you goin' on about, Jessie?'

'His people will come for us, Dawn.'

'Who the fuck are his people?'

'His name is Eugene Brody.'

'Am I supposed to know who that is?'

'Remember we covered organised crime groups in class the other day?'

'Of course I do.'

'My stepfather is a captain in the Brody-Creedon gang. He's one of the Brodys.'

Dawn looked down again at the crumpled corpse.

'Why didn't you say?'

'What difference did it make? I'm not involved in his drugs or his gambling or any of that – neither is my mother. But I've met his

brothers. His nephews. There's no way something like this will be kept out of the news. And they'll retaliate. They'll have to.'

'You could ask for protection.'

'In Ireland, Dawn? Where would they hide us? Because we'd both have to go: my mother would be as much at risk as me. My life would be over as much as that fucker's is. We might as well kill me now.'

Dawn rubbed her eyes, suddenly exhausted. 'So what do we do?'

'We walk away and pretend this never happened.'

'Jessie…'

'Help me get him up the side street.'

'This is fucking mental!'

Together they carried the prone figure off the main thoroughfare and placed him on the ground up the narrow laneway where they had waited for him.

'This is a poor part of Dublin,' Jessie said urgently. 'If we'd been on O'Connell Street or somewhere like that, we would have been caught on CCTV, but there are no cameras in Ringsend, because nobody cares about this place. So no one saw what just went down.'

'You don't know that! Anyone could have been looking out a window or something!'

'I grew up here, Dawn. I know everyone who lives on this road. They're mostly elderly and will have been in bed sound asleep before eight o'clock. No one saw us.'

'That's an awfully big assumption, Jessie.'

'He'll be found in the morning. When the police interview the landlord of the pub he just staggered out of, he'll report my stepfather was blind drunk and in a foul mood. The Gardai will also know Eugene Brody has a lot of enemies, any one of which would gladly beat him to death at the drop of a hat. No one will suspect his well-behaved stepdaughter, who has never been in trouble a day in her life.'

'They will come knocking on your door though, Jessie. Where were you tonight?'

Jessie looked Dawn dead in the eye. 'That's easy,' she said. 'I was with you in your flat listening to Grateful Dead albums.'

And that was the story they stuck to.

As far as the world was concerned, Eugene Brody was killed by person or persons unknown while he walked home from the pub one night in 1992, although it was strongly suspected the killing was gang-related.

The only two people who knew the truth were Dawn Wilson and Jessie Boyle. And they never openly spoke of what had occurred that night ever again.

CHAPTER FORTY-ONE

In the Phoenix Park complex, the press conference concluded and the journalists all filed out, some still speaking urgently into voice recorders, others tapping furiously at the screens of iPads.

Dominic O'Dwyer turned on Dawn Wilson in fury. 'I hope that gambit hasn't cost my daughter her life!'

'I trust Jessie Boyle,' the commissioner said. 'She thinks what you've just said will cause the man holding Penelope to break cover. When he does, we'll be waiting.'

'But I have just insulted him! Called him a pathetic, money-grabbing victim! Won't that goad him into hurting her to get back at me?'

'Jessie and her team think your daughter is much more than just a hostage,' Dawn said. 'She has information they want her to divulge.'

'What information?'

'I don't think that's important, do you?'

O'Dwyer seemed about to say something, then stopped, his mouth opening and closing like a fish.

'Mr O'Dwyer,' the commissioner said, tucking her notes into a leather tote bag, 'if there is any information you have still to furnish us with, even if you think it might be only slightly useful, now would be a good time to share it.'

'I… I don't know what you mean!'

Dawn sighed, shaking her head sadly. 'I think you do,' she said. 'I think you're fully aware of your daughter's connections to a number of very dangerous criminal factions, and anything you can tell us could only be a help.'

'I could have you fired for that, Commissioner,' O'Dwyer said, and she saw he was shaking with temper. Or was it fear?

'Maybe you could and maybe you couldn't,' Dawn said. 'Either way, Penelope would still be missing. When you're ready to talk about it, you know where I am. In the meantime, I've got work that needs doing. We have six days before Samhain. I don't want to waste a second of them.'

And she left him standing there looking sad and uncomfortable.

CHAPTER FORTY-TWO

Terri was enjoying working with Jessie and Seamus.

She knew they'd been unsure of her at first – everyone underestimated her abilities, assumed because she was small and skinny and unattractive she was also slow-witted and incapable. But she had actually learned, over the years, to enjoy proving them wrong. The fact was that hunting for information by following trails through the records was something she found not just easy but fun. It was like a game to her, a game she understood on an almost cellular level.

So, proving that she could not only do what she was employed to do but do so at a remarkably high level was just a matter of course. Once people understood she was going to be an asset, they at worst tolerated her and at best actively liked her.

She felt her two new colleagues fit into the latter category.

Jessie was the more cerebral of the two. When she was in the office, she spent long periods of time gazing out the window at the heaving grey waves of the Atlantic. Terri wondered if she was working on the case in her head, going over details and logging clues, or if there was something else on her mind – her former partner who had been murdered, perhaps. Jessie struck her as someone who carried a lot of pain, a lot of guilt. There was a sadness about her Terri recognised all too well, a melancholy that hung just below the surface but was there, if you took the time to look.

Despite it though, Jessie was kind. Not in grand, overt gestures that meant nothing, but in the smaller things, the things that mattered.

For example, she always listened when Terri spoke, asking questions and acknowledging points to show she not only heard but very much wanted to understand fully whatever point Terri was making. That Jessie clearly struggled with any technology beyond the basic features of a smartphone made her efforts all the more meaningful to Terri, as a lot of what she was doing now involved online records and accessing obsolete accounts. She had a feeling Richard Dunbeg had left a digital footprint, but being an archaeologist, it was likely to be in the virtual fossil records, so that was where she was hunting. Jessie genuinely wanted to understand how Terri was doing it and made a point of never ending a conversation without congratulating her on her work and letting her know how much she valued the skills she brought to the team.

That kind of affirmation meant everything to Terri. She loved Jessie for it.

Seamus was a bit gruffer, but he was funny and quick-witted, and she liked the way he did everything with the enthusiasm of a small boy, while also exuding the confidence and physicality of a man. She liked his accent, the fact that he sometimes dropped into the Irish language without realising it – she was fluent too, although she rarely had the chance to use her mother tongue anymore – and she liked how, when he smiled, his entire body seemed to light up and come alive.

Seamus rarely allowed a thought to cross his mind without sharing it, something that seemed to annoy Jessie but which Terri really appreciated. She had grown up in a world where keeping your feelings and opinions to yourself was the only safe thing to do, so meeting a person who saw no reason not to expound on whatever was diverting him was extremely refreshing. The other morning, Seamus had spent an hour analysing which brand of tomato ketchup he liked the best and telling Jessie and Terri why –

it was Heinz, of course. Terri thought this was one of the funniest conversations she'd ever had, and she thought Jessie had found it secretly amusing too, even if she'd complained bitterly at the time.

Working with Jessie and Seamus was fun. And she felt safe with them. She knew they were good people. And that was a rare thing in the world these days.

Terri was in the office on her own, as Jessie and Seamus were in Tralee interviewing Mervyn Moorehouse. She didn't mind being alone. And she liked the White Elephant. The Department of Justice had rented a room for her in a B & B close by, but she rarely spent time there, not even to sleep. The rooms where she worked felt alive with the energy of the three of them, and when she was here, she relaxed and felt happy. Most nights she just curled up under her desk.

Jessie knew she did it and didn't mind. So she kept doing it.

It was mid-afternoon, and she was about to begin hacking into a database holding the records of a history-based chat room that had been discontinued in 1999, when her mobile phone buzzed. It was a text message. She didn't recognise the number.

Why haven't you called me? I thought we had a good time.

Who was it? It had to be John, but he had given her his mobile phone number, which she had saved to her contacts list. She had been intending to message again or call but had been advised at one stage not to come across as too keen, and to leave it a day or two before getting in touch. She'd wanted to, quite badly in fact, but had fought the urge after he'd failed to respond to her last message.

She texted back:

Who is this please?

Terri waited, her fingers still dancing over the keys but on autopilot as her conscious mind was now completely focused on the phone. Finally, fully ten minutes later, it buzzed again.

Who do you think it is? How many other guys have you slept with in the last few days?

That made her want to throw her phone out the window. It seemed so aggressive, so unnecessarily cruel. She could block the number, she supposed, and was about to do just that, when it occurred to her that maybe she was reading an unpleasant tone in the message that wasn't there. The entire exchange could have been a joke. She decided to bite the bullet, and texted back:

John, is that you? Please stop pretending if it is. I texted you back yesterday, but you didn't get back to me. If I have somehow offended you, please forgive me.

She went back to working, one eye constantly flicking back to the handset sitting on the desk beside her mouse mat. Ten minutes passed again. Fifteen. Twenty, and she was close to picking up the phone and ringing the number John had given her. She was panicking now, deeply upset that an evening she treasured, one she had replayed in her head so many times, was now being turned into something tawdry, a weapon to hurt her with.

Almost exactly twenty-five minutes after she had sent the text, a response came.

I just realised I was using my work phone – no wonder you didn't know who I was! My bad. I'm not good at pretending not to like someone when I do. Want to get a drink again soon?

Seconds later, a second message pinged in:

And this is John Miskella, btw!!! ☺

Terri almost wept with relief. So happy was she, in fact, that without even realising it, she stumbled across the clue that would lead them to Richard Dunbeg.

CHAPTER FORTY-THREE

Jessie suggested Seamus take on the questioning of Mervyn Moorehouse alone, and she observed through the one-way mirror, feeding her partner questions through an earpiece.

Moorehouse was represented by a solicitor named Stubbs, who Seamus knew was on retainer with one of the locally based Eastern European gangs – a man who had long ago sold any ethical scruples he might have had for a yearly six-figure sum. He sat beside the businessman in the interview room in Tralee Garda station, the closest one with interview facilities, and nudged his client every time a question was posed that may incriminate him, to which Moorehouse would intone, 'No. Comment. *Comprende?*'

Seamus decided that dancing around the issue was getting him nowhere and went right for the jugular. 'Mr Moorehouse, a confidential informant working with my team has identified you as someone with several very good reasons to abduct Penelope O'Dwyer. You are currently coordinating the development of a very valuable property, and I believe Penelope has a role in the project also.'

'It's a free country, isn't it?' Moorehouse spat. 'I don't have to explain my business dealings, nor who I'm working with.'

'No, that is true,' Seamus said. 'But you will need to explain them to a judge and a jury of your peers if you end up charged with kidnapping.'

'This is bullshit!'

Stubbs placed a hand on his client's wrist, and Moorehouse shut his mouth with an audible click of teeth. But Seamus could see he was getting to him.

'When we interviewed you in your home, Mr Moorehouse, you indicated that you and Penny were not involved in a sexual relationship.'

'So?'

'I'd like to show you these, Mr Moorehouse. They're screenshots I made of security footage from the Kerry Arms. As you can see from the date stamp, here you are entering Ms O'Dwyer's room at two thirty on the afternoon of the sixth of June. And here you are leaving at six twenty-five. Might I ask what the two of you were doing during the intervening three hours and fifty-five minutes?'

'We were discussing business.'

'Really? According to Ms O'Dwyer's work diary, she'd already had a business meeting with you the night before.'

Moorehouse looked uncomfortable. 'We had more to talk about.'

'Do you know she was visited by Joshua Harding that morning?'

Moorehouse shifted in his seat.

'He only stayed for an hour. Brought a bottle of gin and a bottle of Scotch with him. Alistair Burns was there the day before. Twice. He didn't bring any liquor though. Just himself.'

Moorehouse was visibly shaking now.

'You told me you and Penny were friends. That was the term you used.'

'Yes.' The word came out in a choked tone. It sounded strangled.

'Go back to the other men,' Jessie instructed Seamus. 'Let him know they know about him and don't respect him.'

'Do you know, Harding told us you and Penny were friends. I would guess that means Penny told him. Which suggests she was talking about you. Maybe she told him you'd been "friend-zoned". Is that true? Wasn't she into you anymore?'

Moorehouse looked up sharply at that, and Seamus saw something unexpected in his eyes: it looked like despair.

'You care about her, don't you, Mr Moorehouse? Does it make you jealous to think of her with all those other men?'

The expression of dejection lingered for a moment before being replaced by anger and recrimination. 'Do you have anything other than sleazy rumours and backhanded comments about Penny's social interactions?'

'Bring up the hotel development,' Jessie advised. 'If we're going to get him on the ropes, now is the time.'

'You are spearheading a project to develop a hotel five miles outside Cahirsiveen. According to what I learned this morning at the land registry, you're partnered up with Charlie Doherty on that venture as well as a number of individuals with names I can't even begin to pronounce. Eastern Europeans?' Seamus asked. 'Africans?'

'Both.'

'That seems an awful lot of big fish for one pond. You may be in charge of coordinating the builders and hiring the electricians, but you're hardly the big boss, are you?'

'I'm runnin' the show, so I am!'

Stubbs tried to shush his client, but Moorehouse was fuming now.

'With the information Penelope O'Dwyer has in her head, you could be,' Seamus said. 'I think you tried to control her by embarking on a sexual relationship with her, and when you learned you couldn't do that, because she was having intimate encounters with quite a few other men, you decided to exert control in another way.'

'I don't know what you're talking about.'

'You abducted her. Kept her prisoner. Tried to get account details, passwords, client information from her.'

'Are you going to charge my client with anything, Detective?' Stubbs demanded.

'Your client hasn't answered a single one of my questions yet!' Seamus shot back.

'I have advised him not to, and I continue to do so.'

'When you're at the bottom of the pecking order, you want to feel big, don't you, Mr Moorehouse? You wanted someone to know you had her. You wanted the recognition for it. The accolades. You probably craved the attention. Are you tired of being seen as a little man, Mr Moorehouse?'

'No. Fucking. Comment.'

'Do you feel respected by your peers? Your colleagues?'

'I'm well thought of by everyone I deal with.'

'I don't believe you.'

'I don't care. From here on, my answer to any question is "no comment". Are we clear?'

*

Moorehouse remained in the Garda station in Tralee for a further twenty-two hours, during which time he gave Seamus not one single piece of information.

'We can extend his stay under law for another day,' Jessie told the very tired Seamus.

'I think we need to cut him loose and just watch him,' Seamus said. 'I feel it in my bones: this is our guy. Something about him just doesn't gel for me, Jessie.'

'You may be right,' Jessie said. 'But we're running out of time. It's five days to Samhain, and we're out of options.'

'What do you want to do?'

'Terri says she has something. Cut Moorehouse loose and put a detail on him – maybe we'll have rattled him now and he'll do something stupid. In the meantime, let's you and me go back to the base and see what Terri's been cooking.'

Seamus ruefully agreed.

There wasn't much else he could do.

Jessie was about to hit the road when her phone buzzed with a text message. It was from a number that meant nothing to her and contained no words, just a single symbol:

n

She barely remembered the drive back.

CHAPTER FORTY-FOUR

'It's been under my nose all along; I don't know how I didn't see it,' Terri said to Jessie and Seamus. It was later that evening; the sun was setting across the ocean and the entire room was bathed in a pink glow.

'Tell us,' Jessie said.

Terri handed each of them a printout of an article from the local newspaper, dated 1994.

'I read this three days ago, and I only revisited it this afternoon to cross-check some details on the history of Macgillycuddy's Reeks. I feel a little embarrassed actually. *Gabh mo leithscéal.*'

Seamus looked up at her usage of the Irish apology.

'*Nà habair é,*' he said – don't mention it. 'You've a bit of Irish then, Terri?'

'I studied the language in college as part of my history course,' she said shyly. 'I like to think I'm fluent, but it's classroom Irish really. I… I'd like to use it a bit more…'

'You should've said.' Seamus beamed, putting an arm around her and giving her a side hug. 'It'd be great to have a bit more Gaeilge about the place. Little sis, you and I can talk about Jessie behind her back and she'll never know!'

'I hate to interrupt this cultural love-in,' Jessie said, although her tone showed she was pleased to see her two teammates bonding over a shared interest, 'but can we tune back in to the matter at hand?'

'As you can see,' Terri said, grinning as Seamus winked at her and made a mock-annoyed face at Jessie, 'the article I've printed up relates to a community of New Agers and hippies that settled in the Crann Darrach woods in North Kerry in the mid-nineties. They came to the area initially to protest against the building of an interpretive centre, which was planned as a hub for tourists coming to visit Dedad historical sites. There's a series of passage graves – mounds that contain burial chambers linked by a stone-lined corridor – in a clearing at the centre of the woods, and these were to be renovated as an attraction, with the interpretive centre right next door, complete with a café, gift shop and video suite showing a film about the woods, probably narrated by Stephen Rea or someone like that.'

'It would have been a boon to the area,' Jessie said. 'Brought in lots of funds to the local economy.'

'Yes, but it also meant felling acres of oak forest, digging up land that was unchanged since the tribes walked on it fifteen hundred years ago, and transforming the resting place of what are believed to be Dedad kings and queens into the Kerry version of Disneyland. If you look at the article, you'll see a quote from one of the men who organised the protest. He called the project "the rape of Ireland's natural heritage and social history".'

'These guys were successful in halting the development then?' Seamus asked.

'Oh yes. The dispute went on for more than five years, and it got quite nasty. Construction equipment was vandalised. Some of the crew sent in to fell the trees were beaten up – one was hurt quite badly; he still can't walk unaided. Finally, the local authority relented, and the plans for the centre were moved to another location – to Cahirsiveen, in fact.'

'So the centre just below Sadbh's fort was originally meant for the oak woods?' Jessie asked.

'Yes.'

'Why are you telling us all this?' Seamus wanted to know. 'Like, it's interesting and all, but how does it help us?'

'The community of New Agers who staged the protest set up residence in the woods,' Terri said. 'So by the time construction was called off, they'd been there for half a decade. Legally, they'd been occupying the land long enough to stake a claim on it. To shut them up, Kerry County Council granted them squatters' rights.'

'So they're still there,' Jessie said, finishing the train of thought for her.

'They are. And look at the name of the man the newspapers reported is their leader.'

Jessie did – Terri had highlighted the relevant section of the article in fluorescent green.

'Mr Dick Dunne,' she read.

'Sound familiar?'

'Kind of. You're telling me this is Professor Richard Dunbeg?'

'Look at the second page I printed up.'

Jessie did. It contained a photo taken from the UCC staff prospectus in 1981 that showed a serious-looking young man with a bowl haircut and thick glasses, a bowtie nestling just below his prominent Adam's apple. The panel next to the photo told her this was Richard Dunbeg, Professor of Archaeology.

The photo beside it was grainier and had been clipped from a newspaper article. Terri had marked it 3 June 1997. It showed a crowd of people, some holding crudely made placards, standing in the shadow of what looked to be an earth mover. Front and centre was a long-haired man wearing wire-rimmed glasses. He was dressed in an open-necked shirt and cargo shorts. The caption under the photograph declared him to be Dick Dunne, leader of the protestors.

But it was clearly Richard Dunbeg – even the poor picture quality couldn't disguise the fact.

'We've got him,' Jessie said.

'*Little sis* got him,' Seamus pointed out, giving Terri a thumbs up. '*Iontach*, Terri. *Iontach*.'

Excellent, Terri. Excellent.

Terri beamed with pride.

'You two up for a road trip tomorrow?' Jessie asked.

CHAPTER FORTY-FIVE

Seamus rose at four the following morning, dressing in outdoor gear while it was still dark, pulling on hiking boots and packing a torch, walking poles and a length of rope into a backpack while his mother still slept.

Despite the news Terri had shared the previous day about Dunbeg living locally, Seamus was convinced Moorehouse was Balor – he was fond of Terri, and was impressed she had tracked Dunbeg down, but in truth he did not believe he was the man they were looking for. He felt in his gut that there was something off about Moorhouse. He also knew they didn't have time to wait for the businessman to break his cover or put a foot wrong. That left the detective with only one option: if he could not get to Balor, he would have to approach his apprentice.

And this meant testing another theory of his, one that Jessie had ordered him to discount but which he felt should at least be examined before being ruled out.

What if Coogan, the research assistant who had apparently died in the mountains, had in fact not died at all and was still hiding out up there? It would fit the story some of their clues seemed to be telling, and at least Seamus would be doing something other than waiting around for Moorehouse to stumble. And Seamus reminded himself that Balor had not done anything to reveal his identity in thirty years – why would he do so now?

The apprentice was, he believed, the best course of action.

He'd rung little sis to ask her for coordinates, which she had happily given him, shortly after he'd got home. It had been a while since he'd been into the mountains, but as a boy he'd spent many long hours there with his father, so he was confident he could still find his way about.

It was still dark when Seamus parked his mother's Focus, which she'd given him permission to borrow, at a viewing point and then followed a narrow path through two kilometres of scrub.

It was not usual for Seamus to go rogue, to strike out on his own like this. Yet as he had worked this case, he had begun to feel more and more impotent – Balor was mocking them, taunting them from the shadows. Seamus had never felt he deserved the commendation he'd received after the prison transport shooting, and the plaudits that had been heaped upon him had never felt earned.

When he was referred to as a 'hero' by his mother or his superiors, the word made him feel nauseous.

If he could be the person who brought Penny back from captivity, maybe he would feel he had actually done something worthy. Something really heroic.

As Seamus walked, the path began to climb, and within the hour his shirt was soaked to his back with sweat and his lungs were burning. Seamus liked to tell himself he was at the peak of physical fitness, but it seemed he was wrong – but then, he supposed as long as he didn't have to chase any murderers or gangsters up a mountain, he'd probably be all right.

He stopped to drink some water, looking back over the landscape that spread out before him like a dark tapestry. The Ring of Kerry. His home. Usually, whenever he thought of the place, he was filled with a sense of love and nostalgia, but these past days had caused him to question that devotion. Working this case had shown him an underbelly that cast the place in a whole new light. And not a good one.

He wished he could unsee it. But he knew that was impossible. Putting the cap back on his water, he turned his back on the vista and continued to climb.

Just as the hands on his watch told him it was six o'clock, he reached the place Terri told him Damian Coogan, the man they called Reek, had made camp during his vigil on the mountainside more than three decades ago.

The wilderness had long since reclaimed any trace of the campsite – though he spent half an hour poking about. Shining his torch into copses and under bushes, Seamus could see no sign of human habitation in the area. In fact, the path leading there was largely overgrown, and he had to use one of his walking poles to beat his way through in places, so it looked as if no one at all had been there for some months, at least.

Beginning to think Jessie may have been right and that this was just too long a shot, Seamus inspected the map he had marked up with Terri's help and took a passage upwards, a series of steps that seemed hewn into the bare rock – climbers called it the Devil's Ladder, a moniker Seamus decided not to think about.

If he'd thought the going was hard getting to Coogan's old campsite, this was even worse. There were long sections of the ascent where he had to use hands and feet to make progress, scrabbling over the surface like an insect clinging to the face of the mountain. Forty-five minutes after he began his climb, he came to a low, jagged overhang, beneath which he could feel a chill blast of air that told him he had found the opening to a cave system.

This was where Coogan believed Balor, the Celtic embodiment of the Devil, was buried. And it was as desolate and miserable a place as Seamus could imagine. Clicking on his torch, he got down on his stomach and inched inside, using his elbows to seek purchase.

For about two metres the rocks above him were barely cen-timetres above his head, and Seamus experienced a powerful sense of claustrophobia. As he edged his way further inwards, it became darker and darker ahead, and colder and colder, until the only illumination was thrown by the beam of the torch, and he was chilled to the bone. If it continued like this for much longer, he was going to have to haul himself back out and abandon his efforts. He was about to do just that, the panic building in him to a high crescendo, when suddenly the stone lifted away, and he was struck by a sense of space and majesty as the mountain opened up before him.

He dragged himself out of the channel and entered a world of total blackness. Using the wall behind him to haul himself upright, he swept the beam of his torch left and right and saw he was in a vast natural amphitheatre that stretched for several hundred yards ahead of him and the same at least above.

Straining his ears, he could hear a breeze blowing through cracks and fissures in the rock, and the steady drip of water. Outside of the narrow beam of the torch, all was inky black. He was going to have to move slowly and with great purpose if he was to avoid coming to harm. Training the light on the cave floor, he saw it was pocked with puddles of pale green water but seemed solid enough. Stepping carefully, he started across the chasm, hearing his steps echo in the stony emptiness.

It felt like he was walking backwards in time – moving through a gulf of human existence which he could scarcely comprehend. Seamus was not a man who spent much time pondering his own mortality – such musings could be detrimental to someone who made a living putting themselves in harm's way – so he did his best to shake off the sensation.

But it was harder than he'd expected.

Somewhere to his left, something skittered in the darkness – Seamus assumed it was a rat or some other creature that made this cold, dank place their home. Never one to be squeamish, the detective acknowledged he very probably was not alone in the caves and continued to make his way to the other side, hoping whatever it was kept to its own section of cave and left him to navigate his.

After what felt like an age, he reached the far wall, which sloped upwards at an angle of about seventy-five degrees. At first, he thought his efforts were in vain, as the rock wall seemed impenetrable, but as he shone his torch over the surface, an inch at a time, he saw, about fifteen feet up, an opening, and as he looked closer, he saw someone had hammered mountaineering pegs into the rock face. The pegs were covered in a crust of rust and some kind of pale lichen had colonised them, but he tested the lowest one and found it sturdy. Using them as foot- and hand-holds, he carefully made his way up to the cave mouth.

The opening was a little over seven feet high and probably eight in diameter, and when he got to it, he sat there for a moment, getting his breath back. As he did so, two things struck him simultaneously.

The first was that, on the wall to his right, almost at eye level, were a series of ogham letters in three neat lines. Their placement suggested to Seamus that the person who had written them had sat exactly where he was when they had done so. That this had probably occurred more than a thousand years before he had taken up his place in that stone doorway added to the otherworldly nature of where he was.

He was using his phone to take a photo of the markings when the second thing occurred to him. He could smell something.

It was faint at first, but as he took shallow breaths to better identify what it was, the detective realised he was smelling old woodsmoke: someone had made a fire in the corridor behind him.

Getting tentatively to his feet, Seamus began to feel his way along the stone passageway. As he travelled deeper, the smell became stronger and the ceiling above began to slope downwards, forcing him to stoop until he was bent almost double.

Seamus had never felt so alone in his life. He tried not to consider that every step was taking him further and further away from daylight, that darkness now had him in its embrace and that the passage he was traversing was angling downwards, deeper and deeper into the mountain itself. The air got very thin, as if the memory of fire was sapping all the oxygen from it, and Seamus tried to keep his breathing measured and steady. Each minute seemed to stretch as long as an hour, and he began to worry about the batteries in the torch. The beam seemed to have become dimmer, and while he'd packed spares, the thought of changing them in the darkness scared him. He had his phone, of course, but using the torch on it would eat up the battery on his only source of communication with the outside world, and he was loath to do anything to compromise that.

The passage continued to angle downwards. At one point, he encountered a place where a pile of rocks had fallen, seemingly from the ceiling, and there was just enough room for him to crawl over them. The ceiling beyond this continued to get lower and lower, and to add to Seamus's discomfort, the walls began to close in, so he had to squeeze through columns of rock to make any headway. It was as if the mountain itself was trying to crush him. In a moment of dire panic, he started to fear he would become wedged, stuck irretrievably in the freezing dark, entombed with Balor in a mountain grave.

Seamus stopped where he was, panting from the exertion.

'Fuck you,' he said, gently at first, then louder. 'Fuck you, mountain! You don't scare me, all right? I am not afraid of you!'

The passage was so close there was no echo – the sound of his words was soaked up by the dank rock. But addressing his terror aloud grounded him, made him feel better. He had come to this place of his own volition, and he could decide to leave if he wanted to.

For a moment he allowed himself to stop struggling, to sit back against the stone. What was he doing? What did he hope to achieve? He had come here to see if there was any sign of Damian Coogan, and he had to admit there was not. The smell of fire could have been carried down cracks in the rock from somewhere on the other side of the mountain – sheep farmers burned gorse at this time of year to create grazing for their flock. He was probably smelling that.

It was time to get out of this hellish place.

Seamus was about to go back the way he'd come when he heard something totally unexpected: a voice in the darkness. The sound was indistinct at first, and he thought he must have imagined it. He froze, sweat standing out on his brow despite the coolness of the cave, and listened intently.

At first there was nothing – just the heavy sound of his own breathing in the enclosed space. Then, suddenly, he heard it again, and this time the sound seemed to be travelling towards him. Was it someone singing? It couldn't be – that was too bizarre. He listened again.

Yes, there it was. Deep in an abandoned cave system in a mountain in the middle of the wilderness in Kerry, at seven in the morning, a harsh male voice was singing a song in old Irish: 'Bean Pháidín'. Seamus knew the song well – his mother used to sing it to him when he was small. It was supposed to be a comedic song, about a woman who longs to be the wife of a man named Little Paddy, who is clearly not much of a catch.

Hearing it so out of context in such a strange place was anything but funny though. Seamus thought it utterly chilling.

Am I going mad? he wondered for a moment. *Has the stress of work finally got to me?*

Deciding such self-indulgent philosophising was not going to do him any good, he came to the conclusion that, regardless of the unusual location, he was still a police officer and should therefore act accordingly. Drawing his SIG from the holster clipped to the back of his belt, he called out, 'Hello? My name is

Seamus Keneally, and I am a detective with the National Bureau of Criminal Investigation. I am asking you to identify yourself. I am armed and will fire if given reason to do so.'

The singer, very close now, stopped, and Seamus heard them giggle, a sound both twisted and frightening in the darkness.

'I'm going to ask you one more time to tell me who you are,' Seamus called out. 'I am a Garda, and I am within my rights under the Criminal Justice Act 2016 to request you identify yourself.'

The tunnel veered to the right, a hairpin turn, and at this point the ceiling was so low Seamus was moving forward in a crouch, the torch in one hand, his gun in the other. Whoever they were, they were just around the corner. Seamus could hear them breathing.

He pressed his back against the wall and waited.

'*'S é'n trua, nach mise, nach mise, 's é'n trua nach mise bean Pháidín,*' the voice sang, cracking at the lilting notes as if it was not used to being raised in song. 'It's a great pity that I'm not, that I'm not, it's a great pity that I'm not Little Paddy's wife.'

They're just feet away, Seamus thought. *I can smell them. The smell of burning seems to be coming from them. How is that even possible?*

The voice sounded as if it was right beside him. He could hear breath being sucked in in ragged gulps, saliva clicking in the throat as each new line of the song was begun. It suddenly seemed to Seamus that waiting for his fate to meet him was a poor idea, and before he had the chance to change his mind, he lunged forward around the corner.

In the torchlight he caught a brief glimpse of a thin, ruined face and stringy, dead man's hair before something smashed into his jaw and he knew no more.

CHAPTER FORTY-SIX

'Where the hell is he?' Jessie asked Terri for the fourth time in as many minutes.

She was in a bad mood already. When she'd got out to the MG that morning, someone had scratched Π into the driver's-side door, right beside the handle, so there was no way she could miss it.

Now Seamus was late. Seamus Keneally had many habits Jessie found irritating, but lack of punctuality was not usually one of them.

'He was going to check out Damian Coogan's campsite this morning,' Terri said, giving the same answer she had furnished each time the question had been posed.

'He did not tell me he was planning on doing that,' Jessie said, picking up her phone and speed-dialling her partner, an action she had also done multiple times since he'd failed to show up at the prearranged time.

'No, but he did tell me,' Terri said mildly.

'Didn't I tell him *not* to pursue Coogan?'

'Yes, but he was just trying to help, Jessie.'

'Seeing as you two are thick as thieves now, did he indicate what time he'd be back?' Jessie grumbled.

'He said he'd be here to travel with us.'

'The call still can't be connected.'

'There's probably very little coverage up there,' Terri offered.

'Probably.'

'I expect he found it harder to locate the spot than he thought he would,' Terri suggested. 'He told me he hasn't been up there in years.'

'Well, I'm not waiting any longer,' Jessie said. 'Will you send him a text and let him know we're going on ahead of him? He can follow us if he gets back in time.'

'Yes. All right.'

'And please tell him I am pissed off.'

'Okay.'

'You can quote me verbatim. "Jessie is pissed off."'

'I'll make sure I do.'

'Use caps.'

'Caps. Got it.'

'And any emojis or whatever you think are appropriate.'

'Okay... I'll have to think about that.'

Jessie pulled on her coat.

'I suppose you want to call shotgun?' she asked Terri as they locked up the office.

'Sorry?' The girl looked up from her phone where she had been scrolling through her emoticon collection, puzzled.

'Oh, never mind,' Jessie said.

I never thought I'd miss that, Jessie thought as they walked down to the MG. *Go figure.*

*

Ten minutes into the drive, Terri's phone beeped.

So where are we meeting tonight?

She grinned, in spite of herself, and texted back:

I'm at work now – can I give you a ring later?

She expected a quick response, but she was beginning to get used to the rhythm – or lack thereof – of John's texting. It was like the idea to message her popped into his head, and then he became distracted and forgot all about the fact he had. She tried to tell herself it was endearing.

Jessie fiddled with the stereo in the MG, and some kind of alt-country began to play. It had a driving acoustic guitar front and centre, with an insistent mandolin riff pushing the melody onwards. A male voice came in – plaintive, pained. He was telling someone he would write them a letter tomorrow, as tonight he couldn't hold a pen.

'Who's that?' Terri asked.

'Justin Townes Earle,' Jessie said.

'He's good.'

'I know.'

Her phone beeped again.

Can't we sort this out now? I have stuff to do, and I need to plan my day.

That blindsided Terri. She texted back:

I don't want to mess you around is all, John. I'm out in the field, and I don't know how long I'll be or what time I'll be back in the office. Can I please give you a call later?

She waited, phone in hand, hoping he would tell her that, of course, that was perfectly reasonable. That he was just keen to see her. But no such message came.

As Jessie parked the MG on the outskirts of Crann Darrach woods an hour later, a terse message from John Miskella landed on her phone.

Don't bother calling. I've had a better offer.

Terri wanted to ring him right away, tell him she was sorry, that it was just the nature of the work she did and it didn't mean she wasn't interested. But Jessie Boyle was looking at her expectantly, and there was work to be done, and for Terri, the work was always the most important thing.

So she put her phone away and tried to do the same with her confused feelings for John Miskella.

CHAPTER FORTY-SEVEN

The commune at Crann Darrach looked like something from the pages of a John Steinbeck novel – if the Joads sported dreadlocks and wore hemp sandals, that is. The forest covered an area of twelve square kilometres, all that remained of a vast oak wood that had once covered most of the western coastline.

Colourfully painted gypsy caravans, tepee-style tents, shelters made from branches and foraged wood, renovated storage containers and even a few cannibalised garden sheds were set here and there among the trees, covering an area of several acres. As Jessie and Terri walked through the hodgepodge village, Jessie noted that everyone they saw seemed to be busy: a woman with a baby lashed to her front was washing clothes in a huge basin using an old-fashioned washboard. A man stripped fat and hair off some kind of animal hide using what looked to be a piece of flint, while another was drying strips of meat, all hung on a criss-crossed platform of twigs over an open fire. A group of teenagers – whom Jessie thought should probably have been at school – were weaving baskets from reeds and green twigs.

All about was calm industry. Not a single person was gazing at a screen, nor did anyone appear anxious, hurried or unhappy.

'I thought you said these people were violent,' Jessie said to her colleague.

'They haven't been active participants in the protest movement since the late nineties,' Terri said. 'It seems that as soon as they were given the land, they felt they'd won the fight and didn't need

to agitate anymore. They downed their placards and became…
survivalists, I suppose you'd call it.'

'Maybe that's what it was all about,' Jessie said. 'Forcing the state
to give them a place to settle and do their own thing unhindered.'

Jessie heard the words as she spoke them and wondered if they
sounded cynical. She tried very hard not to allow the work she did
to colour her view of people, but it was hard for it not to happen.

'Maybe,' Terri said. 'I had thought their stance was all about a
cause, but maybe you're right.'

A young man with very long auburn hair approached them.
'Can I help you?'

'We're looking for Dick Dunne,' Jessie said, holding out her
ID so he could see it.

'Dick is down by the river with some of the youngsters,' the
young man said. 'Come. I'll show you how to get there.'

A path that had been laid with wood bark led away from the
encampment through the trees.

'Dick is our camp elder, and as part of his duties, he takes the
children for lessons each day for a few hours,' their host told them.

'What does he teach them?' Terri asked.

'Whatever they need to know,' the young man said.

Jessie laughed. 'As simple as that?'

'Exactly as simple as that,' the long-haired youth agreed,
smiling. 'Wouldn't it be wonderful if every child could have such
an education?'

The river could suddenly be seen shimmering through the trees,
and Jessie found she could actually smell it: a sweet, crystalline
aroma that seemed almost alive. They broke from the cover of the
woods and there it was, brown and bubbling. Sitting on its bank
was a collection of about twenty children of various ages, and at
their centre Richard Dunbeg – or Dick Dunne.

The long-haired youth went and spoke to Dunbeg quietly
for a moment. Jessie saw the older man gazing at her and Terri,

seeming to size them up, and then he stood, brushed himself down and walked towards them. Their guide took his place among the children, apparently continuing the lesson.

'What do you want, officers?' Dunbeg asked them. He did not seem angry at their presence, more resigned to it.

'We'd just like to ask you some questions,' Jessie said.

'We all have questions, Detective.'

Dunbeg motioned with his head, and they began to walk north along the river, away from the group of children.

'I don't know if you've seen the news,' Jessie began.

'The news that is important to me is most likely very different to that which seems relevant to you,' Dunbeg said. 'My days are informed by the seasons, the cycle of nature, the comings and goings of the birds and the animals of the wood.'

'That's great,' Jessie said, 'and it looks like you and your friends have a nice thing going here. I can respect that, I really can. But I'm going to have to ask you to focus on more worldly matters. Where were you on the night of the fifteenth of October?'

'I was here.'

'And I'm sure your neighbours can confirm that?'

'Of course, if they are required to do so.'

Jessie nodded. 'How often do you leave the woods, Mr Dunbeg?'

He stopped and looked at her sternly. He was in good physical shape for a man of his age, and his skin had a natural tan. His hair, which was almost completely grey and thinning on top, was long and tied in a very loose ponytail with what looked to be a strip of hide. He seemed fit, healthy and radiated calm intelligence. Jessie found it hard to believe he was behind a series of abductions. But then, she'd met killers before who presented a respectable face to the world. Jessie Boyle had learned long ago not to trust first impressions.

'Please do not address me as Dunbeg,' the man said. 'I left behind that name more than twenty years ago, as I no longer valued what the person who bore that title stood for, the life he led. I took another name and began a new existence.'

'And how often does that existence take you away from Crann Darrach?' Jessie asked again.

'I haven't left these woods in fifteen years,' Dick Dunne said. 'This is my home. It is where my soul has found peace. It gives me everything I could want, and I see no reason to step outside of its protection.'

'You don't leave the settlement here at all?' Terri asked.

'Once a month one of our men goes into Kilnaughten to pick up the few materials the woods cannot provide,' Dunne said. 'But those are small trifles indeed. We are not strictly vegetarian, but we eat little flesh, and what we need we hunt for. We grow crops and forage for the rest of our plant-based food. We grind our own flour and make our own clothes. We built a mill upstream that powers generators we use at night – the sun provides light during the day. We live a simple life, free from the burdens the modern world has foisted on the masses. And as you will understand if you are prepared to truly look, we are happy.'

Jessie and Terri looked at one another.

It was still possible the man who had once been called Richard Dunbeg was Balor, or had been once before passing on the baton. The two investigators could not definitively eliminate him as having coordinated the abduction of twenty-eight women, the latter half of whom had been taken since he'd set up residence in this wild community, a place without computers, televisions, mobile phones or any of the technologies those who had communicated with Balor had described.

Dick Dunne could be Balor. Or perhaps he knew the person who was.

As slim a chance as it might offer, time was rapidly running out for Penny.

CHAPTER FORTY-EIGHT

While Jessie interviewed some of the other residents of the commune to confirm Dunne's assertion he hadn't left the woods in a decade and a half, Terri sat down with the former archaeologist at a hand-crafted wooden table outside the traditional caravan he called home.

'Mr Dunne, can I ask you something?' she began.

'I may not answer, but that should not preclude you from posing your question.'

'What happened to you during the excavation of Balor's Stone?'

The man did not respond for a long time, but finally he said, 'I heard it calling to me – the stone. As soon as I set foot in that rough field, I could sense its presence like fingers in my brain. Spiders running across my every thought. Quilt was the first to unearth it, but he was just a crude instrument. The stone was waiting for me to come to pluck it from the earth and place it back where it belonged.'

'You believed Balor was real – that the story in the runes was true?'

Dunne sighed heavily, as if he had always known someone would ask him to relive those painful moments of his past.

'Have you read much philosophy, Ms Kehoe?'

'Terri, please. I've read some. It's not really my area.'

'A number of thinkers, going right back to the Greeks of antiquity, spoke of the coming of a superman. Modern readers immediately conjure images of the superhero from the movie and comic books – the muscle-bound oaf in blue and red – and assume the concept to be a benign one, but no one before that saw the figure as anything other than a force for chaos.'

'And you think Balor was one of these supermen?'

'There are many ancient writings that are wholly accurate, that can be seen as true history. Archaeologists have found the ruins of many of the cities described in the Old Testament, for example, and learned that the descriptions in the text are remarkably accurate. Why not, then, the Celts?'

'Why didn't you want the stone brought back to the university?'

'Why do artefacts have to be kept in glass cases in dusty rooms? Why can't they be living, breathing parts of the landscape we all inhabit?'

'Wouldn't the elements destroy it? Wear the markings down to nothing?'

'There are ogham stones in fields all over Ireland. The etchings on them are as vital now as they were a thousand years ago. I wasn't *mad*, Terri, although I was painted as such. I do believe I had a spiritual experience, but I didn't lose my mind.'

'You became obsessed with Balor though, didn't you?'

'Who told you that?'

'It's not true?'

'The stone became my field of study for a few years, but I would hardly say I was obsessed.'

'You lost your job at the university…'

'I resigned. I expect I would have been asked to leave sooner or later, as my heart was no longer in it. And there was the… the incident with Coleen.'

'The woman you assaulted?'

Dunne shifted uncomfortably on his chair. 'I was drunk and frustrated, and I acted abominably. That poor woman treated me with nothing but kindness, and I mistook it for something more and tried to force myself on her. I should have been prosecuted.'

'So that had nothing to do with Balor?'

Dunne looked puzzled. 'Not in the slightest. It had to do with me abusing alcohol and becoming fixated on a pretty young woman who gave me extra-large helpings of apple crumble because she was a nice person and felt sorry for a lonely bachelor.'

Terri wasn't sure what to say to any of that, so she said nothing. She had learned in her short life that silence could often be the most effective tool in a conversation.

'I tried to make it up to Coleen. I wrote her a letter of apology. I sent her money. But she never responded, and I don't blame her. I abused her trust. It's… well, it's one of the main reasons I left my old life behind. Professor Richard Dunbeg was a monster. I was determined Dick Dunne would be a better man.'

'I think he is,' Terri said, and she meant it. 'What you've done here is remarkable.'

'Thank you. I know pride is supposed to be a sin, but I do permit occasional flutters during periods of reflection.'

'There was another member of the excavation team who became fascinated by Balor. Damian Coogan?'

'Poor Damian. Yes. I think he was always a bit psychiatrically fragile, and the furore over the stone tipped him over the edge. I had an uncle who suffered from schizophrenia. I don't know if Damian was ever diagnosed, but I recognised some of the symptoms. He began to see and hear things that weren't there. And the stone – the words written on it became his religion. His creed.'

'He ascribed to the belief that the story on the stone was literally true?' Terri asked.

'Yes. To be clear, I believed Balor was a real, living person who terrified the Celts and probably murdered a lot of them. I find it completely plausible he was treated as a god – complete with sacrifices, human or otherwise – but that the locals decided after a time they wanted rid of him. I suspect he was murdered, but if you wish to entertain the grim idea he was drugged and buried alive in a bottomless pit in the mountains, I won't dispute it.'

'Fair enough,' Terri said, thinking Dunne was much more reasonable than John Miskella would have her believe.

'Damian, on the other hand, believed *every single detail* on the stone. He was convinced Balor was in an enchanted sleep and destined to rise again after the second age of man came to an end.'

'Which would have been at the dawn of the twenty-first century,' Terri said.

'Exactly. Balor, according to Damian, was going to return as King Under the Mountain. Damian wanted to prepare the way for him. He dug out all these old texts – some really nasty occult stuff. Said there was a series of rituals he needed to perform, and that he had to begin by mortifying himself.'

'What did that mean?'

'He started by giving up alcohol, caffeine and tobacco. He starved himself. Cut and burned his skin. I mean, he was deeply disturbed. By the time he moved up into the hill country, he was a shadow of the man I knew. I tried to help him, but it wasn't any good. He was beyond hearing reason.'

'Who was it that started to call him Reek? Do you remember?'

Dunne looked puzzled for a moment. 'They didn't call Damian by that name.'

'Are you sure?'

'I'm certain. Damian was my research assistant for several years. I would have known. No – there was another chap that was called that. Damned if I can recall who though.'

Terri sat forward, willing him to remember.

'Please try, Dick. It's important.'

The former archaeologist closed his eyes. It was as if he was going deep inside himself, riffling through his mental files to find the answer. Finally, though, he opened them and shook his head.

'I'm sorry. It's gone. If it comes back to me, I'll get word to you.'

'I'd appreciate that,' Terri said. 'A woman's life may depend on it.'

'Well then I will double my efforts to remember,' Dunne said. And Terri believed him.

CHAPTER FORTY-NINE

Time was nearly up, and Jessie was fighting not to let panic become her master.

She had to trust in her skills and instincts. That she had got it so badly wrong with Uruz ate at her, but she could not allow that doubt to seep through now. She had to remain resolute.

Jessie had, since they'd begun working on the case, been putting together a profile of Balor.

He presented himself to her piecemeal – she had only caught glimpses of him so far. But a picture was forming.

Her main doorway into his consciousness was through Penny.

The attacks on the women, so many women, indicated severe maternal abandonment issues. That he had taken someone like Penelope O'Dwyer suggested he was drawn to strong, self-assured women. Drawn to, yet also intimidated by. He wanted to possess her energy, destroy it, though he was taking his time to bask in it too. Yet she did not fit his usual profile – many of his previous victims had been women whose lives were in turmoil, or who would not be missed. That someone like Penelope had been chosen, someone with a profile, someone from a powerful family who would certainly look for her, suggested a profound shift in the need the killing satiated.

Penny was different because this murder was different. It would serve something specific. Jessie just wasn't sure what yet.

He was not afraid to take on a leadership role. In fact, he probably had delusions of grandeur: this was a man who had taken on the mantle of a god, after all.

Jessie had, at one point in the dark hours or a night she'd spent in the Barracks, even spent some time examining the possibility that Balor might be Dominic O'Dwyer himself, Penny's father. He fit the profile perfectly.

She discounted the theory eventually, deciding it was too much of a reach, but the pages she had used to outline the hypothesis remained in her desk drawer. She was ruling nothing out until she had a definitive path to follow. And such a path remained frustratingly elusive.

Somehow Balor had covered up his true nature for decades, but violent tendencies like this could not remain wholly dormant. They would seep out into the rest of the individual's life. There would be anger management issues at work, sexual dysfunction.

You would not have to look closely to find these things either. Friends, colleagues and family members would whisper that this person had a hair-trigger temper.

And he had issued a challenge. He wanted her to come for him.

This meant one of two things: either he didn't believe she was good enough to catch him, or he was drawing her to him for another reason altogether.

Whichever was the case, the dance was drawing to a close.

The trip to the woods hadn't brought her to him, but she was starting to believe he would come to her before the end.

CHAPTER FIFTY

They got some sandwiches and ate them back at the White Elephant. Jessie bought two large subs for Seamus, but there was still no sign of him when they sat down to eat.

'All right then,' Jessie said when they were both at their respective desks, food open in front of them. 'We're both agreed that Richard Dunbeg or whatever he's calling himself today isn't our guy. So where does that leave us?'

'All we have left is Reek,' Terri said.

'Whoever the hell he is,' Jessie said irritably.

'There's still the UCC connection,' Terri reminded her. 'That still fits, so I think we need to follow it.'

'But now we're being told we're not looking for Damian Coogan,' Jessie said. 'We're starting at ground zero all over again.'

'Not quite,' Terri said. 'I can still hack into those deleted Instagram messages. And I can ask my contact in UCC to rethink what he told me. He obviously misremembered who Reek was. Maybe if he asks around?'

'It's somewhere to begin,' Jessie agreed. 'Ask your friend first. If he can get a name, it could save us some time hacking records.'

Terri nodded and picked up her phone. She paused for a second – should she do this? John had told her not to ring him, after all. But this was work. So therefore different.

Snapping out of it, Terri dialled the original number she had for Miskella. It rang for about five seconds before it was cut off – the call had been refused. She tried again, and this time the line went dead almost immediately.

'I think he must be in a meeting or something,' Terri said, trying to keep the disappointment from her voice.

'I'm sure he'll call back. Give it some time.'

'Yeah. Maybe I'll start seeing if I can hack into Penny's direct messages while I wait.'

'Can't hurt, I suppose,' Jessie agreed.

Terri had been working on Penelope's Instagram for an hour when her phone rang – it was Miskella's other number, which she had saved to her contacts as his work mobile.

'Hey, John,' she said.

There was silence at the other end for a moment. Terri thought she could hear machinery whirring in the background, but she couldn't tell for sure what it was.

'John, are you there?' she asked, wondering if he'd been cut off.

'Why are you calling me?' he asked, and while she recognised his voice, there was an odd quality to it.

'I need to ask you something, if that's okay.'

A long pause again. Now she thought she heard water running, like a cistern refilling.

'What is it?' came the reply. His voice seemed toneless. Dead. She didn't like it.

'You mentioned when we spoke that Damian Coogan was called Reek – my research suggests he wasn't, that another person had that nickname. I was wondering if you might ask around for me, see if you can find out who it was?'

'Are you calling me a liar?' The question was snarled at her with real venom. 'I tried to help you. I tried to be your friend. And what do you do? You *fuck* me, you don't call, you don't make plans with me and when you do, it's just to squeeze more information out of me?'

'John… I don't think you lied,' Terri said, feeling the blood run from her face and her hands begin to shake. 'It was obviously just a mistake. I only wanted you to take some time and think about it, perhaps see if some of the older staff members might remember differently—'

'I'm busy, Terri,' the voice spat. 'Don't call me again, okay? You're just some reject from a fucking care home anyway. I can't believe I ever liked you to begin with.'

He hung up abruptly, and she sat with the phone still pressed to her ear, tears building behind her eyes.

Jessie watched from across the room.

'I wasn't listening in,' she said, 'but he didn't exactly keep his voice down, so I heard most of that.'

'I… I'm sorry,' Terri said.

'If you don't mind my saying, he sounds like an asshole,' Jessie said.

'He didn't seem to be when I met him,' Terri said, and a tear did roll down her cheek now.

'They often don't,' Jessie said. 'But that's men for you. Most men anyway.'

Terri nodded, and as she did, more tears spilled down her cheeks in rivulets.

'Ah, pet,' Jessie said, and getting up, she went to the girl and held her while she sobbed.

Twelve days ago…

Penny stood outside the Kerry Arms waiting for the man she had arranged to meet there following her dinner with Mervyn Moorehouse.

Her second appointment of the evening told her he would be driving a black Toyota Yaris, and she hoped he'd get there soon, because she was bursting for a pee. She and Moorehouse had downed a couple of bottles of Rioja over their meal, and she regretted not having gone before leaving the restaurant. She knew damn well that if she popped into the Arms to run to the bathroom, he would bloody well arrive and maybe drive on, thinking she'd forgotten or stood him up, and she couldn't have that. It had taken her ages to arrange this meeting, and she was damned if she was going to sabotage it before it had even happened.

So she hopped from one leg to another and waited.

He was late now, and she was starting to get irritated. This ungodly hour had been agreed as a time to meet to accommodate him, after all. So he'd better show.

Penny heard the engine of the Yaris before she saw it. New Street was quiet, no other traffic about, and the large black car cruised up and came to a stop outside the hotel's front door. The passenger-side window rolled down, but Penny couldn't see anyone inside, only darkness.

'You can park on the street over there,' she called in. 'We can chat in the lobby of the hotel. I won't keep you long – I'm sure you've got better things to be doing at this time of night.'

This was met by silence.

'I'll go ahead and wait for you inside,' she said. 'Park up and I'll see you in a moment.'

More silence. Really annoyed now, and a little creeped out, she said, 'Right. I'm going in. Come or don't come, I don't care anymore.'

She spun on her heel and had taken only one step towards the hotel when she felt rather than heard the rear door of the car opening; then something had her by the shoulders in a grip that felt like steel, and she was whipped off her feet and dragged backwards with such force her full bladder gave way.

There was a moment of disbelief and disorientation, but then something was pressing over her nose and mouth, and she couldn't breathe. A face was peering down at her, but it looked odd, as if someone had written strange signs all over it, and then the car began to move, and panic gripped her.

Fuck's sake – how is this happening? *she thought.* This can't be happening to me!

Penny tried to fight, but it was no good.

The last thing she heard as consciousness drifted away was snatched of a song with Irish lyrics: "S é'n trua, nach mise, nach mise, 's é'n trua nach mise bean Pháidín.'

CHAPTER FIFTY-ONE

Seamus came around sometime later. He didn't know how long he had been unconscious or where he now was – at first, he thought the blow he'd received had blinded him, because opening and closing his eyes made no discernible difference, but gradually he understood it was just very dark.

The side of his face hurt badly – he suspected he'd been hit with a rock of some kind, and he knew without having to check that his cheekbone was broken, possibly his eye socket as well. Then he thought he probably should check and found he couldn't: his hands were tied together in front of him, and when he tried to stand, he discovered his feet were too.

He struggled for a few moments to see if he might free himself, but the effort made him dizzy and nauseous, and he thought he might pass out, so he ceased his exertions and lay there in the dark, breathing heavily and trying to calm the panic that was rising in him.

He probably drifted into unconsciousness again for a time, because he suddenly realised he was awake again, but had no recollection of actually waking up. He felt less ill, and where his face had previously hurt, it was now cold and numb, which he thought might be a sign of nerve damage, but there was no benefit in thinking about that so he decided instead just to be glad he was in less pain.

It was time to get his bearings.

He didn't need to be an expert spelunker to know he was still in the cave – that much was obvious. The floor beneath him was hard stone, and there was a wall of a similar texture and solidity at his back. The question was: had he been left where he'd been attacked or moved somewhere else? If he'd been left where he'd fallen, he could probably find his way back out, once he got loose of his bonds. If he was somewhere new, that added a whole other raft of problems to what was an already difficult situation.

He scooted upwards so he was sitting on his bum and managed to get his feet underneath him. Pushing upwards an inch at a time, he finally got himself to a full standing position.

Right, he thought. *I've been moved. There's no way I could do this in that awful tunnel.*

That brought him back to the person who had attacked him.

Who the hell were they?

The only answer he could come up with was that his hunch had been right: Damian Coogan was alive and hiding out in the Reeks. And, from what Seamus had seen during their brief encounter, he had gone completely batshit crazy.

Which was both good news – he could probably out-think someone who was in an altered state – and bad news – someone who was deranged might do anything, so out-thinking them might be a moot point.

As he stood there, leaning against the wall for support, he realised something else – it wasn't completely dark after all. It had taken him some time to get used to the darkness, but now that he had, the gloom was not total. He could make out the shape of a doorway to his left; he could just discern a wall about twelve feet in front of him, and a domed ceiling five feet above his head.

And there, hunched against the wall on the opposite side of the room, was a shape. He peered at it from his one good eye for several long moments before he was sure it was, beyond doubt, a person.

'Hello?' he called.

The shape moved, and then spoke. 'Who's there?'

It was a female voice.

'Penelope O'Dwyer, is that you?' Seamus asked.

'Yes. Please help me! He… he says he's going to kill me.'

'Is it Coogan? Did Coogan tell you that?'

'He's not a man. He's something else. You have to help me!'

'Penelope – Penny – I'm a police officer, and I'm here to take you back to your family, I promise. We will get out of here.'

'I want to go home,' the woman sobbed. 'I want my dad!'

Seamus tried to talk to her, but it seemed the glimmer of hope he'd offered was too much for Penelope O'Dwyer. Within moments she was crying inconsolably, begging the darkness to deliver her from the nightmare she found herself in.

CHAPTER FIFTY-TWO

Jessie spent the rest of the afternoon going back over her psychological profiles, both for Penny and Balor, and she went back over the profile she had constructed for Uruz too and tried to work some of that into her theories. None offered her any clues as to how to move forward though. They had hit a wall, and Jessie was forced to admit that all hope lay in Terri's efforts.

She was also starting to get nervous about Seamus. Her partner was as reliable as a Swiss watch, so for him to still not have checked in made her think something unexpected had happened. And though she didn't want Terri to see how unsettled she was, she permitted herself the luxury of admitting, in her private thoughts, that she was deeply concerned.

When the clock above the door in their office read four thirty, she tried calling him again. And, as had happened all the other times she'd tried, a prim voice told her the phone user could not answer her call at that time, as he had his mobile handset powered off or was out of coverage.

Could her partner still be in the mountains? Policing was a team sport if ever there was one, and having a colleague selfish enough to disappear for hours at a time without so much as a 'by your leave' was intolerable.

'I don't suppose the Boy Wonder answered your text message?' she asked Terri, whose brow was furrowed as she typed furiously.

'Sorry? What?'

'Seamus hasn't checked in with you?'

'Oh – no. Not a dickie bird.'

'Okay. I'm going to give him such an arse-kicking when I see him.'

'Of course you will. I think I'm in, Jessie.'

Jessie pulled her chair over so she was sitting beside Terri.

'Nothing online is ever truly deleted,' Terri explained. 'People tell themselves it is, because it helps them sleep at night believing their secrets are safe, but in reality, every single thing you share, every item you view, every message you send, is all stored somewhere, even the ones you've technically deleted. You just need to know where the right storage containers are located, and how to search the files once you're inside.'

'And you've found the container holding Penny and Reek's conversations?'

'Here they are. Have a look for yourself.'

Jessie had hoped there would be a lengthy interaction between the two but the sequence of messages on Terri's screen was short and cryptic.

Penny: I hear you are the best person to speak to about my project. Are you available to take anyone new on?

Reek: Your reputation precedes you and your work intrigues me. But I need to hear more if I am to consider throwing in my lot with you.

Penny: I have everything with me. I'd be happy to go over details with you.

Reek: I'm very busy at the moment. Could I suggest the inhospitable time of 10.45 p.m. on the evening of October 15th to meet? It really is the only time I have available.

And then the messages they had already seen began, culminating in an agreement to meet after Penny finished with Moorehouse on the night she vanished.

'This doesn't tell us anything,' Jessie said, disappointed. 'They could be talking about stamp collecting.'

'No, but now I'm in the system, I can access Reek's IP address,' Terri said, referring to the Internet protocol address, a numeric label assigned by all Internet providers to each piece of hardware on a computer network. 'With any luck, that'll lead us to him.'

'It'll lead us to whichever machine he used to set up his Instagram account, which isn't the same thing,' Jessie said. 'But it's better than nothing.'

'It might take me a couple of hours. There are a few firewalls I'm going to have to work around, but it's definitely doable.'

'Go for it,' Jessie said and went back to her desk. 'I'll be here if you need me, which I'm guessing you won't.'

'I appreciate the company,' Terri said and went to work.

It would prove to be a long night.

CHAPTER FIFTY-THREE

A slightly anxious Katie Keneally arrived at the White Elephant at nine thirty that night.

Terri was grappling with a particularly stubborn encryption system, and Jessie was going through Penny's emails for the umpteenth time, looking for any references to the leisure centre. It was frustrating, but everything she had so far come across looked to be completely legal and above board. Jessie created a folder of emails and correspondence from Moorehouse and pored over those, looking for the rhythm and cadence of the Instagram messages, but if she was honest she couldn't find it.

Moorehouse's emails read like text messages, while the Instagram missives were much more articulate and florid. Which didn't fit at all.

They both paused in their work at Katie's tentative knock on the door.

'I'm very sorry to disturb you,' the older woman said, stepping nervously inside. 'But I'm wondering if Seamus is here?'

Jessie closed her laptop and Terri leaned back from her workstation.

'You haven't heard from him either?' Jessie asked, trying to keep the building sense of anxiety she was feeling from her voice.

'Not a thing. He asked to borrow my car, and I heard him leave the house at the crack of dawn. He was supposed to drop it back before ten, and he didn't, so I just thought he'd been delayed. I wasn't going anywhere, so it wasn't really a problem.'

'But he had arranged to be back by mid-morning?' Jessie asked.

'He said he'd be done with whatever he was up to at that stage. I wasn't too bothered when he didn't show, but it's not like him to not ring. When he still wasn't home for his dinner and I hadn't had a phone call or a text, I started to get a bit more concerned. If he's away on something confidential, that's fine, but I'd like to know he's all right. Ever since that shooting business, I've become a bit of a worrier.'

Jessie picked up her phone and dialled Seamus. Yet again, that same soulless message.

'Did he tell you where he was going, Terri?'

'He and I mapped out the journey, yes,' Terri said. 'But Jessie, he's gone into the Reeks. It'll be treacherous in the dark.'

'Just give me the location, Terri. I'll drop you home, Katie, and I'll give you a call as soon as I find him.'

'Thank you. I'm sure he's fine, but I'd prefer to be certain.'

'He won't be fine when I get my hands on him,' Jessie said darkly.

CHAPTER FIFTY-FOUR

It was ten forty-five when she found the Ford Focus parked at a viewing point in the lower reaches of the mountain range. It was empty and had not been tampered with, and she had to assume Seamus had just left it and not returned.

Jessie stood beside Katie Keneally's car, leaning against the bonnet of her MG, and looked out into the darkness, the Kerry countryside spreading out below her, shrouded in night. Why would Seamus have abandoned his mother's car? And why would he disappear without making contact with anyone?

Erring on the positive side, he may have found what he had come looking for: Damian Coogan, alive and well and living off-grid much as his old associate Richard Dunbeg was doing at the other side of the county in the Crann Darrach woods. Maybe Coogan had information that was pertinent to the investigation, but the only way he was prepared to share it was if Seamus remained in whatever campground he had established up in the crags, a spot isolated and without coverage. Her partner could be up there right this moment, interviewing the former academic.

It was a nice idea, Jessie thought, but a dim hope. Seamus had been gone now for close to nineteen hours. An informal interview would not take that long, and the more likely explanation for his continued absence and lack of contact was that he had fallen and broken something and was unable to drag himself out or call for help.

That the detective might have come to harm through the agency or design of someone else – that he had been attacked or even abducted – was an eventuality Jessie did not want to think about. Not yet anyway.

She shrugged off her long woollen coat and replaced it with a waterproof anorak she kept in the boot of the MG. In her glove compartment she found the Heckler & Koch handgun she and Seamus had confiscated when they'd made their visit to Ultain Cloney. Putting it in the anorak's pocket and using the torch on her phone to guide her, she began up the path Seamus had taken that morning.

CHAPTER FIFTY-FIVE

Every ten yards or so she called his name.

The night was mild, but the damp air had soaked the bracken, and within ten minutes the lower part of her jeans was wet through, making the upward slog uncomfortable as well as exhausting. At one point she thought she heard movement and froze. In the thicket off to her left she discerned the sound of twigs breaking and something large moving about.

'Seamus, is that you?'

The movement stopped. Jessie stood in the dark, the gun in her hand now, trying not to breathe loudly. The rustling came again, much gentler this time. Slowly, deliberately, she took a couple of steps towards the scrub. Shining the beam from her phone among the undergrowth, she saw nothing at first, but then detected two lights shining back at her. Initially, she couldn't work out what she was seeing, but then to her horror realised the light was reflecting off the twin orbs of someone – or some*thing*'s – eyes. They seemed black and impossibly huge, and terror seized Jessie, causing her to throw herself backwards and bring the gun up.

Something prevented her from firing though, and she lay on the wet mountain path, the H&K aimed on the spot the eyes had been, trembling with tension. Nothing happened for a long, fraught instant, then the undergrowth exploded outwards, and the powerful form of a red deer leaped right over Jessie's prone form and disappeared into the darkness on the other side.

Jesus Christ, she thought. *I am not built for the countryside. I'm really not!*

Picking herself up, she continued her climb.

There was no sign of Seamus at the long-abandoned campsite, and even though Jessie spent close to an hour there and called his name until she was hoarse, no one answered. Once again, she thought she discerned movement on the slopes below her, but the encounter with the deer had made her less jumpy, and while she called each time and trained her light on the area the noises had originated from, she was not rewarded by the appearance of her friend.

Checking her phone, she saw that while coverage was not at full capacity, she did have a couple of bars, and rang Terri.

'I'm about to make for the cave you mentioned,' she said. 'No sign as yet.'

'Be careful,' Terri said. 'I'm making some headway here, too.'

'Good. I'll call again when I get up top if I can.'

'I'd be grateful if you did.'

She slipped twice during the final climb: in the spots where both hands and feet had to be used to progress, she had to put the phone in her pocket and was forced to operate purely by touch in the darkness. For an inexperienced outdoors person like Jessie, this was impossible, so swearing loudly, she decided to hold her handset in her mouth to still have some light, and finally made it to the opening in the rock.

When she got there, she marvelled that anyone would have been inclined to burrow their way in, so narrow and unwelcoming did it look. Getting to her knees, she shone the beam from her phone inside and saw the low fissure continued, a frighteningly narrow passage between two sheets of rock, as far as her eyes could see in the darkness.

So intent was she on peering into the cave that she barely heard the soft tread behind her. Some part of her mind just had time to register the sound when someone grabbed her by the ankles and hauled her backwards with a strength shocking in its power.

CHAPTER FIFTY-SIX

The force with which she was dragged backwards caused Jessie to drop her phone, and the handset clattered off the hard rock and skittered away into the cave. Jessie tried to twist onto her back to better defend herself, but whoever it was had her in a vice-like grip, and all she could do was try and get a hold on the sparse grass and scrub that grew in the thin earth at the cave's mouth to try and halt her passage.

This bought her a second: she managed to snake her fingers under a chunk of stone and tensed her muscles, bringing her slide to a brief halt. The person who had her grunted in surprise, and in that second she got her left hand into the pocket of her jacket and brought out the H&K. Releasing her grip, she allowed herself to be pulled again, and as she was rolled over to her right, aimed blindly and fired.

In the momentary muzzle flash, she caught a glimpse of a ragged, waif-like figure – a scarred face, hollow eyes and topsy-turvy graveyard teeth – but she didn't have time to absorb this information. The person yowled, either in fear or pain, she didn't know which, and dropped her legs. She fired again, but the flash this time revealed nothing, as whoever it was had taken off down the mountain, not using the stone steps Jessie had traversed but instead careening through the scrappy trees that formed a thicket on the uneven rock face – a route Jessie had thought utterly impassable. She pulled herself up and attempted to give chase, but it was useless.

The strange creature had gone.

She went back to the cave – she could still see the light coming from her phone, so knew it hadn't gone far, and she gingerly reached in and got it. Using the light, she searched the grass around and about where she had lain and saw droplets that appeared black in the electric light but which she knew would be red in the sunshine.

At least one of her shots had connected.

The screen of Jessie's smartphone was cracked from being dropped on the stone floor of the cave but was still usable, and she had just enough coverage to make a call.

'Someone made a run at me,' she told Terri when she picked up.

'Are you okay?'

'Yeah, I'm fine. I hate enclosed spaces – I'd try to crawl into the cave to see if Seamus is in there, but I'd be a sitting duck with someone up here gunning for me. It's a non-starter.'

'Do you know who it is?'

Jessie paused before answering.

'I think maybe Seamus was right, Terri. I think I was just attacked by a dead man.'

'Do… do you think he hurt Seamus?'

'I don't know. We have to assume the best and prepare for the worst. Can you ring Tralee on the direct line from the office and ask them to send some men up here? If this is what I think it is, Seamus and Penny are being held hostage. We don't have much time.'

'Give me two minutes, Jessie. I'll call them.'

Jessie held the phone. She could hear Terri speaking urgently in the background.

'Jessie, there's been a major traffic accident between Tralee and Limerick. Twenty cars involved in a pile-up. Multiple casualties. All hands have been redirected to deal with it.'

Jessie felt her heart drop. Was this a coincidence, she wondered, before deciding it didn't matter whether it was or not. She would have to seek help from another quarter.

'I'll call the commissioner,' Terri went on. 'She'll send help.'

'Do, but they won't get here in time.'

'What are you going to do?'

'Get support elsewhere.'

'How can I help?'

'Keep your phone close to hand. I'll call if I need you.'

'I'll be right here, Jessie.'

'Thanks, Terri. It feels good to know that.'

Both women paused, each acknowledging, just for a moment, the closeness of the other, if only just through the phone connection.

'I have the IP address for Reek,' Terri said after a few seconds.

'Could you trace it?'

'Yes. It wasn't easy. The person used a virtual private network, which hides your location and makes it difficult to trace your activity.'

'I'm hearing the word difficult, but not the word impossible.'

'There are ways to circumnavigate VPNs. I know some of them.'

'And?'

'The Instagram account was set up on a machine on University College Cork's staff network.'

Jessie, who was sitting on the ground just outside the cave, laid her head back against the stone, thinking about that.

'Do you know when?'

'It was in 2016. I can probably narrow it down even further, but that'll take more time.'

'I think that'll do for now. I need to get back to the MG. I've a lot more to do before the night's done.'

'Is there anything you need from me right now, Jessie?'

'Get up all the maps you can of Macgillycuddy's Reeks. The more detailed the better.'

'Am I looking for something in particular?'

'Two things. Any roads that are usable by cars that go through the mountains. And any details you can find of cave systems – even ones that aren't used or have been declared dangerous.'

'Okay, Jessie. I'm on it.'

'I'll call back in a couple of hours.'

'I'll be waiting.'

Jessie Boyle, fighting exhaustion and a nagging sense that she did not have time to do all the things she needed to, began to pick her way back down the mountain.

It was two o'clock in the morning, and Samhain was in three days' time.

PART SEVEN

The King Under the Mountain

Three days until the eve of Samhain

'My consuming lust was to experience their bodies.'

Jeffrey Dahmer

CHAPTER FIFTY-SEVEN

As Jessie drove, she rang Ultain Cloney to tell him she was on her way to his compound. Despite the late hour, he answered on the second ring.

'I wasn't expecting a repeat visit,' he growled at her.

'I think we can help one another out,' Jessie said. 'I'll explain when I get there.'

'I'll put the kettle on. Maybe Benson will bake a cake.'

'That'll be nice,' Jessie said and hung up.

The moon, three quarters full, reflected palely on the pools in Cois Donn bog as Jessie crossed the narrow road through the wetland. When she got to the metal gate, it was standing open; Benson, dressed exactly as he had been the last time she'd seen him – except his white shirt showed no bloodstain tonight – stepped out to greet her.

'I'm disappointed to see your arm isn't in a sling,' Jessie said as he approached. 'My friend shooting you was a high point of our last meeting for me.'

'The bullet grazed me is all,' Benson said. 'Your friend's aim needs to be better if he wants to do any real damage.'

'Maybe he hit you exactly where he wanted to,' Jessie said. 'Did that occur to you?'

Benson snorted, as if this was a ludicrous suggestion.

'Mr Cloney says you can bring your vehicle inside,' he said.

'That's progress,' Jessie observed.

'If you say so,' Benson deadpanned, a single strand of his greasy white hair rippling in the night wind.

Cloney, clad in his habitual black coat and hat, met her at the door of the farmhouse.

'Come in and take a load off,' he said. 'To what do I owe the pleasure?'

'I think I met the man who's been taking out your transports tonight,' Jessie said. 'And I believe he's taken my friend.'

'I don't understand all of it yet,' she said when she and Cloney were sitting at the kitchen table, mugs of tea in hand. 'But here's what I know: forty-six years ago, a group of archaeologists from UCC dug up a piece of rock with a horror story written on it. I don't know if some kind of swamp gas was released when they pulled it out of the ground or if the stone itself had radioactive properties, or if it really was cursed; truthfully, it doesn't matter. What is certain is that two, maybe more of those archaeologists became mentally unbalanced because of their contact with that piece of rock. One of them was so disturbed, he left his job and his home and moved into a tent in the mountains so he could be near where the god that the stone told of was buried. Most people believe he died up there, but my partner went looking for him and didn't come back. So he obviously found someone.'

'Why did he go looking for a dead man?' Cloney said.

'Seamus believed he faked his death and hid out up there, waiting for this Celtic demon to come back.'

'Do you think that could be the case?'

'No. I don't reckon a human being could live up there alone for that long. I suspect Seamus met whoever is really taking the women though.'

'This is all fascinating, Ms Boyle, but how does it affect me?'

'I'm glad you asked. You told me your trucks were hit when they used the mountain roads. Hikers have occasionally gone missing too. I think it was this same person trying to keep them away from his killing ground.'

'You're saying some mentally deranged psycho took on my lads and bested them?'

'They never would have seen him coming. Whoever he is, he knows the terrain. Don't diminish what he's achieved, Mr Cloney. He's waged a one-man war for more than forty years and won.'

'And you think he took your friend?'

'Yes. Seamus went up there and never came back.'

'He might be dead,' Cloney said. 'You should consider that.'

Jessie took in a long, shuddering breath. 'I have to believe he's still alive.'

'You think he's got Penny, this person?'

'I do. I'm hoping if we find Seamus, we'll find her as well. You said you wanted her back. It's why I'm here.'

Cloney picked up the teapot and replenished their mugs.

'How can I help?'

'Tell me which roads you used when he hit your convoys. And give me a couple of men who know the area. I'm useless up there on my own.'

Cloney grinned. 'I only have one man on my crew who knows the Reeks.'

'I'll take him.'

'Are you sure about that?'

'I need help, Mr Cloney. I'm not ashamed to admit it.'

'It's Benson.'

Jessie did nothing to hide her distaste.

'Brilliant. Just brilliant.'

CHAPTER FIFTY-EIGHT

Penelope O'Dwyer was in shock. She teetered between hysteria and catatonia, and while Seamus tried to talk to her, most of the time she didn't answer. If she did, it was to plead with him to take her home, and no amount of explaining that he was working on it seemed to make any difference. He told her that his friends would come for them. That no matter where they were, no matter who it was that was holding them, they had not been abandoned.

'Jessie will come,' he told himself, whispering it over and over again. 'Jessie will come.'

He was in a dazed, exhausted sleep when someone grabbed him by the hair. He had not seen the man who had taken him since that awful moment in the tunnel so was surprised when he felt himself being dragged upright.

'The hero is coming, the hero is coming,' that strange voice was saying.

'I'm no hero, but I'll do for you, you weird bastard,' Seamus shot back, showing far more bravado than he was actually feeling.

Through the gloom, the detective saw wild eyes and a gnarled face but little else. The hand that held him aloft was as strong as iron, and he could smell dust and dirt and woodsmoke off him.

And blood.

Has he killed someone, or is he wounded? Seamus wondered. *If he is…*

It was an advantage too valuable to waste.

Crooking his arm, Seamus lashed out with his elbow, driving it into his captor's gut. He heard air escaping in a rush, and a pained groan followed, and he was dropped to the ground. Not wanting to give quarter, he kicked out with his bound legs, hoping to knock the wild man down, but struck only empty air.

Then there was a dull thud and the man was on top of him.

'*Buachaill dána*,' he said. Bad boy. 'Cut you for that. Bleed you.'

'Yeah, well, fuck you,' Seamus said.

The face that was glowering above him cracked into a gap-toothed grin, and then Seamus felt a searing pain in his lower abdomen and realised he'd been cut. The blade carved a groove across the muscles of his stomach and Seamus felt darkness gathering about the edges of his vision, which gradually became pools of blackness.

He plunged gratefully into one of them and knew no more for a time.

CHAPTER FIFTY-NINE

Jessie, Cloney and Benson spent a couple of hours looking at maps of the area, and while they talked, Jessie put Terri on speakerphone so she could listen in and enter all the details into a Google Maps account which Jessie could sign into on her phone.

The spots where the trucks had been hit were all within a one-kilometre radius, and Terri identified three cave openings close by.

'The local caving society has a pretty decent website,' Terri said, 'and I've been going through their newsletter. Two of the caves in the region you're talking about are regularly visited – in fact, they're considered to be beginner-level systems. The other one, though, is a red zone, which means it's not recommended even for the most skilled potholers.'

'That's the one he'll be using then,' Jessie said.

'Can we try and draw him out?' Benson asked. 'I don't like the idea of doing gunwork underground. There's the danger of ricochets and shrapnel, and the percussion of the weapons might bring the roof down on us. It would be better to take the target down in the open, then go in and extract the prisoners.'

He was sitting at the other end of the table from Jessie, methodically cleaning a sawn-off shotgun that was in pieces in front of him. Jessie thought it an interesting contradiction, that such an unsanitary man would be so scrupulous about his weapon.

'I doubt he'll do so much as stick his head above ground,' Jessie said. 'He came out to attack me and was shot for his troubles.'

'How serious a wound?' Benson asked.

'I don't know. It was dark and he ran away. There was blood though.'

Benson shook his head. 'You and your friends need to learn to shoot better,' he said.

'We leave at first light,' Jessie said, ignoring him. 'Terri, is that all entered for me?'

'Just log on to Google Maps like I told you, and it'll be there.'

'Thanks, Terri. Get some rest now, okay?'

'I won't sleep until I hear Seamus is all right.'

'Me either,' Jessie said. 'I'll call you soon.'

Terri hung up. Jessie suddenly felt very alone, now her colleague was no longer a presence in the room.

Oblivious to her unease, Benson started to put his gun back together, locking the sections in place with calm precision. He noticed Jessie watching and winked at her. The gesture made her want to vomit.

CHAPTER SIXTY

Benson insisted they travel in a camouflaged jeep, one of the vehicles in Cloney's storage sheds.

'That sports car of yours stands out like a sore thumb,' he said. 'I can't believe a police officer drives something so conspicuous.'

'I don't use it for stakeouts,' Jessie retorted.

'If you were a man, I'd think you were trying to compensate for something,' he pondered.

'How about we agree there's no need to make conversation?'

'Didn't Sigmund Freud say something about all women wanting to have penises? Is that it? You're a shrink, aren't you – am I on to something there?'

'I will shoot you before we get anywhere near the mountains if you don't shut up.'

While Benson drove, Jessie kept her eye on the satnav on her phone.

'This is the road where the trucks were attacked,' the flaking gangster said as they cruised along a narrow lane, peaks of rock rising on either side to create a canyon.

'We'll reach the point closest to the cave in five minutes,' Jessie said. 'You should start looking for somewhere to park.'

Benson found a gap between two dry stone walls and manoeuvred the vehicle into a field containing scraggy-looking sheep, more wild than domesticated.

'The cave is five hundred yards that direction,' Jessie said, pointing at the slope directly opposite them.

The place felt as isolated as anywhere Jessie had ever been. On either side the mountains rose, making the valley feel hemmed in. The air was very still, and high above, a bird of prey wheeled languidly.

Jessie felt a moment of gnawing panic. *What if Seamus is already dead?* she thought. *Maybe I've allowed this to happen all over again, and we go in there and that bastard has carved him up and left him in some charnel heap with all the others.*

She actually felt tears spring to her eyes and, with a trojan effort, forced them back. She could not show weakness in front of Benson. Luckily, he was paying her no heed, taking weapons and ammunition out of the jeep and stowing them about his person.

'Eastwards it is then,' he said, putting the sawn-off through a loop on his belt and a Glock 17 into a holster at his hip. Today he was wearing a black sweatshirt over charcoal jeans and boots. Despite the fact Jessie knew he had donned the clothes only that morning, the gangster emitted a heavy stench of stale sweat and halitosis, and the upper part of his torso was heavily dusted in dead skin. It was as if whatever toxicity lurked inside him oozed its way out of his pores and was carried on every breath.

He tossed her a large torch with a rubber grip.

'Before we go up here, I need to know I can rely on you,' he said. 'You are police, and therefore too moral for your own good.'

Jessie almost laughed at that. 'You mean I give a shit about what I do?'

'A conscience will not do you any good here,' Benson went on, ignoring the barb. 'The man in that cave is a killer. He has taken life and will again if he survives to do so. He has your friend, and you tell me he has Penelope O'Dwyer.'

'I believe he does.'

'We shall see. If I meet him during this mission, I will shoot on sight, and I am shooting to kill. I advise you do the same.'

Jessie checked the load in her H&K and put it back in the pocket of her jacket. She had a knife – also taken from Cloney's place – pushed through the belt of her jeans.

'I'd prefer to take him in,' she said. 'But if it comes down to him or us, I won't let it be us.'

Benson sighed. 'That does not fill me with confidence.'

'Well, it's all you're getting,' Jessie said. 'Now let's go.'

As they started the climb to the cave opening, Jessie received a text message from an unknown number.

Balor waiting for you. Time for a reckoning.

CHAPTER SIXTY-ONE

The cave opening was wide and high, but the moment they stepped inside they could see a rockfall blocked the passage three metres in.

'Shit,' Jessie said, and panic spiked again.

What do we do now? How do I get to him?

Benson was not so easily dissuaded.

'Hang on a moment,' he said.

Shining his torch on the mound, the thin man pushed this rock here, that one there. They were all solidly wedged, making a kind of uneven wall right to the ceiling. Benson tested a large, square-looking piece that was on the lower-right corner of the structure, and to Jessie's surprise and relief it wobbled.

'Help me,' Benson said.

As it happened, he barely needed help at all. The loose stone was little more than a piece of shale, and they lifted it with virtually no effort. It revealed a hole that could easily be crawled through.

'And so we pass down the rabbit hole,' Jessie muttered.

'After you,' Benson said.

Jessie took a deep breath and crawled head-first into the darkness.

Beyond the obstruction, the corridor was high enough for both of them to walk without stooping. A breeze came from somewhere, and Jessie noticed the floor was completely clear of rocks or any other obstructions.

He uses this a lot, she thought. *It looks like we've come in his front door.*

The passage continued directly into the heart of the mountain. They'd been walking for five minutes, the beams of their torches scything through the blackness, when Benson said, 'Take a look at this.'

He stopped and trained his torch on a tapestry of ogham markings covering the walls on both sides, making the channel in the rock seem like the inside of a pyramid. Looking closely, Jessie saw these were not ancient markings – they appeared relatively recent; some even had stone dust still in them.

'Wonder what it means,' Benson said.

'I don't know for certain,' Jessie pondered. 'But if I had to guess, I reckon he's continued Balor's story. Written his part of it.'

'Pity for him the tale is about to reach its conclusion,' the peeling man said, and they walked on.

They had travelled about half a kilometre under the mountain when a cave opening appeared on their left. Jessie shone her torch inside and almost cried out in shock: the space seemed to be filled with people, all of whom appeared frozen in the midst of bizarre contortions – it was like someone had hit a pause button while they were in the middle of a seizure. It took Jessie a moment to realise what she was seeing, and this understanding was followed by a moment of dread: *What if I find Seamus in there?* a voice inside her head asked. *What if he is among the dead?*

Benson peered over her shoulder.

'Do you want me to check?' he asked. 'I don't really care either way, so it's no problem.'

'No. I need to do this myself.'

The killer shrugged.

'Your funeral,' he said.

Jessie stepped into the mausoleum.

There were close to forty bodies in that space, all moulded in bizarre poses and kept in place by pieces of wire and sticks, then suspended from lengths of cord attached to the roof of the cave.

The effect was macabre in the extreme, forcing the deceased to perform a ceremonial dance for eternity, capering and gyrating to music only they could hear.

Most were little more than dried husks, time having reduced them to paper-thin skin and brittle bone. To Jessie's relief, neither her partner nor Penelope O'Dwyer were among the troupe. Once this was confirmed though, Jessie's attention was drawn to something even more unexpected – and deeply unnerving.

The dancers were arranged in a series of concentric circles, and in the eye of the vortex of death was the being their dance was honouring: a massive skeleton, easily more than seven feet from head to toe. The remains of the missing women had been arranged so it looked as if they were performing a ritual over the giant's bones. Almost as if they were worshipping him.

Did he actually find Balor? Jessie wondered. *Did the crazy bastard go down into the bowels of the earth and bring that thing back up?*

'You done in there?' Benson called to her. 'Some of us have places to be.'

Whispering a silent prayer for the fallen, she went back out to her companion.

'Seamus and Penny aren't in there,' she said.

'Then the mission is still a go,' Benson retorted. 'Which is good – I hate a wasted journey.'

The corridor got wider as they travelled on, and soon it opened into a broad crater. A path had been constructed down the centre, rocks piled on both sides to mark out the trajectory to be followed. Jessie realised the torches weren't offering the only light anymore – the entire place was bathed in a dim glow.

'There's sunshine coming in somewhere,' she said to Benson.

He peered upwards and gestured with the sawn-off.

'There's holes in the roof,' he said. 'It's where the breeze is coming from too. I'd guess rain comes in as well – there's pools of water about the floor here and there if you look. This is his living quarters. We're in his house now, Ms Boyle. Be ready.'

Benson was right. At various points around the cavern more rocks had been laid as if to create the outlines of rooms. In one Jessie saw what looked to be a sleeping bag and books laid out in rows. In another was the remnant of a fire, cold now, and some blackened pots for cooking. In others were collections of assorted junk – tools, pieces of scrap, wood: collected detritus that may come in useful for a man living in the wild.

The path led them to a wall of stone, in which there were three openings.

'What do you think?' Benson asked.

'When in doubt, keep going in a straight line is always my policy,' Jessie said.

'You're the boss.'

'Let's not pretend for a minute that you mean that,' Jessie said.

Benson had started to answer when his left hip exploded in a cascade of red. A boom filled the tunnel, and the man staggered forward, somehow remaining upright. He looked at Jessie as if to ask her what had happened and then toppled over. As he fell, Jessie heard a second boom, the sound of the gun that had wrought the wounds, and knew the shooter must be at the other end of the long chasm that stretched behind them. She dropped to the ground, pulling the H&K from her pocket. The cavern about her filled with manic laughter, followed by singing Jessie at first thought was in gibberish but then realised was in Irish.

She pressed her ear to Benson's mouth – he was breathing, but barely.

'I'll come back for you,' she whispered, and keeping low as she could, she ran for the central corridor.

CHAPTER SIXTY-TWO

The song echoed about the vast space behind her, and as the guttural voice rose and fell, Jessie fought to swallow her fear and searched for that stillness at her centre.

She knew it was there.

She just had to shut out all the other emotions to access what was left in their absence.

The cavern she was in veered left and honeycombed into four more openings. Utterly befuddled now, and terrified of getting lost in the maze of passageways, Jessie put her back to the wall and called out, 'Seamus! If you're here, please answer!'

The singing stopped for a moment, and the sound of a shell being jacked into the chamber of a shotgun reverberated from outside – wherever he had been hiding, her attacker was coming. The song resumed, closer now.

'Seamus, for the love of God, let me know you're alive!'

She heard moaning – it sounded close by – then, weakly, 'What the hell took you so long?'

It's him! Jessie experienced a wave of relief and joy so great it almost overwhelmed her.

'Keep talking so I can find you!'

'You're the one always telling me to shut up!'

'Well now I'm telling you to do the opposite – do you always have to be so difficult?'

He was in the second chamber from the right, deathly pale under a coating of grime and filth. Someone had bound his hands and feet with rough cord, and blood was crusted on his shirt from a wound in his side. She embraced him, realising she was crying, and so was he.

'Don't you ever run off like that again, Seamus Keneally!' she said, cutting his bonds. 'I've only just got used to you as a partner, and I'm not about to start breaking in a new one.'

'You say the nicest things,' he replied. He was doing his best to sound upbeat, but Jessie could tell he was weak and in pain. He gestured to the other side of the cave and said, 'It's Coogan. Do you see? It was Coogan all along.'

Jessie shook her head. It didn't seem possible, but now was not the time to quibble about details.

'I bet you'd like to meet Penny,' Seamus was saying.

In the shadows was another crumpled figure. Jessie shone her torch on her and saw the poor girl was filthy, stick-thin and wide-eyed with terror.

'Penny, I'm from the police,' Jessie said. 'I've come to get you out of here. Can you walk?'

'He's coming,' the terrified girl said. 'You can't get away from him. He's not human. Not a man.'

'I don't think captivity has been easy for Penny,' Seamus said, then his eyes rolled back in his head and he passed out.

Jessie shook the detective gently but to no avail.

'Stay with me, Seamus. Don't you wimp out on me now, d'you hear?'

She rubbed his cheeks vigorously, and his eyes opened again.

'Did I drift off for a moment?'

'You did. Seamus, we need to go. Now.'

Her partner shook his head and gripped her shoulder.

'No point in even trying until you deal with Captain Caveman,' he said. 'He isn't going to listen to reason, Jessie. You're gonna have to put him out of action.'

She noticed the singing had stopped, the caves shrouded in a dense and foreboding silence now.

'Take this.' She pushed the handle of the knife into his fingers. 'If something happens to me, you'll need to finish the job. Get Penny out.'

'Don't be thick,' Seamus said. 'You've got this.'

He grimaced as if seized by a wave of pain.

'I don't suppose you brought food as well as weapons, did you? I'm starving.'

'When we get back to Cahirsiveen, I will buy you all the food you can handle.'

'I'll hold you to that, Jessie Boyle.'

'You ready?'

'You know I am.'

'Okay then. Here goes.'

She stood up, holding the gun in her right hand and the torch in her left, and called out in as loud a voice as she could muster, 'I am speaking to the man who used to be called Damian Coogan. Balor has revealed himself to me, and he is displeased with you. I am here to take your place. Now come forward.'

'I'm not going to lie, I didn't see that coming,' Seamus said.

Then the ceiling of the cave exploded inwards, and something wild, ragged and angry landed on top of Jessie.

CHAPTER SIXTY-THREE

Jessie went down, the full weight of Damian Coogan on her back. Earth, clay and twigs were in her hair and eyes. She understood there must have been a vein within the rock that led into this cave from above and that Coogan had blocked it at some point, only to use it now to get the drop on her.

She managed to keep a grip on the torch, but to her dismay the gun flew from her hand and clattered off into the darkness. Her attacker was like a wild thing, squirming and spitting, jabbering words she could not understand. Fingers dug into her hair, jagged nails ripped into her scalp, and then she felt her head being snapped back before being slammed forward onto the dirt of the cave floor with stunning force.

Stars wheeled in front of her vision, reality swam, and she thought, *I can't fight him. How is he so strong?*

But then the pressure on her was gone, and somewhere in the distance she heard scuffling and swearing, and consciousness slowly returned. When it did, she was lying on top of the torch, but a thin beam of light still emitted from beneath her. In it she saw Seamus grappling with a person that seemed to her little more than skin draped over bone. Clumps of hair protruded about his ears, but the rest of the head was completely bald, and the man was dressed in a pair of ragged trousers and nothing else. The shrunken body was a patchwork of scars, and as she peered through the gloom, Jessie realised they were all in the shape of ogham letters – the same sequence over and over again. Coogan, at some crisis point in his madness, had cut Balor's name into his flesh repeatedly, a physical mantra.

An ancient-looking pump-action shotgun lay on the floor near Penelope O'Dwyer's feet, but it might as well have been half a mile away. The woman was beside herself with fear, cowering against the wall while the detective fought for his life.

Seamus had the screeching, gibbering man in a chokehold, but in his compromised state he was no match for Coogan, who drove one of his bony elbows hard into the wound in the detective's abdomen again and again, causing it to rip further and blood to gush forth. Seamus's grip weakened, and the gangrel creature scuttled away, watching Jessie through sunken eyes as she fumbled in the darkness and found her lost gun, which she grabbed.

'You lie!' it hissed at her. 'You lie!'

Coogan made to spring at Jessie, fingers bared like claws, when the room filled with the booming sound of a gun blast. Half of Damian Coogan's right side disintegrated, and he was thrown against the wall beside Jessie with a wet, smacking sound. Jessie looked about her, thinking it must have been Penny who had fired the shot, but the girl remained almost catatonic.

Gazing about to identify her rescuer, Jessie's eyes came to rest on a figure swaying drunkenly in the doorway, sucking in rasping breaths. Benson, looking like something from one of the seven circles of hell, had the sawn-off shotgun, its barrels still smoking, held loosely in his hand. The wound in his hip glistened in the torchlight.

'Get out of here,' he said in a voice barely above a whisper.

'You're coming with us,' Jessie said, quickly cutting Penny free and helping her to her feet – the woman was compliant but seemed to have no awareness of what was going on. 'No one gets left behind.'

'I'll follow,' Benson said. 'Now go, please.'

He took the keys of the jeep from his pocket and tossed them to her.

Coogan, still alive, was making a mewling sound and trying to stand. With trembling fingers, the wounded gangster fed two more shells into his weapon. Jessie, half-carrying Penny, got her free arm under Seamus's armpit and hauled him upright.

'Leave him,' she said to Benson. 'He's already dead. His body just doesn't know it yet.'

The gangster gazed at her from lidded, bloodshot eyes.

'I can't feel one of my legs,' he said, and she knew each word was an effort. 'Getting the few yards from where I fell to here was agony. My vision is going in and out of focus. Even if I survive the journey back, I won't be who I was.'

'You might be better,' Jessie said, but she could tell he wasn't registering what she said. Benson was locked in his own private torment.

'Go. He and I have unfinished business. My own injuries aside, the lad from our crew who disappeared was my nephew. The debt must be paid.'

Coogan had somehow returned to his feet and was holding on to the stone of the cave wall to steady himself. Jessie didn't know how he was still conscious with so terrible a wound.

'Balor sees all,' he said in a reedy, wavering voice. 'He is coming. You cannot stop him.'

Jessie placed a hand on the gangster's arm, squeezed it once, then dragged Penny and the barely conscious Seamus out of the chamber that had been their prison, taking them towards the daylight.

They were crossing the path through the cavern where Coogan had made his living quarters when the first shotgun blast sounded.

Moments later, there was a second detonation, this one of a different cadence – Jessie thought it was probably a handgun.

One for Coogan, and one for himself, Jessie thought.

To her great surprise, she felt a moment of sadness at Benson's passing.

'Is that it then?' Seamus asked her. 'Is it over?'

She was desperately worried about him: he was bleeding profusely from his side, and his lips had started to turn blue.

'I hope so, Seamus,' she said. 'I really do. Come on, let's take a rest, shall we?'

In fits and starts they made it back to the cave mouth. Once there, Jessie laid her partner down, placing Penelope O'Dwyer beside him, and pulled out her phone. There was a dim signal.

'Terri?'

'My God, Jessie! Are you okay? Do you have Seamus?'

'I have him, but we need help. If I move him any further, I'm afraid he'll bleed out. Can you use the GPS on my phone to get Mountain Rescue to us?'

'Of course I can!'

'Tell them they need to come quickly, okay?'

'I will, Jessie. Hang in there.'

Jessie Boyle wrapped her arms around her partner and held him until the rescue team came.

CHAPTER SIXTY-FOUR

Penelope O'Dwyer was dehydrated, malnourished and psychologically traumatised, but other than that seemed not to have been physically harmed. Seamus, on the other hand, was not so lucky. The detective's heart had stopped in the ambulance on the way to Cork University Hospital, but the paramedic had refused to let his patient go. With CPR and a shock from a crash cart, he was revived and rushed straight to the operating theatre, where his perforated liver was patched up and the vast quantity of blood he'd lost replenished.

Jessie, Terri and Katie Keneally sat together in the family room – the nurses knew better than to debate that piece of semantics with them – and waited on news.

'He's in the recovery room now,' a doctor who looked to be fourteen years of age told them at seven thirty that evening. 'He's lucky he's in such good physical condition. A less robust metabolism might not have survived such trauma.'

'Will he make a full recovery, Doctor?' Katie asked, her face drawn with worry.

'Oh yes, I believe so. We'll keep him under observation for the next forty-eight hours, but unless something drastic happens, you'll be able to take him home in a week or so.'

Jessie was getting her sixth coffee of the evening from a vending machine in reception when Dawn Wilson arrived.

'How's Seamus?'

'He'll live to fight another day.'

'And how are you? You look like shit.'

'That's about how I feel.'

'My driver keeps a bottle of Scotch in the car,' the commissioner said. 'Want to have a wee drop with me? It beats the shite these machines spew out, I can tell you that.'

Jessie nodded and followed her friend to a black Lexus in the hospital car park.

'Take us around the block a few times, Bill, will you please?'

When they were in the flow of traffic, Dawn produced a bottle and two glasses, and poured liberal shots for them both.

'You got her back,' she said. 'It was a fucking impossible case, but you did it.'

'Did we?' Jessie asked.

She had already given her friend a detailed account over the phone of what had happened in the caves, so the commissioner was aware of all that had transpired.

'What do you mean?' Dawn asked, giving her old friend an exasperated look. 'Penelope O'Dwyer is in the loving embrace of her family again. Forensics is picking apart the contents of that nightmarish fucking cave system as we speak – they reckon it'll take months to go through all of it, but the work has begun. You caught the baddie, Jess. Pat yourself on the back and feel proud of yourself.'

'We got Coogan – or at least Benson did. But wasn't he just the apprentice? Balor's still out there.'

'How do we know there ever really was a Balor?' Dawn asked. 'Couldn't it have all been Coogan?'

'I don't think it could,' Jessie said, sipping her Scotch. 'He was living in a cave system in the Reeks for nearly forty years and he was psychiatrically deranged. I don't think he was capable of much organised thought.'

'You don't think he abducted the women then?'

'He abducted them and held them and might even have killed some of them. But he didn't plan it. He hadn't used technology since the late 1980s, so he certainly didn't send videos infected with Trojan viruses, and he surely didn't hack security cameras, and I can promise you Damian Coogan did not have an Instagram account. There was someone else involved. Of that I am absolutely certain.'

Dawn Wilson took another swallow of Scotch.

'And do you have any idea who that person is?'

'Seamus is convinced it's Mervyn Moorehouse.'

'*Seamus* is convinced?'

'He's all we've got really. Any evidence we have points to him. It's all circumstantial but…'

'Your job was to get back the kidnapped girl,' she said. 'You did that. You also retrieved the remains of twenty-eight women whose families can now lay them to rest, along with more than twenty other individual remains we still have to identify. On top of that, the "giant" you found was not a real giant at all but had been constructed from dozens of other remains – some kind of bizarre sculpture made of human bones. With a bit of luck, we'll be able to trace them from their DNA and their families can put them to rest.'

'That is good news,' Jessie said. 'But there's still a loose end.'

'You're not going to let it go, are you?'

'Would you?'

'It's not neat and it's not tidy, but the powers that be are happy we've got our man,' Dawn said. 'Take some time off, get a little rest, and we'll chat again in a few days. Mervyn Moorehouse remains under surveillance, and for now that's as much as any of us can do. You've done some good work here, Jessie. You should let yourself rest and enjoy it.'

Jessie knew she was right.

But rest was to elude her for some time yet.

CHAPTER SIXTY-FIVE

The following day, Terri sat on one side of Seamus's hospital bed, Katie on the other, her son's pale hand held in her own much smaller one as he drifted in and out of drug-aided unconsciousness. Terri was amazed at the emotions she was feeling. She barely knew this man, yet she honestly believed she would never be the same if he did not recover. That her life would somehow be so much the lesser if he was not in it.

She was pondering this surprising truth when her phone beeped. Assuming it was Jessie, she looked down to see 'John Miskella – Work' flash across her screen.

I behaved terribly. My therapist tells me I have serious self-esteem issues, and they make me get very defensive. When I get defensive, I become a total dick. Please forgive me. And if you can find it in your heart to do so, please give me another chance. I would like to come to Cahirsiveen to see you this evening. If you're free, even for a short time, I'd love to meet you for a drink.

Despite herself, Terri felt her heart soar. She was beginning to accept she had misread John's intentions completely, that out of lack of experience and a low opinion of her own merits, she had permitted herself to be manipulated and, ultimately, made a fool of. Perhaps she hadn't been completely wrong about him after all.

I could meet you for a short time. I worked most of last night and all of today, so I'm quite tired. But I would like to see you.

The response came immediately this time.

Excellent. Let me know when and where you'll be, and I'll collect you. I need to earn a few brownie points, so expect me to be chivalrous to a fault this time.

Terri grinned. Maybe things weren't so bad after all. Life was starting to look a little rosier.

CHAPTER SIXTY-SIX

Dawn offered to drive Jessie and Terri back to their respective guest houses.

'Get some sleep,' Jessie said to Terri as she climbed out of the car.

'I will. But I have a date first. I'll finish up early though.'

Jessie gave the girl a funny look. 'You're not going out with that asshole? Whatshisname… Miskella?'

'He texted and apologised. John… he's been through some tough times. He and I have a lot in common actually. If it wasn't for him smoking those awful Woodbines, I'd say we were perfectly matched. I decided to give him one more chance anyway.'

'Well, if you're sure,' Jessie said. 'But if he starts giving you any kind of guff – take my advice and walk away. You deserve better than that, Terri.'

'She's right,' Dawn agreed. 'If I were you, I'd leave it at one drink. If he's genuine, he'll be happy to see you and won't complain. That's my tuppence-worth anyway.'

'Do you think?'

'I do.'

'Okay. Maybe I'll do that then.'

'Have a good night, Terri,' Jessie said. 'I'll be in touch tomorrow.'

'Night, Jessie. Night, Commissioner.'

And they pulled away, leaving the girl standing at the end of the drive that led to her B & B.

Dawn was about to drop Jessie back to her guest house when Jessie turned to her friend and said, 'You brought me into this against my will by calling in a debt you knew I couldn't refuse to pay.'

Dawn looked at her old friend, her expression solemn. 'I did. And I know I should be sorry, but I'm not. A girl's life was saved. Which almost brings things into balance, doesn't it?'

'Maybe it does. But I want you to do something for me now.'

'What?'

'We have one compelling suspect for Balor. Come with me and let's interview him one more time.'

'You seriously want to do this now?'

'I do. What have we got to lose?'

Dawn shook her head. 'I suppose it can't hurt,' she said.

Jessie gave the driver Mervyn Moorehouse's address.

Moorehouse's composure flickered for just a moment when he realised the Police Commissioner of Ireland was sitting in his living room.

'I've said everything I have to say to you people,' he drawled, but Jessie noted a weakness in his voice. 'Either arrest me or leave me alone.'

'We found Penny,' Jessie said, going right for the jugular.

Moorehouse's face went a deathly shade of pale.

'A cave system in the Reeks,' Dawn said, shaking her head in wonderment. 'That, my friend, is a new one for me. You're going to go down in the history of crime alongside the likes of Josef Fritzl for sheer ingenuity. I'm impressed. That's a right set-up you've got up there.'

'You might as well give up now though,' Jessie said with a grin. 'Forensics are already hunkered down in your tunnels. You *will* have left your DNA in one of your kill rooms. You and your apprentice won't have been careful, not up there among the bodies and the darkness.'

Jessie suddenly realised that Moorehouse's lower lip was trembling.

'Is Penny alive?' he asked in a voice cracking with emotion.

'I'm surprised you're asking *us* that question,' Dawn said. 'Did you lose control of your attack dog?'

'Just tell me please – is Penny all right?'

Jessie leaned forward in her chair. 'I'll tell you how she is if you answer some questions for me,' she said. 'What exactly is your relationship with Penelope O'Dwyer?'

Moorehouse shook his head, and now tears were rolling down his cheeks.

'I told you! We're friends, her and me.'

'A friend who has proven extremely uncooperative with the police during our investigation,' Jessie said. 'I would go so far as to say you did everything you could to encumber us.'

'I wanted to help you find her,' Moorehouse blurted.

'You'll have to pardon me when I say I don't believe you,' Jessie said.

'I went to Limerick,' he said. 'I thought she'd been taken by Charlie Doherty's crew. They'd been warring with Cloney, you see, and the hotel project seemed to have raised all kinds of old animosities. I went to see if I could get her back.'

'They didn't have her though,' Jessie said, thinking for the first time that perhaps Moorehouse was telling the truth.

'No. I offered them money. I said I'd work for them. But… it wasn't them.'

'So you sent us to brace Cloney for you,' Jessie said. 'I take it you don't have an in with him?'

'I… I didn't know what else to do,' Moorehouse said. 'I love her, you see. I was just trying to get Penny back.'

And then Mervyn Moorehouse broke down in tears.

Dawn looked over at Jessie and shrugged.

'I hate to state the obvious,' Dawn said. 'But I don't think it's him.'

CHAPTER SIXTY-SEVEN

Jessie was just about to get into bed at seven that night when her phone rang. It was Ultain Cloney.

'You cost me one of my best men,' he said. 'I should be furious.'

'I tried to bring him out with me, but he didn't want to come. He ended things his own way. I wish it went differently – honestly I do.'

'You found Penny. I appreciate that.'

'You know, there will be questions asked about some of her off-the-book clients.'

'I expected as much, but we were prepared. Penny has made sure everything is just the right side of legal. Why do you think she's so valuable to me?'

'We'll see about that. It won't be me coming after you on that count anyway, Mr Cloney. I hope you and I can part as friends on this occasion.'

'As do I. I've had someone leave your car at the White Elephant. Your wee friend, the one with the blue hair, she was there and took the keys. Told my man she was waiting for someone to pick her up.'

'Okay. Thanks, Mr Cloney. For everything.'

'It has been a pleasure, Jessie Boyle. I'm sure our paths will cross again.'

And he hung up.

She had just drifted off to sleep when her phone rang yet again.

She picked it up and put it to her ear without opening her eyes.

'Yes.'

'Ms Boyle? It's Dick Dunne. I'm speaking to you from a pay-phone in a public house, so please pardon the background noise.'

'Hello, Mr Dunne.'

'Are you all right? You sound odd.'

'I have been awake for more than fifty hours, Mr Dunne, so you'll have to excuse me. How can I help you this evening?'

'Do you remember the last time we spoke, your colleague inquired about someone who worked on Balor's Stone who was known among his fellows as Reek?'

'Oh. Yes.' Jessie sat up in bed. 'Have you remembered?'

'I have actually. There was a young man, he'd come to us initially as part of one of those programmes for children from disadvantaged backgrounds. He'd been in care, and Dr Quilt took an interest in him – he was technically too old to be fostered, but he moved in with Quilt, became a sort of surrogate son for him. It was him they called Reek. It was because of the cigarettes he used to smoke – those awful Woodbine things. He always used to say they reeked, but they were strong and cheap.'

'Miskella,' Jessie said. 'You're talking about John Miskella.'

And she was out of bed and throwing on her clothes before she had even hung up.

CHAPTER SIXTY-EIGHT

Terri messaged John and asked him to pick her up at the White Elephant, offering to give him directions. He told her he knew where it was though and that he'd see her at eight.

A man came and dropped off Jessie's MG – Terri accepted the keys, told him she worked with Jessie and gave him her name. He rang someone on his phone, clarified it was okay to leave her in charge of Jessie's classic, then strolled off in the direction of the town.

Terri was just about to go back upstairs when a black Toyota Yaris turned in from the road, and she saw John behind the wheel. She waved, and he returned the gesture.

'So this is where you work?' he asked as he got out of the car. 'Isn't this a tourist office or something now?'

'We just rent a few rooms upstairs. If you give me two minutes, I'll lock up and we can go and get a drink and chat about everything.'

'Sounds ominous,' he said.

'Doesn't have to be,' she said. Reaching up, she pecked him on the cheek before running in and up the stairs to their work room.

She had just logged out of her laptop when she heard the door swinging open, and turning around, saw he had followed her.

'I'm just coming,' she said, trying to keep her voice light. 'Um… you're not really supposed to be up here. Confidentiality and all that… I'm sure you understand.'

But he ignored her completely, his eyes on the photographs of the missing women she had fixed to the wall.

'I've never seen them together like this,' he said, and his voice had a strange sing-song quality to it, each word seeming to hit a lower register, as if someone was turning a dial as he spoke. 'They dance, under the mountain. Did you know that, Terri? They dance forever and ever.'

'John, you're scaring me,' she said. 'I'd like to go now please.'

'Balor moved from Quilt to me when the old man died. He started it, but it was my job to complete the task.'

Terri suddenly felt very cold.

'John... what are you saying?'

She tried to edge towards the door, but he stepped in her way.

'Coogan became my apprentice. Quilt had others, but he never told me who they were. I sought Damian out in the Reeks, and he was only too happy to help. It was my idea to stage his death. Wasn't that clever of me?'

Terri looked around the room desperately. Her eyes fell on Seamus's hurley stick, leaning in the corner behind his desk. Slowly, one step at a time, she backed towards it.

'He caught them and brought them into the caves beneath the mountains, and I let him play with them for a while before I killed them. Penelope was supposed to be the last one,' he said. Terri noticed for the first time that there was a knife in his hand. 'She and Jessie were meant to be the final sacrifices. The hero and the maiden.'

As she watched, he was changing: his posture became straighter, his movements slower and more purposeful, his facial expressions more languid. It was as if she was looking at a different person. And his voice: lower, deeper, guttural and raw. It didn't seem possible a voice like that could come from a human being.

'Penelope was to be my greatest work. My masterpiece.'

He was very close to her now, and Terri could feel heat radiating from him in waves.

'Quilt was a wonderful foster father. He allowed me to study whatever I wanted, actually encouraged me to become a computer hacker. It's amazing what you can find out online these days. I learned how to build Trojan Horse software to send untraceable videos that would self-destruct. And do you know that shutting down security cameras is ludicrously easy with only a minimal amount of know-how? The police have been dumbfounded by it all, but it wasn't difficult.'

'John, you're not making sense,' Terri said.

'Jessie and Penny's sacrifice was going to finish it,' he went on, ignoring her. 'It would have released me, manifested the power I need to establish my kingdom.'

'John, I don't think you're well,' Terri said, and as she did so, she reached for the hurley, felt its comforting weight in her hand.

'John's gone, Terri,' the thing that had once been John Miskella said. He smiled, and Terri thought she was going to scream.

Then he lunged at her with the knife, and she did.

CHAPTER SIXTY-NINE

It took Jessie ten minutes at a sprint to make it from her B & B to the White Elephant. By the time she got there it was ten minutes past eight, she was soaked with sweat and her lungs felt as if they were ready to burst out of her chest. Her MG and a black car of some kind were side by side in the car park, but she barely registered the fact, slamming through the door and taking the stairs two at a time.

Jesus, please let me be on time, please let it not be too late, she prayed.

But she feared she might be. Someone was screaming in their work room, and below that it seemed an animal was snarling. She drew the H&K as she hit the last step, and as she did, she heard Terri scream from inside, 'Get your fucking hands off me!'

There was a crashing, crunching sound, and the growling turned into a gurgling whine, and then it stopped.

Jessie kicked open the door in time to see Terri Kehoe swinging the round *bas* of Seamus's hurley stick onto the head of a man who was lying face down on the office floor. The girl lifted the weapon to hit him again, and Jessie called to her, 'Terri, it's okay, love. He's gone. You're safe, pet.'

The girl, wild-eyed and sobbing, looked at Jessie, and then down at the fallen man.

'He… he was going to kill me, Jessie,' she said. 'Only… he wasn't *John*. He was something else.'

'I know, Terri. I know.'

She walked over and took the hurley from her friend, using the sleeve of her jacket in the absence of a glove, and kicked the knife so it was out of Miskella's reach. She then squatted and checked the pulse of the fallen man. It was steady: he was unconscious but still alive. Terri was still making hysterical sobbing, gulping sounds.

'Terri, hun,' Jessie said as she handcuffed Miskella's hands behind his back, 'I'd hug you, but forensics are going to need your clothes. Can you go into the kitchen and bag them while I call for backup? You can put my coat on when you've got it done, okay? It'll keep you covered.'

Terri nodded and went to do as she was asked.

Jessie paused for a moment, looking down at the man who was behind so much pain and mayhem. If Balor had been in that room only moments ago, he was gone. Seamus Keneally's hurley had driven him out.

Heartened by the thought, Jessie dialled 999.

CHAPTER SEVENTY

One week later

Seamus was sitting up in bed, eating some kind of green jelly. Jessie thought it looked like something that might grow on a pond that had been left untended. Her partner, on the other hand, seemed to be relishing every mouthful, which she supposed was a good thing.

'The Instagram messages between Reek and Penny,' Jessie told him, 'and we know now that Miskella *was* Reek – they were all referring to a research thesis she wanted to do on the Dedad forts on her father's land.'

'No one told us she was into history,' Seamus said.

'I'm not sure she really was. She's still very traumatised, but from the brief conversations we've been able to have, she wanted to employ someone in the history department in UCC to complete the research. She was going to get the end result bound and give it to her father as a present. Which brought her into Miskella's orbit.'

'And the rest is history,' Seamus said, winking at her.

'Not funny, Seamus,' Jessie said, although she secretly thought it was.

'So this guy, Miskella, who Terri was kind of dating, was Balor all along?' the detective asked incredulously.

'Not all along. Quilt, the man who uncovered the stone first, he took on the personality to begin with. Started the killing. When Miskella came to UCC as part of a programme for disadvantaged youth, Quilt took an interest in him. John Miskella was abandoned by his parents – he was literally found in a carboard box on the steps of a church in Ennis, so the care system was all he knew. According to social services, he had some horrific placements where he was routinely abused. Quilt ended up as a sort of foster father, and I do think it was all done with the best of intentions at the start. But then the stone came into his life and… well, everything went to hell. Literally.'

'Is Miskella talking?'

'Miskella isn't – Balor is. The Balor personality has completely taken over. But it seems to know everything that happened, and it's pretty boastful. We've been able to put together a good picture. The psychiatrists are saying it's a form of multiple personality syndrome, probably caused by suppressed childhood trauma. He's not demonically possessed obviously, but he believes very strongly that he is.'

'What do you think it was about the stone that made all this happen?' Seamus asked, scraping the bottom of the plastic bowl with his spoon.

'I have no idea. I wondered if there was some sort of radioactive compound in the rock, or if something gaseous was released from the soil, which was boggy, by all accounts. Both would explain hallucinations and altered states of consciousness, but not over such a prolonged period of years. In the end, we'll never know. All we can say for sure is that Quilt and Coogan were both broken by it, and Miskella was probably already emotionally damaged from his time in care.'

'And they thought the stone wanted them to murder all these women?'

'It was part of a plan to pave the way for Balor's return,' Jessie said. 'Thirty sacrifices were needed, all focused around different Celtic festivals and holy days. The final two had to be the daughter of a king and the hero sent to rescue her. The male and female energies that exist in us all.'

'Why didn't Coogan kill me and Penny when he had us then?'

'It had to happen on the Eve of Samhain,' Jessie said. 'So he was waiting for that. But also – I don't think they expected you to come.'

'No?'

'I think Miskella was waiting for me.'

Seamus put the empty bowl down on his bedside locker and looked at it sadly, as if he thought it might spontaneously replenish.

'But you're a… um… well, you're a girl, like. So wouldn't that be two female energies?'

'It wasn't about my gender. It was about my role. What I was there to do. And of course, we can't forget Uruz's involvement. He and I have unfinished business. This was his way of getting closure: have one of his friends kill me.'

'You reckon Uruz and Morgan and him planned the whole thing?'

'I do.'

'That's kind of messed up, Jessie.'

'Doesn't make it any less true though.'

'And the drug convoys being hit? That was just to keep people away from Coogan's hideout?'

'Well, it was a little more than that, according to Miskella.'

'Or Balor.'

'I feel weird calling him that. Forensics have been all over the caves, and Miskella's house has been searched, and no sign of either drugs or money or anything else have been found. According to Cloney, he's lost millions in product over the years. And other gangs were hit too before they all stopped using roads through the mountains.'

'So where's all the loot?'

'I said they didn't find drugs or money. Miskella's basement, however, is full of every kind of computer gadget and networking doohickie and communications amplifier and I don't know what else money can buy. I'm told it's a set-up that a university lecturer's wages could not have paid for.'

'So he spent it all on tech stuff?'

'That's just the start of it. It looks as if he and Coogan did some work in the cave systems too, shoring up some of those tunnels the cavers believed were too dangerous. That would have required funds and equipment, which he would have had to smuggle up there, one piece at a time. But that still doesn't account for all of it.'

'I think you have a theory about that,' Seamus said, grinning.

'We have to remember, he's a hacker. He could well have the money converted into some kind of cryptocurrency by now.'

'Crypto what?'

'You've heard of Bitcoin?'

'I've heard of it, but I haven't a clue what it is.'

'It's digital money. That's all you need to know. The tech boys reckon he converted the bulk of the money he stole into that and has hidden it on the web. Which is a very, very big place.'

'So it may well never be found.'

'It was dirty money anyway,' Jessie said. 'So it's probably no great loss.'

She paused for a moment before continuing, 'You know how Benson, Cloney's enforcer with the skin complaint, went up there to help me, and we had to leave him behind?'

'Didn't he shoot himself?' Seamus asked. 'I mean, he was dying anyway, but…'

'They never found his body,' Jessie said.

'They found Coogan's though, right?'

'Oh yes. They did. Benson's should have been in the cave with it. But it wasn't.'

'Do you think…' Seamus asked.

'That he survived somehow?'

'Yes. I mean, is it possible?'

'I don't know,' Jessie admitted. 'But if I'm honest, a part of me hopes he did. He was a bad man but… without him, I don't think we'd have made it out of there, you, Penny and me.'

They said nothing for a while as they thought about that.

'How exactly is Morgan mixed up in all this?' Seamus asked after a while. 'Why did he tell us about Balor in the first place? I mean, what did he want?'

'I think he was bored and wanted to play with us,' Jessie said. 'And I think Miskella was in touch with him. And Uruz too.'

'And do you reckon he wanted out of the Central Mental Hospital?'

'I do.'

'To forge a relationship with his niece?'

'Call me a cynic, Seamus, but I don't believe it for a minute. I find it hard to believe anything that comes out of that man's mouth.'

'I think he sent you to Kerry to be a sacrificial lamb,' Seamus said. 'He's a twisted, dangerous man, Jessie. And he is right where he should be. Locked up.'

Jessie nodded and sighed.

'Uruz is still out there though,' she said. 'And he's still watching. And waiting.'

'And so are you,' Seamus said, reaching over and taking his partner's hand. 'And you're not alone anymore. If… when… he makes his move, we'll be ready.'

'Thank you, Seamus.'

'And who says we have to wait anyway? Let's start bringing the fight to him. Morgan says these guys are all connected – if that's the case, by chasing these killers, we're chasing Uruz too.'

Jessie looked at her partner, and he saw concern in her eyes.

'There's one other thing though,' she said. 'John Miskella is going to be in there with Morgan. And I don't like the idea of that one bit.'

EPILOGUE

Three weeks later

'It's always darkest just before it goes totally black.'
John 'Hannibal' Smith, the A-Team

Seamus Keneally looked thin and was still pale, but the spring was back in his step and Jessie had not seen him without food of some kind in his hand for several days. Terri still had rings under her eyes and was quiet and watchful, even for her, but she assured Jessie that she was doing okay. Jessie wasn't sure she believed her, but there wasn't much she could do other than be there for the girl.

Which she had every intention of being. For as long as she could.

The three investigators were in the meeting room in Harcourt Street, with Dawn Wilson at the top of the table, looking as if she had something to say.

'You three make a pretty good team,' she began. 'Individually, you're all pretty good at what you do. But together, you are much more than the sum of your parts. You create something unique.'

'Is there a point you're trying to make in the middle of all that?' Jessie wanted to know.

'I'd like you to continue to work together as a special investigative unit,' Dawn said. 'Answerable directly to me. My go-to team, if you like.'

'Sort of like the A-Team?' Seamus piped up.

'They were mercenaries on the run from the law,' Jessie said. 'That's totally different.'

'What about Robert McCall, *The Equalizer*,' Terri offered.

'Wasn't he a vigilante who was paid to balance the odds when people were being bullied or oppressed?' Dawn asked. 'And he was, like, really old.'

'I always liked *Knight Rider*,' Seamus said. 'Do we get a car that talks and can do cool jumps?'

'Don't you just borrow your mam's car?' Jessie said mischievously.

'She's happy for me to use it,' Seamus said defensively.

'We're just us,' Terri said. 'I'd like to keep working together.'

'Me too, little sis,' Seamus said, giving Jessie a pointed look.

'And me,' Jessie agreed. 'I'm not ready to part company with these two quite yet.'

'Good,' Dawn said. 'Because I have another case for you.'

'Please tell me this one is in a city,' Jessie said. 'If I never see a mountain again, it'll be too soon.'

'I'm afraid not,' Dawn said. 'A traveller family was camping in a forest in County Leitrim, and they stumbled across what seems to be a burial site spread across a very large area of the woods. Some of the remains are very old… but others are recent.'

'Have the bodies been matched to any known missing persons?' Seamus asked.

'Well, that's the point,' Dawn said. 'There have been no reports of missing persons locally, and the remains don't seem to fit any outstanding cases on the books either. The truth is, we don't know who they are.'

'Do the local Gardai have any thoughts?'

'They're at a loss. Leitrim is the least populated county in Ireland. The local boys are good at tracking down cattle thieves and dealing with the Continuity IRA, but this is something very new.'

'New how?' Terri asked.

'The bodies were buried across a timeframe of more than five years, and they were all killed in different ways – gunshots, stab wounds, asphyxiation. One was even buried alive.'

'We're probably looking at different killers,' Jessie said.

'Possibly,' Dawn said. 'But there's more. I had a look at other files and reports relating to the area where these bodies have been found, and I discovered something alarming. There are a dozen unsolved murders directly linked to those woods going back more than a decade. It looks as if something nasty has been going on in that part of Leitrim for a while. I want you to see if you can't find out what it is.'

'Brilliant,' Jessie Boyle said. 'Just brilliant.'

A LETTER FROM S.A. DUNPHY

Dear Reader,

I want to say a huge thank you for choosing to read *Bring Her Home*. If you enjoyed it and want to keep up to date with all my latest releases, just sign up at the following link. Your email address will never be shared and you can unsubscribe at any time.

www.bookouture.com/sa-dunphy

I hope you loved *Bring Her Home*, and if you did, I would be really grateful if you could write a review. I'd love to hear what you think, and it makes such a difference helping new readers to discover one of my books for the first time.

I love hearing from my readers – you can get in touch on my Facebook page, through Twitter, Instagram or my website.

Many thanks,
S.A. Dunphy

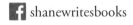 shanewritesbooks

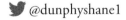 @dunphyshane1

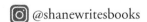 @shanewritesbooks

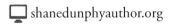 shanedunphyauthor.org

ACKNOWLEDGEMENTS

Writers often get asked why they wrote a particular book or series of books, so let me get in there right away.

I *had* to write the Boyle and Keneally series. These characters and the world they live in called to me, and I had no choice but to answer.

In 2019, I published the last book in the Dunnigan crime series, a dark quadrilogy of books charting the quest of a criminologist to find his niece who had been abducted eighteen years previously. The novels received a lot of positive attention, and the research I did while writing them put me in contact with a number of people who worked alongside the police force in Ireland who were not, in fact, police officers themselves.

I met psychologists, social workers, hackers, accountants, profilers, medics, ammunition experts and countless others who were part and parcel of the world of crime prevention but who had never gone to the police training academy in Templemore.

So even though David Dunnigan, the protagonist from my previous series, was on hiatus, I wasn't done with these civilian consultants yet. I felt compelled to spend more time with them.

In tandem with this I wanted to write a modern crime series that possessed the atmosphere and creepiness of folk horror. The horror genre has always fascinated me as a medium. All kinds of themes can be explored through the lens of the fantastic, and folk horror gave me the opportunity to examine the effect history has on the present. I wanted to explore the idea that layers of human experience exist all around us, and their reverberations can still be felt.

That the series would be set in Ireland, where I've lived for most of my life, was a given. And my protagonists were all going to be outsiders: most writers consider themselves to be a little separate from the mainstream, and having spent my adult life working in social care and child protection, what other kind of people was I going to write about?

Jessie and Seamus, Terri and Dawn all strutted onto the page as if they belonged there, and before very long they were leading me to the mountains of Kerry and a frightening and claustrophobic cave system where awful things had happened.

I've already grown very fond of all of them. I hope you have too. Because they have lots more stories to share with you. Believe me, Jessie and the gang are just getting started.

And there are some people I need to thank on their behalf, without whom you would never have met them.

Ivan Mulcahy, my literary agent, is a man whom I am deeply indebted to. He is one of those rare people who actually does what he says he is going to do. Every single element of the plan he and I made for my literary career when he took over as my agent three years ago has come to fruition, and I can honestly say I have never felt more satisfied, valued and nurtured as a creator. He is, to put it in the simplest terms possible, not just a colleague but a dear friend. Thank you, Ivan, for everything you do.

Everyone I have met and worked with at Bookouture has been a joy. It may seem a no-brainer that a publishing house should place the author front and centre, but I can tell you from years as a jobbing writer, it is not always the case! With Bookouture I found a group who understand the process of creating a novel, but even better they are experts in framing and establishing a series with a view to ensuring it will run and run. Their grasp of what crime readers want is profound. They are completely au fait with which tropes work and which don't, and they can school you on how to market and promote a title across all media. Rarely have I received such encouragement and positive feedback on my work.

I especially want to take a moment to thank my editor, Therese Keating, who made the process of writing this book so much easier, and actually brought a real sense of fun and excitement to the editorial process. Therese has a sense of humour and a love of language that permeates everything she does. Some of her notes on the first draft of *Bring Her Home* made me laugh out loud, while others really got me thinking and gave me perspectives on the characters and the story I had never considered. By seeing the book through her eyes, I was able to explore the world of the novel in new and interesting ways. Thanks so much, Therese.

My friend and fellow author Emily Clarke was kind enough to read some of the early chapters of the novel and give me feedback on pacing, atmosphere and character development that really helped in those uncertain first days of writing. Emily's amazing grasp of plotting and her instinctive sense of how characters interact were invaluable, and she also taught me a valuable lesson in how important it is to name each of your characters thoughtfully – the right name can make all the difference! It's a lesson I won't forget. Emily, you're a true friend.

I read lots of books during my research for this novel, but the one I went back to time and again was *Early Irish Myths and Sagas* by Jeffrey Gantz (Penguin, 2000). If you have an interest in any of the Celtic history and mythology discussed in this novel – and I didn't make up any of it; it's all real and waiting to be discovered – then that's the book for you.

Cahirsiveen is very much a real town in County Kerry, and I should really thank all the people who live there. During the writing of *Bring Her Home*, I visited the area, but as it was during the Covid pandemic and therefore in the middle of lockdown, everywhere was closed and I didn't get to chat to anyone. But the majesty and beauty of the place were still evident, and I was able to stand outside the White Elephant, which is a real building exactly as I described, and imagine Terri and Jessie working there late into the night.

Macgillycuddy's Reeks are real too and well worth a visit.

To finish, I'd like to thank you, dear reader, for taking the time to read this book and for staying with Jessie and her friends right to the end. I hope you enjoyed the journey and would like to come back for the next one. Because there's a mystery waiting in County Leitrim, and it's going to test Jessie, Seamus and Terri's skills to the last.

You don't want to miss it.

I can promise you that.

Printed in Great Britain
by Amazon